ABOUT ELIZABETH HOLLAND

Elizabeth Holland is a writer of romance novels. She enjoys the escapism of picking up a book and losing herself in a new world. Elizabeth is a keen advocate for mental health and often speaks out about her own struggles. She writes to escape her own thoughts. When Elizabeth isn't writing, she's usually outside walking the dog. Her favourite walks are when it's cold and rainy, so she can work on her next plot.

The Cornish Vintage Furniture Shop

THANK YOU

A big thank you to Deborah Klée, Chris Towndrow (Chrissie Harrison), and Rebecca Chase, all of whom helped to shape this book.

They're all wonderful authors, and I'd really recommend their books.

CHAPTER ONE

Mabel shivered as another droplet of rain landed on the back of her coat. It slid below the neck and slivered along her spine. With a huff, she dropped the screwdriver. It fell to the concrete floor with a loud thud. The screws were stuck on the Art Deco dressing table she was working on, and it was what felt like the hundredth day of rain. Her workshop was damp, and even the radio couldn't drown out the sound of rain pounding on the corrugated roof. She grumbled and stood, stretching her aching joints.

"I need a holiday in the sun," she muttered as she picked up her umbrella and stepped out into the dismal day. Since a holiday was outside her budget, she decided to go into Port Isaac for a hot chocolate.

Mabel's walk down the cobbled road to the harbour was slippery. The wind blew a gale, and rain pelted down at an angle, meaning her brolly was completely useless. Below, the sea crashed ferociously. Despite being soaked, Mabel paused by the wall to look at the harbour. Wave after wave crashed against the shoreline as the wind blew the sea foam onto the beach. It was a dismal day, yet there was beauty in the ferocity of Mother Nature. Mabel continued her descent and smiled as she walked past the ice cream shop, which would be buzzing in the coming months. She couldn't wait to order a triple chocolate ice cream cone with a flake. It would melt in the midday sun, leaving a sticky trail across her hands.

By the time Mabel reached Fisherman's Brew, she was wet through to the skin. Hair was plastered to her face, and her feet squelched in her boots. She pushed open the door and sighed as warmth wrapped around her shivering body.

"Mabel, dear." Betty spotted her as she walked in. "Leave your umbrella by the door and come sit by the fire. Do you want your usual?"

"Yes, please. Thank you." With chattering teeth, Mabel peeled off the dripping coat and hung it on the stand by the door. The coat claimed to be waterproof, but it seemed that didn't extend to the Cornish rain.

The windows had steamed up, and a handful of people sat inside, warming themselves with a drink and a slice of Betty's Victoria sponge. A gentle hum of conversation wound its way around the cafe, interspersed by the hiss of a milk frother. Mabel scraped her wet hair into a plait, allowing a few wispy tendrils of blonde hair to frame her face. There was an empty table by the fire, and Mabel took the chair closest to the flames. The cafe was cosy and homely, filled with memories. On the opposite wall was a sideboard Mabel had refinished for Betty. It was a beautiful, hand-crafted piece with delicate carvings and mouldings. Mabel had painted it sage green to match the cafe's decor and added gold to highlight the Rococo mouldings. It was pretty, and in the dim light of the cafe, the gold shimmered. Mabel had stripped the top back to raw wood, knowing the piece would be heavily used. Betty displayed cutlery, napkins, and condiments on it. Everyone always complimented it, and Betty would proudly tell them about Mabel and her business.

"Here we go. A hot chocolate with cream and a flake," Betty announced. Thick hot chocolate filled a glass cup, swirls of freshly whipped double cream bobbed on top, and a milk chocolate flake balanced across the glass, slowly melting. Mabel's mouth watered at the sight.

"Thank you. I don't know what I'd do without your treats." Mabel smiled at the elderly woman who had run the cafe for as long as she could remember. In her twenty-eight years, Mabel's order hadn't changed. Once old enough to speak, she always begged her mother for one of Betty's 'melted chocolate drinks'.

"What are you working on?" Gwen called from a couple of tables over. She always sat near the counter so she could chat with Betty. Gwen was one of Port Isaac's well-known residents. She knew everyone and everything. Each morning, Gwen sauntered into the harbour, her hair perfectly coiffed into a French chignon, and her outfit would always match the season. Today, she wore black trousers, walking boots, and a cashmere grey jumper. Despite the weather, Gwen looked elegant. Not a single hair out of place, or a hint of a crease on her clothes.

"I've got a beautiful Art Deco dressing table. It's got those typical curved sides, and a huge, round mirror. I've been struggling with getting the handles off this morning. My client wants to replace them, but the screws have all rounded and are proving to be a nightmare." Mabel scooped cream onto the flake as she watched Gwen visualise the piece.

"What have they asked you to do to it?" Gwen asked, her lips pursed.

"They're keeping the burr walnut veneer drawers, but are replacing the handles as they've been damaged."

"What about the body?" Gwen drummed her fingers on the table.

Mabel scuffed her shoe on the floor as she readied herself for an argument. "The veneer is beyond saving. The client has opted to paint it instead of recovering the piece."

Gwen's face contorted. "Painted furniture," she muttered. "It's an abomination."

"You know my process, Gwen. I ensure everything is done properly so in the future, the piece can be returned to its original form with a new veneer." Mabel rehashed the same conversation they'd had countless times.

Mabel sipped her hot chocolate and waited for Gwen's next barb. It was eleven o'clock and Mabel should have known better than to visit the cafe. Gwen would be there until the early afternoon to revel in the gossip that flew in with the lunch rush. Mabel assumed it was because Gwen was lonely.

"I met a man yesterday," Gwen announced. Mabel coughed as her drink went down the wrong hole. It had been the very last thing she'd expected to come out of Gwen's mouth. Gwen's husband passed many years ago. He had been the love of her life, and Gwen had never shown an interest in anyone else.

"Poor man," Betty muttered. She'd wandered over with a cup of tea and sat opposite Mabel.

"Not for me! He's buying the pub."

"Our pub?" asked Mabel.

"Yes. The Fisherman's Rest."

"After all these years, it still amazes me how you know everything, Gwen. You're the first to hear of anything that happens in Port Isaac, sometimes even before those involved. I wonder what this man's intentions are," Betty said.

Mabel shared a concerned glance with Betty. The Fisherman's Rest closed a year ago after the pandemic depleted the owner's finances, and it became an unviable business. Mabel had arranged a fundraiser to help, and all the locals turned out, but it hadn't been enough to save the heart of their community. Toby closed Fisherman's Rest a few weeks later and the residents of Port Isaac lost their pub. Betty had hired more staff and opened later into the evening, but it didn't fill the pub-shaped hole in the community.

"Maybe it's a good thing?" Mabel said.

"Yes. I could do without the evening trade, to be honest. I'm not getting any younger and people don't want coffee and sandwiches at that time of night," Betty agreed.

"Nothing good will come of this," Gwen muttered. By now, everyone's attention was on her.

"Who's buying it?" someone called from near the entrance. Mabel turned and spotted her brother in the doorway, his coat dripping onto the floor. His short fair hair was covered in raindrops, which dispersed as he ran a hand through it.

"Michael! Come sit with Mabel. I'll get you a coffee in a moment," Betty called him over.

Mabel waved but turned her attention back to Gwen as the cafe waited with bated breath for her answer.

"Thinks he's Port Isaac's answer to Rick Stein," Gwen said.

"What do you mean?" Mabel asked. She broke off a piece of flake and offered it to Michael, who was staring longingly at it.

He shook his head, so Mabel ate it.

"The man buying The Fisherman's Rest. He's a fancy chef from London. Waltzed in and offered the asking price." Gwen shrugged.

"He's not turning Port Isaac into a playground for his rich London friends," an angry local called.

"Here, here," came the affirmation from the rest of the cafe.

"We'll have to wait and see what happens." Gwen's eyes danced with glee as questions poured in for her to answer. "Oh, Mabel? He needs furniture for the pub, so I recommended you to him. You don't mind, do you, dear?"

Mabel's mouth opened and closed, but no words emerged.

"Thanks, Gwen," Michael said, noticing Mabel's struggles.

"I can't work for this man," Mabel whispered across the table. Betty had gone to make Michael's drink, and the rest of the cafe's attention was firmly on Gwen. "I fought to keep the pub in the community. It goes against everything I believe in to help someone turn it into a fancy place that out-prices the locals. This is just the beginning. His London friends will move in and buy property, and we'll all be left without homes."

"Mabel, stop for a moment and catch your breath. You haven't even met the man yet. For all you know, he could have connections to the area. Do you believe Gwen's gossip?"

"It sounds like she's met him." Mabel scooped a mouthful of cream.

"Don't jump to conclusions, okay? I know you're not in the position to turn down work." Michael had always been the calmer and more logical one of them. Despite being twins, they were each other's opposite. Where Michael excelled in his career as an accountant, Mabel had inherited all the creativity.

"I need a new accountant." She slurped her drink.

"Good. I can finally replace you with a client who actually pays."

"I pay. I pay you in childcare." She stuck her tongue out. Michael had two little girls whom Mabel adored and often looked after when Michael and his wife wanted an evening out.

"Your skinny, decaf latte," Betty said, screwing her nose up.

"That is offensive." Mabel's expression mirrored Betty's.

"It's Elowen's idea. We have to be role models for the girls."

"The girls aren't here," Mabel pointed out.

"I know, but it's a lifestyle change."

Mabel's shoulders shook as she held back a chuckle. Michael sounded exactly like her sister-in-law.

"Whatever," he huffed. Betty shot Mabel a wink and returned to the counter to serve a group of tourists who had wandered in.

"Do you want a sip of mine? I won't tell Elowen."

"No. She'll find out. Gwen will probably tell her." Michael glared at the contents of his mug.

"Cheer up. Milly's six and Mia is four, so you've

only got another fourteen years until Mia is off to university and you can drink hot chocolates again."

Michael groaned and plonked a sugar cube into his coffee. "Don't you dare tell El."

"My lips are sealed. What are you doing out and about on a workday? I thought you'd be chained to your desk."

"I wanted to speak to you. Don't you ever answer your mobile?"

Mabel pattered her pockets, but she didn't have the phone on her. "You know I'm useless with technology."

"You give me so many sleepless nights. What if you fell and hurt yourself? You'd need to call me."

"Michael, I'm twenty-eight. I'm not a ninety-year-old living alone with ten cats."

"You do own a cat."

Mabel kicked him under the table. "Sorry, my foot slipped," she said with a sickly grin. "Why were you trying to get hold of me?"

"Do you want to come for dinner tomorrow night?"

"Is it healthy?"

"Mabel, it won't hurt you to eat a vegetable occasionally."

"I'll come if you promise Elowen won't cook a lentil shepherd's pie again. Who swaps mince for lentils? It was the most depressing thing I've ever eaten."

"It was pretty awful. I can't promise what it'll be, but you have my word it won't be lentil shepherd's pie." Michael held his hand out and Mabel shook it. They stared sternly at one another before dissolving into a fit of giggles.

"It's like having you two in here as children," Betty commented as she squeezed past them to put another log on the fire. "Your parents are very lucky."

"They are," Gwen added from across the room. For a brief moment, her expression softened and a small smile crossed her face before she cleared her throat and turned her attention back to a table of tourists.

"Thank you, Betty," Mabel said.

"How are they?" asked Betty. She leaned her hip against the table. Betty was older than their parents, but didn't have children. Instead, she'd devoted her life to the little cafe and the community. Betty was like an aunt to Mabel and Michael.

"They're okay. Granddad came out of the hospital yesterday," Mabel said. She'd spoken to her mother last night. Granddad Thompson had been in hospital for the past two weeks after a nasty fall. Their parents had rushed to Kent and had been there ever since. During last night's phone call, Mary, Mabel's mother, announced they were putting Granddad Thompson's house up for sale and he'd be coming home with them. She didn't know how long it would take to sort everything, so they were staying for the foreseeable. Mabel's father, Martin, had called out in the background to send his love. It had been a difficult conversation, and Mabel missed them.

"Your poor mother. It'll be good to have them home," Betty said before returning to serve another customer.

"I need to go. I've got a meeting in half an hour." Michael downed his coffee, wincing as he swallowed. "See you tomorrow."

Mabel sat back in her chair and sipped the dregs of her hot chocolate. She could still hear worried locals asking Gwen questions, but she tuned them out. It was something she'd worry about another day. Buoyed by her sugar rush, Mabel paid and left the cafe, ready to spend the afternoon battling with screws.

CHAPTER TWO

Mabel chewed on her bottom lip as she unlocked the barn. The rain had slowed to a drizzle today, but she was still concerned about the roof. A few buckets were strategically placed beneath leaks, which had appeared over the last few weeks. Mabel checked the buckets and was relieved to find only a few shallow puddles of water. It would have to be fixed before next winter, but Mabel's savings were rather sparse. With her coat zipped up to her chin, Mabel switched on the heaters. Despite the dismal weather, she needed to work on the dressing table. The commission had a deadline, and she was already behind schedule. Mabel opened the cabinet where she kept her sandpaper. She selected one with a high grit and put on her mask. This was the less-than-glamorous side of refinishing furniture.

As she scuff-sanded the areas she would paint, Mabel shed her coat and threw it over a chair in the corner. It was a messy job. Dust coated every inch of her and had burrowed its way into the depths of her hair despite it being tied back in a bun. Once the surface was rough enough for paint to adhere, she began the arduous task of cleaning. She had to ensure the barn was spotless, so the dust didn't mix with the paint. Mabel's phone vibrated in her pocket. Michael had texted her, reminding her she was having dinner with them tonight.

"I'm not *that* forgetful," Mabel grumbled. She wrung out a wet cloth and wiped the dressing table. It was much warmer now, so Mabel cracked open the barn door. Outside, it was still grey and drizzly but it was nice to have some fresh air blow in. Next to the doors were towering shelves littered with various paint pots. Mabel's nieces were fascinated with her wall of colours. All the shades under the rainbow were on those shelves, and if the exact hue wasn't there, then Aunty Mabel could mix it for them. Mabel plucked the tin of Jet Black from the row. With the help of a screwdriver, the lid popped open. Mabel plucked a paintbrush from the shelf and dipped it into the pot. She cursed as she caught a stray strand of hair, coating it with a streak of paint.

Hours passed as Mabel painted the piece, careful not to let the black paint bleed onto the areas that were being left natural. Mabel's body ached as she stood from the stool. Her back hurt from hunching over, and she had cramp in her fingers from gripping the paintbrush. A glance at her phone told her it was past lunchtime. Mabel washed her brushes in the sink and headed back to her cottage to shower. She was covered in dust and splodges of black paint.

Once washed and dressed in jeans and a jumper, Mabel went in search of lunch. Her fridge was nearly empty, with a single tomato and a bottle of out-of-date milk in there. She pulled on her raincoat and headed into Port Isaac to buy a few bits.

"Morning," her neighbour called.

Mabel waved but didn't stop to speak. She loved Mrs Lavender, but the woman could chat for hours without stopping once for breath.

The drizzle had stopped, but grey clouds still lurked above. At the heart of the harbour was a small corner shop, one of the few independent ones left in the area. In preparation for the upcoming season, Port Groceries's exterior had been painted a forest green and local artist, Zoe, had repainted the sign above the door. Despite its glossy exterior, the old wooden door stuck as Mabel walked in.

"Good afternoon, little Mabel," Mr Trelawney called from behind the till. He had owned Port Groceries for as long as Mabel could remember.

"I'm not very little these days, Mr Trelawney," Mabel said as she picked up a basket. They had the same conversation every time she popped by.

"You'll always be little Mabel to me, my love."

Mabel smiled as she chose a bottle of milk, cheese, and bread. The inside of Port Groceries was as charming as the outside. Dark green tiles covered the floor. They'd been there for as long as Mabel could remember and had come back into fashion. The original shelves lined the walls with products neatly displayed.

Mabel trailed a finger along the shelf, wondering how many times she'd been inside this shop. Too many to count. The community of Port Isaac was proud of their little grocery store. Whenever anything went wrong, someone would step in to help. Like last week when a disorientated seagull had flown into the window, cracking it. Within a few hours, it had been replaced, and the shop was open again while the bird was nursed back to full health by the local vet. Port Isaac worked like that. Everyone looked out for one another.

As Mabel moved to the next aisle, she noticed a stranger. He was tall, handsome, around her age, and standing right where she wanted to get to. "Sorry, can I get there?" She pointed to the tin of beans hidden behind his broad shoulders.

He grunted and moved a step to the left. "Thank you," Mabel said in an overly cheery voice. She picked up the first tin and added it to her basket.

"Is that all?" Mr Trelawney asked as she put the basket on the counter.

"Yes. I'm having dinner with Michael and Elowen tonight, so I only need lunch."

"I have comics for the girls. Hold on a minute." Mr Trelawney slowly made his way into the back room.

As Mabel waited, a shadow fell over her. The man from the aisle had joined the queue behind her.

"Is nobody serving?" he huffed.

"There is. He's nipped into the back to get something for me."

The man sighed and crossed his arms. Mabel glanced at the shelf behind him, her gaze lingering on him in passing. He must have been six foot tall with short, dark hair. His brow was furrowed and his stare was steely. Despite his surly manner, he was good-looking. He wore a chef's white shirt and black trousers. A dusting of flour covered his cheek, with a few flecks caught in his long lashes which framed his eyes. Mabel stifled a laugh at the solitary carrot clasped in his hands.

"Found them," Mr Trelawney announced. He held a stack of comics. "The girls asked me to put them to one side if they didn't sell. They mentioned cutting the pictures out for their scrapbooks."

"That sounds like an activity Elowen would encourage." Mabel glanced dubiously at the pile of comics.

"Indeed. I'll pop them in a bag for you so they don't get wet."

There was a huff from behind, and Mabel whirled on her heel. "Sorry, are we keeping you?"

"Yes. You are," the stranger ground out.

"I'm terribly sorry to keep you from Fluffy's lunch," Mabel quipped, staring at the solitary carrot.

"Mabel," Mr Trelawney warned.

"Why don't you go ahead of me?" Mabel stepped back to look at the bars of chocolate. Elowen was anti-sugar, so there wouldn't be a rich chocolatey dessert tonight. Mabel picked a bar for later.

The stranger's carrot was weighed and paid for.

"I hope Fluffy enjoys it," Mabel called after him.

"Mabel Appledore, please don't tease my customers." Mr Trelawney tutted.

Mabel grinned and stepped up to the counter.

"*You're* Mabel Appledore? The furniture restorer?" the stranger asked. He'd stopped with one hand on the door.

"The one and only."

"Do you sell furniture?" He stepped back into the shop.

"I upcycle and sell furniture."

"Can you buy it, restore it, and sell it?"

Mabel nodded, wondering where this conversation was going. Mr Trelawney had stopped scanning her items and was listening in.

"Good, I need some."

There was a pause.

"Some what?" she asked.

"Furniture," he said slowly, enunciating every letter as if she were stupid.

"Obviously. What kind of furniture? What kind of finish? What's your budget?"

"Oh, erm. I'm not sure."

Mabel let out a slow breath. She was used to indecisive customers, but this was the worst she'd encountered. "Well, where is the furniture for?"

"The pub. Sorry, I should have introduced myself." He pocketed the carrot and walked towards her, holding his hand out. "I'm Finn Hart. I'm re-opening the pub."

Mabel shook his hand and narrowed her eyes as she looked him over, reassessing now she knew who he was.

"Gwen suggested you might be able to help me," he said after a few moments of silence.

"She shouldn't have promised anything."

"Sorry. I'm sure I can find an online shop to order from. I thought it would be nice to keep everything local." He shrugged and went to turn, but Mabel reached out and grabbed his arm.

"Hold on!" She liked the idea of keeping everything local. Perhaps he wouldn't be an evil out-of-towner. "Why don't you visit my barn tomorrow, say eleven o'clock?" Mabel pulled a scrunched-up business card from her pocket. They'd been Michael's idea. He'd printed them last summer, and this was the first time Mabel had found a use for them.

"Okay. See you tomorrow." He walked out, all the while looking at her business card.

"Seems like an okay chap," Mr Trelawney commented once it was just them.

"Hmm, we'll see. I ought to get back so I can tidy before tomorrow." Mabel tried to keep her workspace clean and organised, but more often than not she found herself so caught up in the process she forgot to put things away. Michael said the barn was a representation of how her mind worked.

"Take care, little Mabel." Mr Trelawney waved

her off.

The walk home was uphill, and Mabel was laden with comics. It was beginning to spit and her hands were too full to pull her hood up. She tipped her head back and exhaled as fat droplets of rain rolled down her face.

CHAPTER THREE

"Maple Syrup!" two high-pitched voices squealed from behind the door. Mabel braced herself for the incoming whirlwind of her nieces. When Milly started speaking, she got Mabel's name wrong and called her Maple. From there, Mabel had assumed the creative nickname Maple Syrup.

"My little M and Ms," Mabel called as the door opened and her nieces threw themselves into her embrace.

"I wish you three would pick healthier nicknames," Elowen said from the doorway.

"There's my favourite sister-in-law." Mabel extracted herself from the two young children and greeted Elowen.

"I'm your only sister-in-law. It's lovely to see you, but why are you dressed as a sweet wrapper?"

The girls snickered from behind their mum and Mabel glanced down at her outfit. She'd thrown a red and white gingham jumpsuit over a cream jumper, with matching red trainers. Her blonde hair was scooped up into a messy bun with a scrunchie that matched her outfit.

"I hadn't realised." Mabel chuckled and handed Elowen a bunch of flowers. "Thank you for having me round."

"Michael said you only accepted the invitation on the promise that dinner wouldn't involve lentils." Elowen gestured for Mabel to follow her. As Mabel trailed behind with the girls holding her hands, she considered Elowen's outfit. She wore a pair of white jeans and a black silk blouse. Her hair was neatly tied back into a chic ponytail. It was put together and organised. Very much like Elowen. Mabel wouldn't last two minutes in white jeans without staining them.

"I didn't say a blanket ban on lentils, just lentil shepherd's pie," Mabel muttered. She let the girls lead her to their play area in the open-plan kitchen. Their toys were all made of sustainable wood and were beige and bland. Every Christmas, Mabel tried to sneak in some garish plastic tat, but it would always go mysteriously missing.

"I've made a tofu salad instead," Elowen said. She bustled around, putting the flowers in a vase.

Milly and Mia looked at Mabel, and their faces mirrored her horror.

"Yum," Mabel said while making a retching face.

"My thoughts exactly." Michael chuckled as he

walked into the room.

"Daddy!" the girls shouted and ran to him.

"Only just finished work?" asked Mabel.

"Afraid so. Can I get you a drink?" he offered.

"Yes, please. Do you have any wine?"

"We're doing dry June. There's elderflower cordial or water," Elowen said.

"I didn't realise dry June was a thing." Mabel raised her eyebrows at Michael, who was struggling to hold back a laugh.

"I'm doing it with my pilates group."

Mabel nodded as though she understood what went on in a group of women who met up weekly to do a torturous exercise class. She loved her sister-in-law, but sometimes Elowen needed to lighten up.

"I'd love some water, please."

Half an hour later, Mabel was sitting on the floor playing with the girls' dolls. Her back ached, but she didn't want to disappoint her nieces. A few years ago, Mabel had made little dresses for their dolls from fabric scraps. They still wore them, but they were rather tatty. Mabel made a mental note to get some new fabric.

"I met the new owner of the pub today," Michael said. He'd left Elowen to prepare dinner and was sitting with Mabel.

"So did I. He's a right pillo—idiot." Sometimes Mabel forgot little ears were around and would pick up on anything she said.

"What's a pillo, Maple Syrup?" Mia asked and climbed onto her lap.

"I was going to call him a pillow."

Michael's shoulders shook, and Mabel poked him in the ribs.

"Dad, you're such a pillow!" Milly giggled.

"Thank you, Mabel. Why do my children always learn new words when you visit?"

"Dinner's ready," Elowen called.

They sat around the dining room table. Mabel had her nieces on either side. Elowen had made a tofu salad and sweet potato chips. Despite her reservations, Mabel had to admit it tasted good.

"Did you make a good impression on Finn?" Michael asked. He was sitting across the table and had his stare trained on Mabel.

"Maybe? He took my business card, so that's a good sign, right?"

Michael groaned. "Mabel, you really need his business."

"I'll be perfectly polite. He's popping around tomorrow to discuss what he wants."

"Do you want me to be there?"

"Michael, I am capable of running my own business, but thank you."

"Is this the infamous Finn Hart?" Elowen asked.

Mabel turned to her sister-in-law, who had been quietly listening to the conversation. "Infamous?"

"He worked at a very successful restaurant in London. Well, so I've heard. Some mums were talking about him when I collected the girls from school tonight."

"He certainly seemed to know the business when I met him. I offered to do his accounts, but he declined, saying he already had an accountant."

"That's rude. He told me he wanted to keep everything local. I'll have a word with him tomorrow."

Michael groaned and held his head in his hands. "Mabel, do not have a word with him. The last thing we need is for both of us to lose his custom."

"Fine. Your loss." Mabel shrugged.

Milly and Mia monopolised the conversation over the rest of dinner, each recounting their days.

"Don't forget to turn Mia's night light on," Elowen called at the bottom of the stairs. Michael had taken the girls to get ready for bed. They'd dragged their heels, not wanting to say goodbye to Mabel, but had eventually given in.

"So, what does this Finn Hart look like?" Elowen asked. She took the tea towel from the side and dried the dishes Mabel had washed.

Frowning, Mabel tried to recall her meeting with him. She remembered him being attractive, but her attention had been focused on his rude manner and solitary carrot. "I think he was tall," she offered.

"Mabel, you'll never get a boyfriend if you don't even notice a hot chef right in front of your nose."

Mabel flicked soap suds at Elowen. "El, I don't want a boyfriend," she whispered.

"Oh, Maple Syrup." Elowen pulled her into a

hug. "Not everyone is like that ratbag. You deserve to be happy."

"I am happy." Mabel sniffed. She leaned her head against Elowen's shoulder and closed her eyes.

"I know you are, but you don't have to do everything on your own."

"I tried it with someone, and it didn't end well." Actually, it had ended with Mabel's entire life crashing down around her. The man she thought she'd spend her whole life with cheated on her during the most stressful time of her life. Mabel had failed her university exams and returned to Port Isaac as a pale imitation of the girl she once was.

"Do you fancy a chocolate?" Elowen said.

"Aren't you anti-chocolate?" Mabel moved to the island and sat on one of the stools.

"For the girls, yes."

"And Michael?"

"And Michael," Elowen confirmed. Mabel chuckled as she watched her sister-in-law open one of the top cupboards and pull out a box of chocolates hidden behind a pile of organised Tupperware. They were dark chocolate and organic, but Mabel wasn't in a position to be fussy.

Elowen made them each a cup of tea and sat beside her. "It's decaf."

"Perfect." Mabel needed her beauty sleep. It was a shame she hated tea. "He's popping around tomorrow to discuss what furniture he wants. I'll text you and let you know what he looks like."

"Do you think you could get a sneaky photo?"

"No!" Mabel laughed around her mouthful of chocolate. Despite being polar opposites, Mabel had always loved Elowen. From the day Michael introduced them, they'd enjoyed each other's company. It was in their spare room where a broken-hearted Mabel rebuilt her life.

"What's going on here?" asked Michael, his gaze on the box of chocolates which Mabel had almost demolished. There were a handful of strawberry-filled ones left.

"We were having a chat," Mabel said, poking her tongue out at her brother.

"Where did those come from?" Michael had wandered over to inspect the box.

"They were a gift from one of the mums at school after I collected her daughter last week," Elowen explained.

"Why didn't we share them in the evening?" His voice had a child-like whine to it.

"I was saving them for a special occasion."

Mabel nibbled the edge of a strawberry-filled chocolate as she watched them bicker. Occasionally, at times like this, she regretted her decision to remain single. But then she would remember how her entire life had been destroyed and knew it wasn't worth the risk.

"I'm ready to go home now if you can drive me," Mabel piped up. She was looking forward to getting home and snuggling under the duvet with a hot chocolate and the latest series she was binge-watching.

It was still light outside as Michael drove through the harbour. Mabel's cottage was on the other side at the top of the hill.

"Don't mess up your meeting with Finn tomorrow," Michael said. "You're barely making your mortgage repayments."

The reminder was like an anchor around her heart. Mabel was very aware of her dire financial situation. Before the pub closed, she worked there part-time to top up her income. However, since its closure, she'd relied heavily on her furniture and was struggling to make ends meet.

"I'll be on my best behaviour," Mabel promised.

Michael drove her to the door of her single-storey home. *Bluebell Cottage* overlooked the harbour, and despite it being a little tired and draughty, Mabel adored it. She'd bought the cottage because of the barn, but as she'd slowly made it her home over the last few years, she'd fallen in love with it.

"Let me know how it goes," Michael called as she climbed out of the car.

"Will do. Thank you for dinner and the lift home. Love you."

"Take care."

Mabel kicked off her shoes and threw them onto the pile by the door. She went straight to put the kettle on. The kitchen was basic, but she'd made the most of it. When Mabel had moved in, the cupboards had been painted a horrible shade of lime, so she'd stripped them back to their original oak.

They looked pretty now, with the new sage handles Mabel had added. It was small, with just enough space for a fridge and a washing machine, but Mabel didn't mind since it was only her.

While the kettle boiled, she went to change into a pair of pyjamas. The cottage was one bedroom, and the bed took up most of the space, with a small bedside table squeezed in on her side. She'd hung plants from the ceiling to take away from the bland white walls. Mabel had wanted to wallpaper in there but hadn't got around to it. Her bed was made with a pretty floral duvet and a thick knit throw. A rug covered most of the floor and kept her feet warm during the winter months. It was cosy and all hers.

Not wanting to stand over the hob while she heated milk, Mabel made a hot chocolate with hot water and instant powder and took it back to bed with her. She flicked on the television while she Googled Finn Hart.

CHAPTER FOUR

Googling Finn Hart had been a terrible idea. As it turned out, he was a famous chef, earning a name for himself after working for the famous Lachlan McLeod in Mayfair. Mabel was anxious at the prospect of him visiting her barn today. She'd made an extra effort with her outfit, picking out a pair of jeans and an oversized shirt with only a few splatters of paint. The barn was as clean as she could get it. Mabel had spent half an hour scrubbing a patch of pink paint from the floor but gave up when she realised it was making no difference. It was as she headed back to the cottage with a bucket of dirty water and wearing luminous yellow rubber gloves that Finn walked up the garden path. He hadn't spotted her yet, which gave Mabel enough time to give him a once-over. Now she knew of his background at a fancy London restaurant, she could see his polished manner. The last chef the pub had hired was a man in his late forties with questionable hygiene standards, thinning hair, and a penchant for sneaking out the back for a cigarette. Finn Hart was immaculate. His towering frame loomed over her cobbled path. His jeans moulded to his legs and his smart coat looked like it had never seen a droplet of rain. It was a warm day, and his hair shone in the sun, but even from afar, Mabel could see the storm brewing in Finn's expression.

Mabel picked up her feet as she watched him approach her front door. "Morning!" she called. He turned to look at the same time as her foot caught on a stone. The world tilted towards her and Mabel shrieked as the bucket of dirty water sloshed all over her. With a thump, she landed on her bum on the cold, hard cobblestones. Wet clumps of hair stuck to her face, and her shirt clung to her body. A chill blew across the garden and Mabel shivered.

"Here, let me help." Finn held out his hand.

Mabel cringed but accepted. He helped her to stand and picked up the empty bucket. "You should get your shirt in to soak or it'll stain." He was staring, and to Mabel's horror, she realised the white shirt had turned see-through.

"I need to get changed. Why don't you come in and make yourself a drink?" Mabel didn't wait for a reply. She squelched to her front door. It was unlocked, Mabel never locked it, despite the countless lectures from Michael.

Finn silently followed. "The kitchen's through there. I'm going to jump in the shower and change.

I'll be with you in five minutes. Make yourself at home."

It wasn't until Mabel was in the shower, scrubbing the pink remnants from her skin, that it dawned on her she'd let a stranger into her home without thinking twice. Albeit, he was a semi-famous chef.

With wet, but clean, hair, Mabel pulled on a jumper and leggings and went to see what Finn was doing. He stood in the middle of her kitchen, frowning at the kettle, which was still boiling.

"It's broken. It'll never click off," Mabel said, manually switching it off.

"I did wonder. Do you have any coffee? I had a quick look but couldn't find it and didn't want to rifle through your cupboards."

"I don't drink coffee."

He frowned. "What about when you have guests?"

"I don't have guests." It was true. Mabel couldn't remember the last time anyone had popped to hers for a drink.

"Okay. Well, what do you have?"

Mabel went to the cupboard and pulled out an industrial tub of hot chocolate powder. "Hot chocolate?" she offered.

"I haven't had hot chocolate since I was a child." He rolled his eyes and Mabel fought the urge to throw him and his superior manner out of her cottage.

"You're missing out."

"Go on then. Show me what I'm missing out on."

Never one to back down from a challenge, Mabel pulled out two mugs and spooned the powder into them.

"Isn't it better to use melted chocolate?" Finn asked. He'd moved out of her way and leaned against the sink.

"Yes, but that's a treat. This is everyday hot chocolate."

"I didn't realise there was a distinction."

Mabel got the milk from the fridge and noticed him watching her with a small smile playing on his lips.

"I'll make these and show you over to the barn." Mabel needed to get this business meeting back on track.

"Have you lived here long?" Finn asked as she handed him a mug.

"Long enough. Why?"

"Oh. I saw the boxes and thought maybe you'd recently moved in." He inclined his head to the stack of cardboard boxes in the living room. They took up most of the floor space and Mabel had to squeeze past them every time she wanted to get to the kitchen.

"They're supplies. The barn's temperature is too changeable, so I keep them indoors."

Finn nodded but kept glancing towards them.

"Shall I show you examples of my work and you can tell me what you're looking for?" Mabel gestured towards the door. She was eager to get him away from her home.

Mabel led the way to the barn, along the overgrown path which wound behind her cottage. She was too overwhelmed by the morning's events to fill the silence with pointless chatter. They reached the barn doors and Mabel juggled her hot chocolate as she heaved open the towering wooden door. Light flooded into the space and a flush of pride overcame her as she looked at her half-finished pieces.

"This is where the magic happens," Mabel announced and stood aside so he could walk ahead of her. He raised a brow but stepped inside.

Mabel rested against the doorframe and sipped her drink as she watched him wander around the space. She was working on four pieces and had taken the protective sheets off of them that morning. Each one was at a different point in the process.

"What is it you're looking for?" she asked.

"I need furniture," he said, glancing around. "Nothing too fancy or frilly like this." He jabbed a finger at a towering, early eighteenth-century armoire. Mabel had been commissioned to paint the piece a pale pink and to decorate it with floral decoupages. She was halfway through the project and it looked stunning. It was for a local hotel opening in Padstow-on-Sea. They'd asked her to design bespoke items for each room. The armoire was the last piece. They were yet to pay her invoice and so work had stalled.

"Lucky for you, that piece is not for sale."

"What do you do with all this…stuff?"

Mabel fought the urge to kick him in the shin. *Stuff*. Nobody had ever spoken about her bespoke furniture like that.

"The armoire and the dressing table are commissions." She didn't mention the dispute over payment. "Then the dressing table and bed frame are pieces I got at an auction. Once I've finished, I'll sell them."

"Do you have any finished pieces I could see?"

"Not here. I could get together a portfolio to show you." Nobody had ever asked for proof of Mabel's excellent work before. Word of mouth had spread amongst the local areas and work had dribbled in enough to scrape together her monthly bills.

"Yes, please."

They lapsed into silence as he wandered around, taking everything in. Mabel sipped her hot chocolate and watched him. She still couldn't believe he was a semi-famous chef. What was he doing here?

"So, what brings you to Port Isaac?" Mabel asked. She needed to know his intentions before she agreed to work with him. Despite Michael's worries about her financial position, she wasn't, hypothetically speaking, about to get into bed with the enemy.

He stared, and Mabel felt his gaze bore into her. She looked away and glanced at her mug.

"I'm reopening the pub," he said and turned back to the Art Deco dressing table.

"I know that, but why?"

He cleared his throat. "I've been looking for a new challenge and this opportunity almost fell into my lap. It seemed like the right time and the right place." He shrugged. "If you believe in stuff like that."

"Do you?"

"Perhaps. Anyway, I need to get back. I've got things to do."

"Got to get back to feed Fluffy?" Mabel couldn't help herself but instantly regretted the dig.

"The carrot was for a dish I was trialling." His face showed no hint of amusement.

"A single carrot. You might want to review your market research for the local custom."

He sighed. "It's been lovely to meet you, Mabel. I'll be at the pub all day tomorrow. Why don't you pop in with your portfolio? Then I should be able to give you a comprehensive list of what I need." He'd snapped back into formal mode.

"Yes. I'll see you tomorrow."

He handed her his mug and left without another word. Mabel watched him leave before looking at the full mug. He hadn't touched his hot chocolate. She sipped it and went inside to pull out her laptop. First on her to-do list was to Google how to create a portfolio.

"How did it go?" Michael asked. He'd popped in on his lunch break for a debrief.

"It was fine. He looked around my barn and asked about my portfolio." She decided not to mention the incident with the bucket of water, or that she'd forced a mug of hot chocolate on him.

"That sounds positive. How's it coming along?"

Mabel made a non-committal sound.

"Mabel." Michael's voice was stern.

"I got distracted and ordered an Edwardian display cabinet."

"Mabel." Michael rubbed a hand across his chin.

"It's a bargain. Will you help me pick it up at the weekend?"

"Perhaps. I'll have to check the girls' schedules. Hand me your laptop and I'll help you create a portfolio."

"Thank you. Do you want a drink?"

"Do you have anything other than hot chocolate?"

"I have water."

"I'm fine. Sit next to me and I'll talk you through this. What would you say are your best pieces?"

An hour later, Mabel had a folder on her desktop filled with images of the pieces that best showcased her talents. Once she'd focused on the task, it had been easy. Michael had also suggested she bring her sketchbook, which was filled with ideas for furniture.

"Your work speaks for itself, Mabel. Please, don't say anything to offend Finn, and you should have this contract in the bag." Michael glanced at his watch. "I should go. I'm picking the girls up from school."

"Where's Elowen?" Mabel closed her laptop and put it on the coffee table before stretching. She wasn't used to sitting for such long periods.

Michael's stare was focused on the empty fireplace as he answered. "She's got a job interview in Padstow-on-Sea."

"A job?"

"We need the extra income," he admitted and when he turned to look at her, Mabel realised how drawn he looked and the wrinkles on his forehead had deepened.

"Michael, why didn't you say something?"

"You're struggling yourself. I didn't want to worry you."

Mabel grasped her brother's hand and squeezed. "I'll get this job. I promise. Then I'll pay you like I would a normal accountant. No more twin rates. I want to pay my way."

Michael sighed. "That would really help. Thank you."

Things must be bad. Michael hadn't even attempted to dissuade her. She'd tried to pay him when he started doing her accounts, but he'd resolutely refused and told her if she felt so passionately about it, then to donate the money to a charity of her choice. Mabel had set up a direct debit to the local cat sanctuary.

"Come on. I'll walk down to the school with you." Mabel ran to her kitchen and pulled out four small chocolate bars. If Elowen was away at a job interview, she would never know.

CHAPTER FIVE

Mabel was awake bright and early the following morning. She'd added another coat of paint to the Art Deco dressing table before the birds had risen. Now, with the soft hum of bird calls and the sea crashing below, she wandered to the harbour for an early morning swim. Mabel had dressed in her favourite bright red swimming costume and had shoved a towel into her bag. It was her most cherished time of the day when the streets were quiet and Port Isaac was readying itself to rise for the day. She propped her bag against the wall and removed her clothes. It was still early in the year and the sea was cold. She hissed as it lapped at her legs. With a deep breath, Mabel plunged into the chilly water before coming up and gasping for air. A giggle escaped her as she splashed around. Needing to warm up, she swam out to the harbour entrance and back. There were no boats at that time of the day. She was easy to spot in her red costume, but the fishing boats had already left and the tourists wouldn't descend until later.

The worst part of her morning swim wasn't getting into the water, it was getting out. Goosebumps covered Mabel's skin as she jogged across the beach to her towel. Once wrapped in it, she poured hot chocolate from a flask. The village was waking and Mabel relished being in the middle of it. She sipped the warm, thick drink and leaned back against the rock.

"Are you okay? Have you spilt something down yourself again?" a gravelly voice called from behind.

Mabel counted to five before she turned to Finn Hart. "I've been for a morning swim," she explained. He wore running shorts and a fresh sheen of sweat glistened on his forehead.

"A swim sounds like a fantastic idea." He looked wistfully towards the sea.

"You should try it." Mabel could imagine the group of school mums dropping the children off early to get a glimpse of Finn in his swim shorts. It was a sight even she was eager to see. A flush crept up her neck and she pushed away the thoughts.

"Perhaps. Not today. I've got a Zoom meeting in twenty minutes. Are you still popping by later?"

"Yes. I'll head home, get ready for the day, then walk back in."

"Brilliant. See you later." He gave her a smile before disappearing through the passageway to the back entrance of the pub.

Mabel's shoulders sagged, and she finished the last of the hot chocolate. Steam poured out of a window above and Mabel gulped as she realised it was coming from the pub. "Time to go," she muttered, throwing her clothes over her damp costume.

Shop doors were opening and coffee machines whirled as Mabel walked up the hill. She shared a few good mornings with those she recognised. By now, everyone knew Mabel went for an early morning swim and they were used to seeing her traipse through the streets with dripping hair.

⟫⟫⟫⟫ ⟪⟪⟪⟪

Mabel stared at the contents of her wardrobe and did her best to channel her inner Michael. What would he approve of for her business meeting? She flicked through the hangers before settling on a sage linen jumpsuit over a white t-shirt. It was one of the smartest outfits she owned, and by smart, she meant it didn't have paint or furniture varnish splattered across it. Once satisfied she looked somewhat professional, Mabel gathered her laptop and sketchbook and set off into Port Isaac. It was a lovely day with a warm sun appearing in between a handful of fluffy white clouds. Gwen was heading to Fisherman's Brew and Mabel stopped by the community noticeboard so she didn't bump into her. The older woman would want to know where

Mabel was off to, and in a few minutes, she would have wheedled an invite to the business meeting.

Once the route was clear of nosey neighbours, Mabel continued her walk to Fisherman's Rest. The front doors were boarded shut, so she slipped down the side alley. She wandered past the lobster and crab mural which had been there for as long as she could remember. A back door was wide open and Mabel knocked, but nobody greeted her. She walked into the industrial kitchen and poked her head around the next door to find a hallway with a set of stairs.

"Hello?" she called, but there was still no answer. Having worked at the pub, Mabel knew her way around the warren of hallways. She took the door on the right, into the bar area. It was empty, so Mabel set up for their meeting. She swiped a finger along the bar to check it wasn't sticky before she put her laptop and sketchbook down. The pub was stripped of all its contents. Mabel had been there on the final day when the community had created a human chain and passed chairs and tables along and onto the back of a van so the owners could sell them. Now, The Fisherman's Rest looked very sorry for itself. The dirty carpets could be seen in all their glory and the walls were stained yellow. Mabel cringed. It was probably the nicotine seeping through from the days when smoking in pubs was allowed.

"How did you get in?" Finn appeared.

"The back door was open. I did knock and call

out." Mabel kept her back to him as she continued to assess the room.

"There's a lot to do," Finn said. His voice had lost the accusatory edge, and Mabel could detect a weariness.

Mabel chewed her lip. She couldn't deny it. The place looked tired. "What are your intentions, Finn?"

"What do you mean?"

Mabel turned. Finn was on the other side of the bar with his elbows propped on it and his chin resting on his hands. "What are your plans for the pub?" She dragged an empty barrel to the bar and sat on it.

"I want to open a bustling pub which serves both the locals and tourists."

Mabel narrowed her eyes. "That sounds very bland and rehearsed." She stopped herself before she could say anymore. If Michael had been with her, then the conversation would never have gone this far. She was on thin ice and needed to tread carefully or else she'd lose the contract.

He rubbed a hand across his face. "I want this pub to be the thrumming heart of the community."

"Good. You shout that from the rooftop and you'll have the help of the entire village behind you, Finn Hart."

"Do I literally have to shout it?"

"Of course not."

"I wouldn't have put it past you." He held up his hands and Mabel chuckled.

"I'll let that one slide. Finn, if you need help,

then it's right outside your door. This pub was the heart of Port Isaac, and we were bereft when it closed. If you plan to give it back to the community, then they'll support you through it. I could pop next door to Betty's right now and by lunchtime, she'd have a team ready to come in and clean the place from cellar to rooftop."

"You're certainly the girl around town to know." Finn looked lost in thought, so Mabel turned back to the pub. She'd missed the view. The pub was on the edge of the beach and elevated, so its big windows overlooked the sea.

"Mabel, will you help me get the community on board with the reopening?" Finn's expression was pleading. "Nobody will talk to me, and everyone glares when I walk by. I don't know where to begin."

Mabel clapped her hands and swivelled back to him. "You've made an excellent decision. I'll text Betty and the clean-up can begin."

"Brilliant." He smiled and Mabel mirrored it. His face had lit up, and he was very attractive once his surly manner had dissolved.

Before Mabel could switch her laptop on, Betty had texted back to say she would be there when Fisherman's Brew closed, with a group of willing volunteers.

"Okay, back to the matter at hand." Finn had picked up her sketchbook and was flicking through the pages. Mabel's heart thumped in her chest. She didn't usually allow anybody to look at her sketches.

"These are stunning," he said, opening the

book to a drawing of a baby grand piano which she'd repurposed into a drinks cabinet. Mabel had been enjoying a drink in one of the pubs in St Ives when she spotted the piano in the corner with a thick layer of dust coating it. She'd reached for her pencil and began sketching before her consciousness had caught up. Mabel had the idea of turning the piece onto its side. She'd used its existing legs but changed the placement. A few tweaks to the inside and shelving could be fitted to house bottles of wine or spirits. With a lift of the lid, it would unveil a useful purpose and would be a focal point, rather than gathering dust in the corner. Mabel had shown her sketches to the owner and given him a quote to which he had rudely thrown her out.

"I liked the idea, but it was a little out there. Most of the sketches in this book haven't seen the light of day. They're a few sparks of creativity from the deepest depths of my mind." She shrugged it off.

"You're very talented." He flicked to the next page and a soft gasp escaped him.

"Is everything okay?" she asked as he stared at the open page.

"Yes. Sorry, it's just this piece brought back a memory." He turned the page around to show Mabel a Mid Century vinyl cabinet. "My mum had one," he added.

"I restored that one. It had belonged to a couple, and the wife had died a few years before. The husband wanted it restored to its former glory to remember her."

"I wish I had known you when my mother died." Finn's voice was thick with emotion. "I threw out all of her furniture because it was damaged and I didn't know what to do with it. She had a vinyl cabinet like this one and some evenings she'd let me choose the record and we'd dance together." He sniffed and closed the book. "You're very talented, Mabel."

"If you ever find one similar, I'd be happy to restore it for you." She squeezed his hand and jumped slightly when her skin tingled. His eyes met hers, clouded with sadness, but a small smile tugged at his lips. Mabel shook herself off and pulled her hand back, ignoring the emptiness at the loss of his touch. "Let me show you some pieces that are similar to furniture you might want." She busied herself with the book, flicking through the pages.

An hour later, Mabel discovered Finn didn't have a vision for the pub's interior. He'd watched avidly as she clicked through pictures of past projects. Occasionally, he noted a colour or style he liked, but nothing matched.

"Finn, you need to find inspiration. This weekend, visit local pubs and see what they're doing. Work out what you want, and then we can discuss your budget."

"That sounds like a good idea. Will you come with me? I'm free on Saturday."

Mabel blinked and spluttered for words. She hadn't expected an invite. "I suppose I could come with you. Let me check my diary." Mabel got her phone from her pocket and opened the calendar app. Every weekend for the next six months was free, but she wasn't about to admit that to him. "Yeah, I can do next Saturday."

"Brilliant. Shall I pick you up at around ten? We can go for brunch, then move somewhere else for a coffee, and continue until we run out of pubs or can't stomach any more food or drink."

"Okay." Mabel stacked her sketchbook on top of her laptop. Was it a date, or a business meeting? Mabel wondered how she could ask him without it being obvious, but the moment was ruined when Finn spoke.

"Mabel, do you happen to know any of the local fishermen? I need fish, but they don't seem inclined to talk to an outsider."

"Why don't I arrange a meeting with the community? It'll be good for people to hear your intentions for the pub. Then you can also network with them."

"Yes, please. Thank you."

"Here, put your number in my phone. I'll text you a time and place."

"Mabel, this is supposed to be a business meeting," shouted Michael from the doorway.

"Get your mind out of the gutter, Michael. I'm setting up a meeting between Finn and the community." Mabel's cheeks blazed. "I don't usually ask men for their phone numbers," she explained to Finn, who chuckled and handed her back her phone.

"How can I help you?" Finn turned his

attention to Michael.

"I came to find out how your meeting was going." At least he had the grace to look sheepish.

"It went fine. Come on, you can walk me home and I'll tell you all about it." Mabel linked her arm through Michael's, leading him out of the pub. "See you soon," she called back to Finn.

"Goodbye Mabel, and Michael."

"How did it go?" Michael finally asked once they'd put space between them and the pub.

"It went well." Mabel replayed the meeting in her mind. Finn had been very complimentary about her work. His gaze had flickered between the laptop screen and her. Mabel cleared her throat and continued. "I've asked Betty to gather a team to help Finn clean."

"Is that a good idea?" Michael frowned.

"Why wouldn't it be?" They'd reached the top of the harbour and paused by a wall to catch their breath. The sea was calm today and sparkled a deep blue.

"We don't know what his intentions are. You need this work, Mabel, but I don't know if you should involve the entire community."

"He told me he wants to open the pub as the heart of the community again, and I believe him."

"You don't have the best history of knowing who to trust."

Mabel's stomach dropped. "How dare you bring that up!" she cried. "You're older than me by four minutes, Michael. That doesn't mean you can tell me how to live my life or dictate who I should or shouldn't trust. You need to back off." Mabel pushed away from the wall and walked away.

"Maple syrup," Michael called after her, but she didn't turn. He couldn't use her nieces' cute nickname for her to undo what he had said.

The walk home was slow as Mabel processed the pain Michael had unearthed. He was right. She hadn't been a good judge of character, and it was how she'd ended up with a broken heart and a future in shreds. But she was older now, and wiser. Plus, Finn Hart had kind eyes.

Once home, Mabel put out some food for Ethel, her ragdoll cat. At the sound of dinner, Ethel lazily wandered in from where she'd been asleep in the bedroom. A small patch of sun shone through the window onto Mabel's pillow and Ethel could often be found sleeping in it.

"Hello, you," Mabel greeted her, running a hand along her back. Ethel meowed and went straight for her food bowl. "I won't disturb you." Mabel went to make herself lunch when her phone vibrated. It was a text from Elowen. Michael must have already told her what he'd said. Elowen was asking if she wanted to meet for a coffee tomorrow morning. Mabel wouldn't hold Michael's behaviour against her sister-in-law and texted back to say she'd meet her at Fisherman's Brew.

CHAPTER SIX

"I ordered you a peppermint tea," Elowen said. She stood to hug a stunned Mabel.

"Thank you," Mabel eventually spluttered out. She pulled out the chair opposite Elowen and sank into it. Fisherman's Brew was busy this morning with parents popping in after the school drop-off. Mabel glanced longingly towards Betty, who bustled past with a tray of hot chocolates for the table in the corner.

"I love what you're wearing," Elowen said, pulling Mabel's attention back.

Mabel couldn't remember what she'd thrown on, so she glanced at herself. She'd opted for black leggings, a vest top, and a denim shirt over it. Nothing fancy. Meanwhile, Elowen was perfectly put together. She wore black skinny jeans which clung to her slender figure, a white silk blouse, and a grey blazer over it. Her hair fell in perfect curls framing her face and her make-up was flawless.

"Thanks," Mabel muttered. She knew what Elowen was doing and was not about to fall for it.

"I'm sorry for what Michael said yesterday," Elowen started.

"It's not your place to apologise for him. He's your husband, Elowen, not another child." Mabel's tone was harsh, but she was still angry.

"I know. He's under a lot of pressure at the moment." Elowen's gaze flickered around the cafe. Gwen's head suddenly snapped in the opposite direction.

"Is this a conversation that calls for a day out?"

"Definitely."

Mabel considered her to do list for the day. She'd woken up early and put a coat of paint on the Art Deco dressing table so she couldn't do anything more until it dried. "Why don't we drive over to Padstow-on-Sea? There's a new vintage jewellery shop I'd love to snoop around, and The Little Coffee Shop by the Sea does amazing hot chocolates."

"A new vintage shop?"

"Well, it's been open for a while. I sold the owner a refinished desk and promised I'd visit, but I haven't had the chance."

"Drink up and we'll make a move." Elowen sipped her peppermint tea and Mabel scrunched up her nose as she drank hers as quickly as possible, without lingering on the taste.

"Yum," she grimaced and put the empty cup down.

"It's an invigorating way to begin the day." Elowen rolled her shoulders before standing and stretching. "Let's go then."

They piled into Elowen's car and she drove them along the pretty lanes to Padstow-on-Sea.

"I should look into driving lessons the next time I get a big commission," Mabel commented as she grasped the seat. For all of Elowen's sensible ways, she drove like a racing driver.

Padstow-on-Sea was busy, and they had to drive around the car parks several times before finding a parking space. The water was a deep blue and calm. A steady flow of people walked towards the harbour, some stopping to read the menu at the fish and chip shop. The air was already filled with the smell of chunky chips and battered fish. Mabel's stomach rumbled, but convincing Elowen to have such an unhealthy lunch would be impossible.

"It's only going to get busier," Elowen commented.

"The poor residents. I'm glad Port Isaac hasn't produced a famous chef wanting to turn our home into a playground for their ego."

"Let's hope Finn Hart is one of the good guys."

"I think he is."

Elowen linked her arm through Mabel's as they followed the tourists to the heart of the harbour. "Do you have a soft spot for him?"

"Of course not. He seems like a genuine guy. I think he has the community at the heart of his plans."

"He's also very good-looking. Rumour has it, he jogs every morning. Occasionally shirtless."

"I've only ever seen him wearing a top."

"That's a shame."

Mabel laughed at Elowen's genuine disappointment. It had been ages since they'd had a trip out without Michael and the girls in tow.

"Do you want to jump straight into a chat and then wander around?" asked Mabel. Even with Elowen's upbeat mood, she could tell something was brewing under the surface.

"No, let's have a mooch around first. I want to forget my worries for an hour or two."

They popped into a few shops before they reached The Cornish Vintage Jewellery Shop. Mabel's heart picked up as she peered through the window at the rows of sparkling vintage and antique jewellery.

"The Cornish Vintage Jewellery Shop," Elowen muttered, looking thoughtful. "Does that make you The Cornish Vintage Furniture Shop?"

Mabel chuckled. "I suppose it does. I'll have to update my website and business cards. Come on, let's go in."

"Do you need moral support to stop you from buying anything?"

"I have a teeny tiny budget." She didn't, but Mabel knew walking away from this shop without a small trinket would be impossible. Besides, she almost had a contract with Finn, so she could afford to be a little frivolous.

"Good morning," Belle called, followed by a short bark from a little dog hidden behind the counter. "Sorry, please ignore Pearl. We've had a few customers feed her treats, so now she expects it from everyone."

"Oh, how adorable. Your shop is gorgeous," Mabel said, looking around.

"Thank you and thank you so much for the refinished desk you sold to me. It fits my office perfectly."

"I'm so happy to hear that." Mabel introduced the women.

"Enjoy your visit and give me a shout if you need any cabinets opened." Belle beamed at them.

Mabel wandered over to the antique diamonds. Each shimmered in the natural light pouring through the window. They were stunning, but even the smallest one was beyond her budget. Slowly, she moved over to the cheaper section.

"I love these bracelets," Mabel said, picking up a matching pair of gold bracelets from the shelf. They were like delicate daisy chains.

"Aren't they lovely? They're only gold-plated and are quite small, but they're from the eighties," Belle explained.

"They're gorgeous. Elowen, would you mind if I bought them for the girls?" Mabel turned, expecting to find her sister-in-law behind her, but instead, she was across the room admiring a cabinet filled with rubies. Mabel left the bracelets with Belle to wrap and went to see what had stolen Elowen's attention.

"Look at that ruby bracelet. Isn't it stunning?" Elowen whispered as Mabel joined her. It was a delicate gold bracelet with small, round-cut rubies all the way around. Each one glowed in the warm light.

"It's gorgeous. Your birthday's next month. Why don't you drop a hint to Michael?"

Elowen's face fell at the suggestion. "We couldn't afford it," she muttered and moved on to the next display.

Mabel glanced at the price tag. It wasn't too expensive. She'd seen Elowen and Michael spend similar amounts on each other without a second thought. Michael had said they were struggling, but it seems he'd hidden the extent from her. "Why don't I buy these for the girls and then we can get lunch and chat? My treat."

Mabel left the shop with a little paper bag. They walked slowly to the coffee shop. Elowen seemed lost in her thoughts, so Mabel enjoyed the buzz of the crowds. Inside the cafe, Mabel directed Elowen to find a seat outside in the courtyard while she ordered for them.

"Mabel! What can I get you?" Jada asked. She owned the coffee shop, and Mabel had met her through a local business networking group.

"Hi, Jada. Your pastries look amazing. Could I get a couple?" Mabel's mouth watered at the sight of the croissants and pain au chocolats displayed behind the glass case.

"Of course. They've been a hit ever since I introduced them. What can I get you to drink?"

"A hot chocolate and a peppermint tea, please."

Jada raised her brows as she used a pair of tongs to select two pastries.

"The peppermint tea's for Elowen."

"That makes a lot more sense."

Mabel took the tray of food and drinks outside and found Elowen sitting in the corner. She'd taken the seat in the shade. The courtyard was beautiful and had recently opened. Jada had employed a local builder to put down decking and build bespoke wooden seats and tables. Between the tables were pots of flowers filled with peonies and poppies. The smell was soft and subtle, and the gentle hum of bees floated through the air. It was a small haven amongst the heaving harbour outside.

"I got us a couple of pastries to share," Mabel announced. She had expected Elowen to turn her nose up, but instead, she tore off a piece of croissant and smothered it in marmalade. Mabel's stomach flipped at the sight.

"What's going on?" asked Mabel.

"Michael lost another client yesterday. We're already struggling to meet our mortgage repayments. Last night, we went through our finances. It's bad, Mabel." Elowen looked up from the pastry and Mabel could see the dark circles under her eyes. She'd tried to cover them with make-up, but they were still visible. "We might have to sell the house."

Mabel dropped the pain au chocolat. "You can't move! You love that house. It's the girls' home. All their memories are there." Mabel's voice was getting louder, so she stopped to take a deep breath. "But, Elowen, there are no houses in the village for sale."

Silence shrouded their table, and Elowen reached across to squeeze Mabel's hand. "We'd have to move further out to get something cheaper," she whispered.

Mabel was aghast. "You can't do that. Your entire lives are in Port Isaac. The girls love their school and all their friends. No, Elowen, you can't move. We'll find another way." It was Mabel's turn to squeeze Elowen's hand. There was a hollowness in Elowen's expression and a deep sadness in her eyes. "I'm going to get this contract with Finn Hart, and I'll help you."

"Mabel, you're barely making your mortgage payments."

"We're a family, Elowen. We'll do what we have to do to survive this. Leave it with me, I'll figure it out. You and Michael have supported me through my hardest days. It's time I repay that."

"Thank you. Shall we try to enjoy the rest of our day? We have another hour or so until we need to head back to pick up the girls." The emotion had cleared from Elowen's face and she tore off another piece of croissant. Elowen was good at compartmentalising emotions, and Mabel always found it a little disconcerting.

CHAPTER SEVEN

As promised, Mabel had arranged a meeting between Finn and the community. She'd hired the school hall and put notices around Port Isaac. Now, she was setting out chairs for the meeting to begin in the next hour. The hall was as Mabel remembered it when she was a pupil at the school. It was a big room with a high ceiling and polished wood floors with several nicks and dents depicting the years of use. There was a musty smell from a pile of mats stacked in the far corner, so Mabel had thrown open all the windows. Not knowing how many people to expect, Mabel put out fifty seats in rows. She'd rather have too many than not enough. They were those horrible, straight-backed, plastic chairs, but the only other option was to sit on the floor.

"Sorry I'm late," Finn said as he strode into the room.

"No worries. I'm almost finished here." She put

down the last chair and turned to him. He wore black trousers and a chef's shirt. It set his eyes alight and Mabel's heart fluttered.

"Where shall I put the food?" He gestured to the serving platter he held. An aroma of cumin and garlic emanated from the plate.

"Oh, um. I didn't realise you were bringing anything. Let me find a table." Mabel scrambled to divert her attention to the matter at hand. She lined up a few tables by the back wall and instructed Finn to lay the food out there.

"There's more in the van," he said.

"I'll help you. What did you make?" asked Mabel as she trailed along beside him. He towered above her, a strong presence by her side.

"I didn't know whether there'd be anywhere to refrigerate things, so I kept it simple. There's a beetroot salad with maple walnuts, a red pepper orzo salad, and a falafel and caramelised onion hummus salad."

"Lots of salads then." Mabel held out her hands to take a serving platter.

"Yes. I thought it would be refreshing. Did I misjudge it?"

Mabel's brow furrowed as she fought with her conscience. "I'm not sure, Finn. The older residents are probably more set in their ways. I'm sure the younger crowd will enjoy your salads."

"I'm going to offend them before I even open my mouth." Finn sighed. He put the platter down and scrubbed his hands across his face. He looked tired.

Mabel put her hand on Finn's arm to comfort him and was pleasantly surprised to discover the tense muscle underneath her fingers. "Don't jump to conclusions. Let's see how it goes, but be prepared to reassure people that you still intend to serve pub classics."

He opened his eyes and caught Mabel's gaze, and her heart stammered.

"I'm impressed. It's more than the solitary carrot you last cooked with."

"It was an ingredient." Finn gave her a stern look, but his eyes shone.

"What's this? I was hoping for an egg sandwich." Gwen had wandered in while they were talking.

"I was worried about egg in this heat," Finn said, quickly switching to a professional manner. Mabel took the opportunity to station herself by the door to greet people as they arrived. Poor Finn would be talking with Gwen for a while, so somebody had to oversee the smooth running of the meeting.

Once everyone had arrived, Mabel wandered back to the food table where a crowd had gathered. As she had suspected, there were grumbles about the food Finn had brought.

"Is this what you intend to serve at our pub?" Pascoe had asked, peering at the bowls through his spectacles.

"No. I want to serve local produce, but nobody will talk to me." Finn focused his surly stare on the elderly fisherman.

"Shame about that." Pascoe held Finn's gaze for a moment before wandering off.

"Well, I think it's lovely," Elowen said. She'd filled a plate for herself.

"Elowen." Mabel hadn't seen her arrive. She'd texted her and Michael to let them know about the meeting, but they hadn't been sure they'd get a babysitter.

"Michael's watching the girls, but I thought I'd come along and show support for our new publican," she said, beaming at Finn.

"Finn, this is my sister-in-law, Elowen," Mabel introduced them.

"Lovely to meet you. I've met your husband a couple of times. Most recently, when he collected Mabel from our meeting." Finn's expression danced with mischief.

"I'm very sorry about him. He's very protective of our little Maple Syrup."

Mabel groaned as Finn's face lit up.

"Maple syrup? What a wonderful nickname."

"Okay. Enough. Let's get this meeting started." Mabel strode to the front and clapped her hands to get everyone's attention. This wasn't the first time Mabel had held a community meeting.

"Thank you all for coming," she began. "There's been rumours floating around about the pub, so I thought it best to hear it straight from Finn Hart. We met earlier this week and Finn reassured me of his intentions to keep the pub at the heart of the community. There's lots to do to get the Fisherman's Rest back to its former glory, and Finn would like the community's help."

"Then why isn't he standing up there asking us for it?" someone called from the back row of seats.

"Thanks, Mabel. I'll take over now." Finn shot her a dazzling smile, and she stumbled into the closest empty seat.

Finn drew the room's attention as he introduced himself. "Thank you all for coming," he continued. "As Mabel said, I want to re-open the pub and keep it at the heart of the community. I intend to keep you up to speed with the plans. I'll be honest, for the pub to succeed financially, we need to attract some tourist trade."

The room filled with moans and protests. Mabel moved to join him, but Finn gestured for her to stay where she was.

"If you work with me, we can plan a future together. Right now, the cost of running a pub is astronomical; without outsider trade, we'll be bankrupt in a few months."

"What are your plans to bring in outside trade?" Elowen asked. She was sitting behind Mabel.

"I don't want to overcomplicate things. First and foremost, I'm a chef and that's how I want to attract people. Good quality, local food and alcohol. I know there's been complaints about the dishes I've served tonight and I'm sorry. A few things out of my control meant my options were limited." Finn glanced towards where Pascoe and his crew were sitting.

"You'll need fish," Mabel said, jumping up from her seat. It went against her nature to sit and watch the meeting unfold, and she'd finally spotted an opportunity to contribute. "Pascoe will pop by tomorrow afternoon and discuss his catch and what he can offer." There were a few grumbles from the fishermen, but Mabel noticed they didn't say no. "I can put you in touch with the local farms for meat and vegetables. What else is there?"

"I know a builder who could help," suggested local artist, Zoe.

"That's wonderful. The pub needs redecorating and new floors put in," Mabel said and looked to Finn, who nodded.

"His name's Nick Penhale. I'll scribble his number down for you at the end of the meeting."

"Fantastic. What else?" Mabel pulled out her phone and scrolled through the list she'd prepared earlier. "Ah, yes. Do you have dinnerware? Mugs? Cutlery?" she asked Finn.

He looked overwhelmed by her barrage of questions. "I don't think so."

"Brilliant. Zoe, you've recently been getting into pottery, haven't you? I spotted your mugs at The Little Coffee Shop by the Sea. They were gorgeous, by the way."

"Could you pop by tomorrow afternoon and we can chat?" Finn jumped in before Mabel could arrange anything.

"I'd love to. Shall I ask Nick if he can join me?"

"Yes, perfect. I'll open the pub up tomorrow and if you think you have anything to contribute, pop by and we can chat."

There were murmurs of appreciation from the crowd, and Mabel's body finally relaxed. It looked like they'd achieved the impossible and won the community over.

⫸⫷

People lingered, trying the new salads once the meeting was over. Mabel stacked chairs as Finn wandered around the last strays, talking to them and telling them about his background. Mabel longed to know more about him, but she was too far away to hear.

"He's even hotter in person," Elowen whispered and Mabel jumped, dropping the chair on her foot.

"Ouch," she cried.

"Mabel, are you okay?" Finn had darted across the room and helped her to sit.

"It looks like you're in capable hands and I need to get back to Michael and the girls. Are you still coming for dinner on Sunday?" Elowen asked.

"Yes, I'll see you then," Mabel said through gritted teeth. Her foot throbbed and Finn knelt in front of her, slowly pulling off her trainer.

"Do you think it's broken?" he asked.

"I don't think so. It'll just be bruised." She wanted to tell him to stop, but his touch was gentle and it was nice to be looked after by someone.

"It looks okay, but you'll need to ice it. Did you drive down?"

"I don't drive."

"I'll give you a lift home." He went to gather the empty serving platters before she could argue. "Don't move. I'll get these loaded and then come back for you."

Mabel scoffed but did as she was told. She took out her phone as he tidied around the hall and said goodbye to the final few people.

Unsurprisingly, Gwen was amongst them. "Taking you home, is he?" She winked.

"Yes, I've hurt my foot." Mabel gestured to the chair where Finn had propped up her foot.

"What an ingenious idea. It's like something I would have done when I was young." With another wink, Gwen left an open-mouthed Mabel staring after her.

"Do I need to do anything else to the hall?" Finn asked.

"No. The cleaner will pop in early tomorrow to give it a once over before the children arrive for school." Mabel braced herself on the side of the chair and stood. She let out a squeak of pain as she put weight on her injured foot.

"Here, let me." Finn wrapped an arm around her waist and supported her. "You might have to hop."

"This is so embarrassing," Mabel complained as Finn helped her to his van.

"Not at all. I really appreciate all your help, Mabel. Without you, I'd still be at square one, wondering where to begin."

He held open the passenger door and helped Mabel into the seat. She noticed a few people hanging around after the meeting. They were watching her get into Finn's van. The van must have been sold with the pub since it had the Fisherman's Rest logo on the side. There was no mistaking whose van it was.

"I'm guessing nothing happens around here without someone else knowing," Finn commented.

"Nope. It'll be all round the harbour tomorrow morning that you drove me home."

"Perfect," he sighed.

"I'm sorry. I'll try to nip it in the bud."

"It's not your fault. I could just do without the local gossips spreading rumours about my love life." His tone was harsh and his hand gripped the steering wheel.

"I'm sorry," Mabel muttered. She hadn't considered whether he was single or not. What if his girlfriend, or wife - she glanced at his hand but there was no sign of a ring - arrived to rumours of him going home with Mabel? "I'll make sure people know you drove me home because I was injured."

"Here we go. I'll help you inside." He swung the van into her unused driveway and came to help her out.

"I'll be fine from here," Mabel protested, but he wouldn't hear it. He helped her to the sofa and insisted on fetching a bag of frozen peas from her freezer. Mabel would have preferred if he hadn't, as she'd planned to use them for tomorrow's dinner, but he insisted she needed them to stop the swelling.

Mabel rested her leg on the coffee table while she waited for Finn to fetch the frozen package. She hissed in pain.

Finn was taking a while in her tiny kitchen. "Everything okay?" Mabel called.

"Yes. Sorry, I didn't realise you had a cat." He reappeared and settled the bag of peas on her foot.

"Be careful, she might scratch you. Ethel isn't a big people person." She only tolerated Mabel because she fed her.

"She was fine with me in the kitchen. Even enjoyed a good scratch under her chin."

As if on cue, Ethel wandered in and wound herself around Finn's legs, purring in happiness.

"I've never known her to take to someone like that." Mabel watched as she discovered another side of her cat.

Finn cleared his throat. "I should get off. Will you be okay?"

"Yes, I'll be fine. If it's bad in the morning, I'll call Michael or Elowen. Thanks for your help."

"Take care, Mabel." Finn gave Ethel a last scratch on the head before he left.

CHAPTER EIGHT

Mabel swung her legs off the bed and tentatively shifted her weight to her injured foot. A whoosh of breath escaped her as she felt the smallest twinge. She texted Elowen to let her know she was fine and didn't need help. After a slow breakfast of chocolate porridge, Mabel threw on her painting clothes and headed to the barn. She was still working on the Art Deco dressing table and the deadline was looming. Today she needed to add a clear lacquer to the painted areas and polish the exposed wood. It looked lovely. The black paint contrasted beautifully with the walnut veneer, highlighting its red hues.

It took Mabel a couple of hours to finish the piece. She'd spent a long time making sure there were no roller marks from the lacquer and then buffed and polished the wood and mirror. Dappled sunlight filtered through the trees and into the barn, making the buffed surfaces gleam. The air was filled with the smell of furniture varnish and wax. Mabel took a picture and sent it to the customer to let them know it would be ready once the final layer had cured. With that, she glanced around the barn and was painfully aware of how badly she needed more business. Michael had sent another email yesterday chasing payment for the armoire, but they hadn't received a reply. With nothing more to do, Mabel decided to wander into Port Isaac and ask Betty if she needed any help in the cafe.

Mabel closed her front gate as her neighbour called her name.

"Did your guest leave early this morning?" Mrs Lavender asked. She was leaning over the garden wall, a basket of clippings beside her. Mabel wondered how long she'd been outside for, waiting for Mabel to emerge.

"What guest?" asked Mabel, feigning ignorance.

"My milkman said his wife had heard Finn Hart went home with you last night."

Mabel let out a long, slow breath, and reminded herself that she loved her home, even if the residents of Port Isaac were overbearing. "He drove me home last night after I hurt my foot, but he only stayed for ten minutes." Whilst Mabel didn't appreciate explaining herself to nosey neighbours, she had promised Finn she would do her best to limit the gossip.

"That's not what I heard." Mrs Lavender sniffed.

"Sorry to ruin your morning." Mabel waved and set off before her neighbour could ask any further questions.

The day was pleasant and Mabel wandered slowly down the hill to Fisherman's Brew. Her foot throbbed with every other step and she was in a foul mood now. By the time Mabel reached the cafe, the lunchtime rush had dispersed. A few tables were occupied, but on the whole, the cafe was quiet. The season would begin in a couple of weeks, and then it would be difficult to get a table. With the change in weather, Betty had brought in the 'summer' decor. Little pots of lavender adorned each table, and the plain white linen tablecloths had been switched for pale blue ones. Butter-coloured napkins were folded at each table setting, and the mugs had been swapped for Zoe's handmade ones, with pretty floral designs painted on them.

"Afternoon, love," Betty called from behind the counter. She was taking payment from a young couple.

"Had a leisurely morning in bed, did you?" Gwen piped up from her usual table.

"I've been working." Mabel hobbled over to the table near the fire. It wasn't lit today, which was a blessing. The cafe was warm enough with the coffee machine working overtime and the oven filled with cakes for the following day. With so much spiralling out of her control, she needed the familiarity of Fisherman's Brew.

"Do you want lunch, dear?" asked Betty.

"Just a hot chocolate, please," Mabel said, thinking of her dwindling bank balance.

"Finn took her home last night," Gwen announced.

Mabel sank in her chair as a few locals glanced her way. "I hurt my foot, and he gave me a lift home."

"The woman who cleans for me was out walking her dog and saw Finn carrying you to your cottage."

Mabel grasped the edge of the table. She loved the community in Port Isaac, but sometimes she wished she could have the odd secret. "I couldn't put any weight on my foot, so Finn made sure I got indoors safely. He got a bag of peas from my freezer, gave Ethel a scratch under the chin, and then left. Would you like to pop along to the pub and check our stories match?"

Gwen pursed her lips and patted her neatly coiffed hair.

"Mabel," Betty chastised.

"Sorry. I'm stressed. All Finn did was make sure I got home okay. For all we know, he has a girlfriend. We mustn't spread rumours. Finn is giving Fisherman's Rest back to the community. The least we can do is show him a modicum of respect."

"He's single," Gwen announced.

Mabel groaned. Everything she had said, and that was all Gwen took from it.

"How do you know?" Betty asked. She brought over a hot chocolate and a slice of Victoria sponge. "It needs throwing out by closing."

Mabel knew it wouldn't go to waste. Any leftovers were bagged up at the end of the day and Betty's niece drove them to the local homeless shelter.

"Thank you," Mabel said and tucked into the cake.

"I asked him," Gwen announced. Her grin stretched across her face.

"You can't go around asking people if they're single," Mabel said around a mouthful of cake. It was deliciously light and fluffy, and the tart jam went perfectly with the sweet sponge.

"Oh, you young people are so sensitive. Back in my day, there was no harm in asking. You've been single for ages. It wouldn't hurt you to put yourself out there a bit."

"I don't want to put myself out there," Mabel grumbled. She wished she hadn't left the cottage today.

Gwen stared at her for a moment. "In my day, you would have been considered a spinster by now."

Mabel choked on her mouthful.

"I think that's enough, Gwen. Didn't you say you had a delivery coming this afternoon?" Betty prompted.

"Yes. I must go. It's my new garden furniture. See you tomorrow."

Mabel bit her tongue as Gwen left, not wanting to say anything she might regret.

"She means well." Betty leaned across the table to pat her hand.

"Could have fooled me," Mabel huffed. "Sorry, I'm stressed at the moment."

Betty pulled out the seat opposite Mabel. "Do you want to talk about it?" she asked.

Mabel pushed a piece of cake around on her plate. She did want to talk about it. Normally, she would have called her mother, but she had enough to worry about. She wanted to share her worries, but she couldn't. Half of her stress was Michael and Elowen's situation, but it wasn't her place to share it. Besides, as lovely as Betty was, she enjoyed gossiping almost as much as Gwen.

"Work's slow," Mabel admitted.

"I thought you were doing the furniture for the pub?"

"We haven't agreed to anything yet. Finn's still deciding what he wants."

"There's nobody around here as good as you, Mabel. See what happens. If nothing comes of it, I can move the rota around and give you a few shifts."

"I don't want to put you in a difficult position, Betty."

"Don't be silly. I could do with a few days off, so it wouldn't be a hardship."

"Thank you."

A customer came in and Betty left Mabel to finish her cake. Mabel felt as though the weight on her shoulders had lifted a little. She'd lain awake last night thinking about the situation and had already resolved to convince Finn he should employ Michael as his accountant, and then she would suggest

Elowen work some shifts in the bar or restaurant while the girls were at school. Finn Hart was going to be the answer to all her problems. But, if all that failed, she would accept Betty's offer of a part-time job at Fisherman's Brew.

After saying goodbye, Mabel wandered down to the sea. She hadn't risked her foot with an early morning swim, but she missed it. With the worries swirling around her head, a swim was what she needed. Instead, she removed her shoes and socks and rolled up her trousers. It was cold but refreshing. The water was crystal clear. Mabel walked out a little way and tiny fish darted around her, barely missing her feet. She breathed in the salty air and, for a moment, all her worries were silenced.

CHAPTER NINE

Mabel woke Saturday morning with a bubble of nerves in her stomach. She barely knew Finn, yet she'd agreed to spend the day with him. It was a long time since she'd spent time with a man. After her relationship ended and she returned to Cornwall, she tried dating, once. It had begun with the man staring at her cleavage and ended with her pouring a pint of beer over his head. Mabel started her day like any other and made a hot chocolate. As it was cooling on the side, her phone buzzed. It was her best friend, Adele.

"Hi, Del. What time is it there?" Mabel squinted at the time on her microwave and tried to do the maths, but she wasn't quick enough.

"It's only seven. I'm going out for dinner soon, but I wanted to call you first."

"I love hearing from you. I haven't got long, as I'm popping out soon."

"Are you going over to Michael's?" Del asked.

Was that all she did on a weekend? "No, I'm doing some research with a potential customer."

"Sounds exciting. I'll call you later in the week to see how it went. Look, I called for a reason." Del paused. "Mabes, I'm coming home!"

Mabel let out a squeak of excitement. "Really? Are you sure now's the right time?" Del travelled to Australia at eighteen and had worked her way around the country. She'd had a fantastic time and was always trying to persuade Mabel to join her, but it wasn't Mabel's kind of thing. She loved her home too much.

"I've got a job offer."

"I'm so happy for you, Del. When do you leave?"

"My notice period is three months, but I can use what's left of my annual leave, so I should be back in Cornwall by the end of summer."

"That's the best news I've heard in a while," Mabel said. "What's the job?"

"Marketing for a big chain of pubs. I know it's the kind of thing you hate. I'm sorry."

"It's okay. If they're bringing you home, then I can forgive them."

"Exactly. With my experience in breweries here, it makes sense for me to go in that direction with my career."

"I'm so happy for you, Del. Look, I really should go, as I've not even jumped in the shower yet."

"Of course. I'll speak to you in the week to tell you more and I want to hear all about you. Love you,

Mabes."

"Love you, Del. Speak soon." Mabel hung up and all her worries for the day were forgotten. Del always knew how to make her smile. They'd met on the first day of school when Mabel had been in tears after dropping the flower she'd picked and Del had sat beside her and hugged her. Del had gone home with Mabel that evening and they'd picked flowers in the garden and Mabel's mother had helped them arrange them in old jam jars. They'd been inseparable until Mabel went to university and Del flew to the other side of the world.

Mabel showered and dressed. She put on a pair of jeans with wildflowers embroidered on the back pocket and tucked a white t-shirt into them. With a clip, Mabel pulled back the front strands of her hair but left the rest down. A beep outside signalled Finn's arrival. Mabel gathered her phone and keys and ran out the door before he could come in again. She was surprised to find Finn waiting in a fancy four-wheel drive.

"How's your foot today?" he asked.

"It's okay. Thank you." He'd texted her yesterday evening to see how she was and whether she needed anything, but Mabel had declined his help. "This is a very fancy car," she commented.

"It's a loan from a friend while I find my feet. I stayed with him in Scotland while the purchase of the pub went through, and he insisted I borrow it."

"Nice friend." Mabel raised her brow. "Where are we off to?" she asked, keen to move the conversation along.

"I've found a pub between here and Padstow-on-Sea that does brunch, so I thought we'd head there first. Their website looks quite modern, and the menu sounds delicious."

"Brilliant." Despite the air conditioning blowing on her, Mabel undid her window a fraction to allow the fresh air in. "How did your meetings go yesterday?"

"They went well. Thanks for arranging it. I think the locals have everything I need to get the pub up and running again."

"Happy to help." Mabel beamed. She had been right to trust Finn and bring him into the community.

The first pub wasn't far. Finn pulled the car into a parking spot in the near-empty car park. From the outside, the pub looked like any other. Finn placed a hand on Mabel's back to guide her. She could feel his warm fingertips through the thin material of her t-shirt.

They were greeted at the door by a perky waitress. "Good morning. Table for two?"

"Umm, yes. Two, please," Mabel stumbled over her words as her mind focused on Finn's touch.

As the waitress led them to a table, Finn removed his hand and Mabel's senses returned. She looked around the interior. It had been done beautifully. A neutral colour palette had been used to create a warm atmosphere whilst keeping everything fresh and modern. The tables were oak and had been left unvarnished to allow the pale wood to blend into the colour scheme. Mabel ran her finger along the grain of the wood. It was perfectly smooth.

"Mabel?" called Finn.

"Hmm?" Mabel pulled her gaze from the wood and blinked a couple of times as her eyes adjusted.

"Shall we order our drinks now?" Finn was watching her, his brow furrowed.

"Of course. Can I have a hot chocolate, please?"

"Would you like cream and marshmallows?" asked the waitress, who was staring at Finn, not that he'd noticed.

"No, thank you. Finn?"

"A black Americano, please." He shot the girl a smile before he turned to the menu.

"Thank you," Mabel said, pulling the girl from her daze. "We'll decide what we want, so we're ready to order when you return with our drinks."

"What do you think of the menu?" asked Finn once they were alone.

"I haven't looked yet. I've been looking at the furniture and the decor. Remember the whole reason we're doing today's pub crawl?"

"Of course. Sorry, I've got a bit of a one-track mind and everything usually comes back to food or cooking." He put the menu down and looked around the pub. "This is nice. What do you think?"

"I love the warm neutral colours and the exposed wood, but I think it's a little devoid of soul."

"I suppose that's where we can bring in pieces

from locals. Like artwork, pottery, and so on," suggested Finn.

"Perfect. We can keep the decor relatively neutral and allow the locals to shine."

"We have the start of a plan, but I have one caveat."

"What is it?" Mabel leaned across the table towards him.

"I want your furniture to shine too." He held her gaze and Mabel blushed. She pressed the back of her hand to her cheek; as she suspected, it was warm.

"It doesn't need to shine." She played with the edge of her menu.

"I think anything you do will shine," he said.

They were interrupted as the waitress came over with their drinks. Mabel hadn't looked at the menu yet.

"Sorry, could you give us another five minutes?" she asked.

"Hold on," Finn said. "Do you trust me?" His eyes sparkled as he waited for her response.

"Yes?" It came out as a question.

"Can we have two of the vegetable omelettes, please?"

The waitress scribbled down their order and shot Finn one last flirtatious smile before leaving.

"She likes you," Mabel said, blowing on her hot chocolate.

"She's just being nice." He shrugged.

"Do you have a girlfriend back home?" Despite

Gwen's assurance, Mabel wanted to check for herself.

He shook his head and sipped his coffee. Mabel decided not to pry anymore. She'd already asked more than she had intended to. Instead, she sipped her hot chocolate. It tasted delicious, but the mug spoiled the experience. The plain white, thick-rimmed cup was boring, and too corporate for the pub's style. Finn was now tapping away on his phone, and she needed a distraction from watching him, so Mabel allowed her attention to wander. She could imagine similar oak tables in Fisherman's Rest, and a big country dresser, stripped back to the bare wood, used to display Zoe's pottery. Everything would be functional, but at the same time, it would look pretty. There also needed to be a cosy element. In those harsh winter months, when tourists are few and far between, the pub had to be a welcoming space for the locals.

"Two veggie omelettes," the waitress announced, putting the plates in front of them. Mabel was almost certain her plate had been plonked, rather than placed.

"Thank you." She smiled sweetly at the waitress, who ignored her.

Finn didn't acknowledge the woman as he continued to tap away on his phone. Mabel picked up her cutlery, which was another disappointment, and took a bite of the omelette.

"Mmm, that's amazing," she declared. The egg was soft and fluffy, the vegetables full of flavour, and there was a cheesy tang to pull it all together.

"Isn't it?" Finn had put down his phone and taken a bite. "I was reading their menu and they claim all the ingredients are from a ten-mile radius."

"Wow. You can really taste it." The rich flavours assaulted Mabel's tastebuds, and she savoured each bite.

"I think we're off to a good start."

"We had a lot of omelettes growing up," Mabel said. "My mum wasn't a very good cook, and it was the only thing she could make from scratch."

"An omelette was the first dish I learned to cook. My mum often worked late, so from a young age, I cooked for myself."

"Do you have any siblings?"

"No. It was only me and my mum." Finn's tone was laced with sadness as he looked up. "Although it was just the two of us, I was never lonely. Well, not until she got sick. When she was well, she made me feel like the centre of her universe and I could never have been lonely then."

"I'm sorry, Finn," Mabel said. She'd watched the way his face had clouded with pain as he spoke about his mother.

"Thank you. She'd have loved Cornwall. By now, she'd have the entire pub decorated and would be dragging you around local auctions to find furniture."

Mabel longed to hold his hand, but she didn't. What if her skin tingled again? No, it was for the best if she didn't touch Finn Hart.

He cleared his throat. "What was the first thing you upcycled?"

"It was a bedside table that someone was giving away at a boot sale. They'd put a note on it saying it would go to the tip if nobody took it. Even at ten years old, I couldn't bear the thought of it being destroyed. It held memories of past lives and I thought that was something to be celebrated. When I dragged my mum over to it and asked if we could take it home, she gave me a very odd look." Mabel chuckled and Finn's warm laugh mingled with hers. "My dad's shed was filled with paint, so I picked my favourite colour and smothered the piece in it. Needless to say, it looked awful, but my parents still gave it pride of place in their bedroom. I redid it for them a few years later when I knew what I was doing."

"You're lucky to have such supportive parents." Finn's tone suggested there was something beneath his words, but Mabel didn't pry.

"I am, but the business didn't begin from there. Upcycling was a hobby until my life fell apart. It was all I'd ever known and so, out of necessity, I turned it into an income. I wouldn't change it now, but it was difficult."

"Nothing worth having is ever easy," he said, and winked.

CHAPTER TEN

They left the first pub and drove to Padstow-on-Sea. It was a beautiful day and, being the weekend, everywhere was busy, but Finn had effortlessly navigated the Cornish roads.

"I'm so full I can't eat any more food right now," Mabel groaned. Two hot chocolates in one morning were too much, even for her.

"Let's go for a walk instead. I've got a call in an hour, so I need to make sure I have signal."

They left the car in the main car park and walked to the harbour. It was busy, so Finn kept close, his arm brushing against Mabel's. His skin against hers sent Mabel's pulse racing. It had been a long time since she'd been anywhere near an attractive man.

"It's nice," Finn commented. They'd reached the harbour, and he paused to take in the surroundings.

"Is this your first time here?"

He nodded, and Mabel tilted her head to the side. "You're a chef. You've bought a pub in Port Isaac, and you've not visited the famous food spot half an hour down the road?"

Finn scratched the back of his neck and squinted across the water. "I haven't had time to be honest. Taking on the pub was a bit of a last-minute decision."

"How so? Come on, let's wander or else we'll be swept up in a wave of angry tourists." People were tutting as they blocked the path.

He followed her. "I opened a restaurant in Mayfair last year," he said, trailing behind.

"That's exciting. A completely different vibe to Cornwall, I'd imagine?"

"Very different. I thought I knew it all after working in a successful Mayfair restaurant. It took two years to find financial investors, then I had to find premises and employ interior designers. By the time we opened the doors, I'd re-mortgaged my flat, and spent every penny from the investors, and still, the restaurant needed money. It was a complete disaster, and we closed the door after a couple of months." He was walking by her side now, but Mabel could tell from his body language that his thoughts were far away.

"I'm sorry." She reached out to touch his arm, and he jumped. "Sorry," she whispered, pulling back her hand.

"No, I got distracted by the memories. Anyway,

enough about me. I take it you've been here before?"

"Of course!"

"Then I'd love a tour."

They wandered around, popping in and out of the little shops. Mabel was in her element showing Finn around and telling him stories about her childhood, like when she and Michael caught the wrong bus home from school and ended up in Padstow-on-Sea. They hadn't worried and had enjoyed fish and chips on the sea wall while they waited for the correct bus. Meanwhile, their mother had been frantic with worry when they hadn't arrived home.

"I should find somewhere quiet to take this call. Will you be okay?" Finn asked.

"Of course. Call me when you're done and we can meet up." Mabel gave him an awkward wave and wandered into the crowd. It was a warm day, and they'd been walking for the past hour, so she decided to head to The Little Coffee Shop by the Sea. The queue was out of the door, but she knew the wait was worth it.

"Hey, you," Zoe called from a table in the corner as Mabel made it through the door.

"Hi," Mabel greeted her.

"Come join me once you've ordered," Zoe insisted.

The queue went down quickly and Mabel ordered an iced chocolate milkshake and went to join Zoe while she waited for it to be made.

"How was your meeting with Finn?" asked

Mabel. Zoe had a few sketchbooks scattered across the table with drawings of mugs and plates.

"It went really well. Thank you so much, Mabel. This is what I needed to help me and Jada with a deposit for our own place."

"You're moving in together?"

"Yes. I'm letting go of my studio in Port Isaac. I've been living at Jada's, but having all my stuff at the studio is difficult, and Jada's flat isn't big enough for me to bring anything back."

"I'm so happy for you." Mabel didn't voice her worries, but she wondered how Finn was funding this. He said he'd lost everything in his Mayfair restaurant, so how had he bought the pub, and how was he spending a fortune refurbishing it from the cellar upwards? Fear nibbled away at her insides. Had Mabel been too quick to trust him?

Finn's meeting lasted almost two hours. Mabel kept herself busy chatting with Zoe, and eventually, Jada joined them for her break. When Finn called, Mabel was on her second glass of tap water and felt she was distracting Zoe.

"Sorry, that took a lot longer than expected," he explained.

"It's okay. I've kept myself busy." Mabel waved goodbye to Zoe.

"Are you ready to try our next location? We might be too late for lunch, but what about afternoon tea?"

"Sounds wonderful. I'll meet you back at the

car."

Finn was looking decidedly dishevelled when Mabel joined him. His hair was sticking out in all directions as though he'd been running his hands through it, and deep lines were etched across his forehead.

"All okay?" Mabel asked.

"Just boring business stuff." He shrugged and pulled the car out of the space before Mabel had even put her seat belt on.

Finn didn't offer any conversation on the journey, and Mabel didn't push. It was obvious his call hadn't gone well. They reached the next pub. It was a large whitewashed building in the Cornish countryside with blooming hanging baskets on either side of the entrance.

"This place has a stunning garden, but I think we'll sit inside so we can enjoy the decor," Finn said as he led the way.

It was as beautiful inside. Unlike the last pub, this one had soul. While it leant into the trend of raw wood, it also had splashes of colour in the upholstered chairs, the artwork on the walls, and even the napkins were hot pink with a gold scalloped edging.

"I love this." Mabel spun on the spot, taking it all in.

"It's different to this morning's one. I think we need a middle ground. This style will be too much for the locals, but the last one was too bare."

Mabel stared at him, wide-eyed. He'd hit the

nail on the head and she was impressed.

"I completely agree." She nodded, unable to look away from him. He smiled and the lines on his head smoothed.

"We have to order at the bar. Shall I get a cream tea for two?"

"Yes, please, but no tea for me."

"What do you want to drink?"

Mabel considered her options. "Will you ask if they'll do a glass of chocolate milk?"

Finn froze halfway through standing up. "A glass of chocolate milk?" he asked, his face a vision of horror.

"Yes, please." Mabel grinned.

"You have the tastebuds of a five-year-old." He tutted and wandered off to the bar.

While he was gone, Mabel cleared her mind of the niggling worries. It would do no good to focus on them this afternoon. They'd still be there tomorrow. Besides, she didn't want to be distracted in case Finn revealed any further reasons to distrust him.

"I think we know what you're looking for. Now we need to discuss the budget and see what second hand furniture is out there," Mabel said when Finn returned. They'd given him a large shell with their table number written on it.

"Can I get back to you on the budget? I need to have a chat with my investors."

Mabel held a neutral expression. This was the first time he'd mentioned investors for the pub. "Of course," she said and made a mental note to do some digging. The sinking feeling in the pit of her stomach was growing heavier.

Their cream tea arrived, and Finn's eyes lit up. The scones were perfectly risen with glazed browned tops. Little pots of clotted cream were beside them, rising to peaks where they'd been decanted. The jam contained juicy raspberries and was a deep, vibrant red. It looked delicious but was let down by the plates they'd served it on. They were plain white, thick plates like the last pub.

"This looks amazing," Finn said, cutting the scone in half.

"It does, but it's a shame about the plates. A cream tea should be served on pretty, delicate china."

He paused and looked at her. "You know, I was so busy admiring the food, I hadn't considered what it was served on. You're right, a cream tea is more than the food. It's an experience."

"I saw Zoe's sketches today. You'll have no trouble creating an experience with her pieces." Mabel loved to see Finn's passion as he surveyed the food. He dipped his knife in the cream and spread it across the scone. "What on earth are you doing?" Mabel screeched.

Finn's knife clattered onto the tabletop, and heads turned their way.

"Sorry," Mabel mumbled to those around them. She kept her head down.

"What did I do wrong?"

"Has everyone stopped staring?" Mabel asked.

"Almost. Are you going to tell me what happened?"

"We're in Cornwall, Finn." Mabel looked at him, but his face was blank. She shook her head and sighed. "We put the jam on first."

"Is that it?"

"What do you mean 'is that it'?"

"It's only cream." He shrugged and picked up his knife again.

"I don't think I can sit at this table with you if you're going to put cream on first."

He let out an exasperated sigh. "Mabel, after the phone call I've just had, I only care about shovelling this sugary treat into my mouth. I couldn't care less about the jam or cream order."

"Well then, if you couldn't care less, pop the jam on first."

Finn rolled his eyes but did as asked, spreading the jam on the scone. They sat in companionable silence as they ate. The soft hum of conversation filled the air, and the clatter of cutlery echoed throughout. Being in a pub with a tangible atmosphere was nice, and Mabel couldn't wait until Port Isaac's reopened.

"Where does your love of food and cooking come from?" Mabel asked as she scooped the last bit of clotted cream out of the pot and onto a bite of scone. She needed to know more about Finn and his past.

Finn chewed his mouthful before he answered. "My mum. During the day, she worked as a school cook. I know it might sound silly, as she was only cooking for children, but food was her passion. No matter how tired she was after cooking all day at school, if she wasn't at her other job in the evening, she'd always have the patience to cook with me."

"That's lovely. She must have been proud of you when you opened your own restaurant."

"She came to the opening of my restaurant, but by then, her dementia was so bad she didn't recognise me. It was just a month before her death." He paused, but Mabel didn't say anything. His gaze was far off, lost in his thoughts. "She still enjoyed the food. So much so that she asked the waiter to give her compliments to the chef. It meant a lot."

"I'm sorry. My grandma had dementia. It's heartbreaking to lose them bit by bit."

"It was always me and my mum. My dad was never around. Growing up was tough, but my mum never took it out on me. It was us against the world." He smiled, and it was clear he was lost in his thoughts. "She was over the moon when I studied food at college. I worked my way up in kitchens, but by the time I got the opportunity to work under Lachlan McLeod, her memory had already started deteriorating. She just about remembered me on good days. I never got the chance to show her how well I'd done." The pain in his eyes was palpable, and Mabel ached to comfort him.

"My grandma, on my dad's side, lost her memory while I was at university."

"It's awful, isn't it? To feel them slip away when

they're still physically with you. You grieve and lose the person they were, and then you do it all over again once you lose them."

"Truly awful. It was the first and last time I left Port Isaac. I returned to my life crumbled around me. Everything about my life was a mess, and then I lost my grandma. I took it as a sign never to leave again." Mabel rolled her shoulders. She hadn't meant to be that honest with Finn.

He sniffed, and his expression shifted. "Sorry. I don't usually divulge so much personal information during a business meeting."

A business meeting. The words replayed in Mabel's mind. She had thought they were friends, but if he wanted to remain professional, she could do that. It was like a cold bottle of water thrown over her after sharing such personal thoughts and feelings. "In my defence, I don't have many business meetings," she pointed out.

"There's something about good food and good company that can make people open up." Finn shrugged.

Mabel fought a smile at the mention of good company. She squared her shoulders and sat up a little straighter. "I shouldn't have pried. Shall we call it a day and head back? We have a better idea of what you want for the pub. If you can crunch numbers and get back to me with a budget, I'll begin looking for furniture."

Finn was all too eager to take her home. They drove in silence, allowing the radio to steal away any chance of conversation.

"Thank you for today," Finn said as he pulled up outside Mabel's cottage.

"It was the best market research trip I've ever been on."

"How many market research trips have you been on?"

"One."

Finn chuckled. "Well, I'm glad it was your best. I'll email you the budget on Monday and we can go from there."

"Sounds great." There was an awkward pause as Mabel considered how to say goodbye. She opted to lean across the car and place a kiss on Finn's cheek. She regretted it as soon as her lips met his soft skin. He jumped backwards and cleared his throat.

"Sorry. I'm too used to Elowen dropping me off." Mabel's attempts at a joke fell flat. "Anyway, I look forward to receiving the budget." She held out her hand, and he shook it. His grip was firm and decisive.

"Speak to you soon, Mabel," he called after her as she climbed out.

CHAPTER ELEVEN

"How was your date with Dishy Finn?" Elowen asked as Mabel climbed into the car. She had planned to walk to Michael and Elowen's for lunch, but it was pouring down, so Elowen insisted on collecting her. Mabel suspected it was so she could press her for gossip without little ears around, rather than saving Mabel from a wet walk.

"It wasn't a date. It was a business meeting." Mabel's tone was harsher than she'd intended.

"Was it a late one?" Elowen stared as if she could coerce the information from her.

"No. I got back about four, then I spent my evening working on the armoire I'm yet to be paid for." Truthfully, Mabel had needed the monotonous task of hand-painting flowers on the armoire to help sift through her concerns. She had resolved to keep her guard up with Finn until he had confided in her about his mother. At that moment, her resolve had crashed down. She'd found her heart warming to him and sparks of attraction fizzing in the pit of her stomach.

"That's disappointing." Elowen switched the car on.

"Finn made it very clear it was a business meeting. If he doesn't want me as a friend, that's okay. I have plenty of other friends in Port Isaac."

"It's his loss."

"El, you know I don't date." Mabel fiddled with the gift bag on her lap. She'd found it while wandering around Padstow-on-Sea yesterday. It had mermaids all over and she'd bought it to put the bracelets in for the girls.

"That doesn't mean you can't date. One bad experience doesn't have to shape your life."

Mabel took a deep breath. She knew her sister-in-law made sense, but her heart couldn't be vulnerable again. "Maybe one day, El, but not with Finn Hart. It was a business meeting, and we really need his business right now. I don't want to do anything to jeopardise the contract."

"Mabel, we appreciate and love you, but please don't risk your happiness for us." Elowen gave her a stern look, which she usually saved for the girls.

"Don't mother me, El," Mabel warned.

Elowen broke first and laughed before Mabel joined in. "Just promise me you'll put yourself first."

"I promise." Mabel kept her fingers crossed behind the gift bag. Her family and the community were her world, and would always come first.

Elowen put the car into gear as she told Mabel how the girls brought a frog into the house last night and tried to bathe it. Mabel chuckled, but her mind was distracted by thoughts of Finn. Despite her determination not to get close to another man, she could feel the attraction towards him growing.

Inside, the house was chaotic. Michael was juggling different dishes in the kitchen. Meanwhile, the girls were zooming around indoors, unable to go outside to burn off their abundance of energy.

"Maple syrup," they cried and threw themselves at Mabel as she walked through the front door.

"Hello, my little bumblebees." They wore black and yellow striped tops and their hair was in pigtails.

"I'll go see if Micheal needs a hand." Elowen slipped into the kitchen, leaving Mabel with the hyperactive children, so Mabel did the worst thing possible.

"I have presents for you," she announced, holding up the gift bag.

"Presents," the girls screamed, and Mabel held her hands over her ears. For such small people, they made a lot of noise.

Mabel ushered the girls into the living room and sat on the sofa. Their legs bounced and their arms flailed, but it felt like a small victory.

"You have to be careful because they're very delicate and vintage. Here you go." Mabel handed the girls each a thin, long box, which held the bracelets she'd bought them. Little gasps filled the room as the girls discovered their gifts nestled inside.

"Thank you, Mabel," said Milly.

"Thanks, Maple Syrup," Mia whispered. She held the bracelet to the light and giggled as the gold shimmered.

"What flowers are these?" Milly asked.

"They're daisies. Do you remember last summer when we picked the ones in your garden and made a necklace with them?"

"They were pretty," Mia whispered, her eyes wide.

"Now you can wear them all year round." Mabel wrapped her arms around both girls.

"Who do you think wore mine?" Milly asked. She was struggling with the clasp.

Mabel did it up for her and then turned to help Mia. "I'm not sure. They're not very old. Only from the eighties."

Mia gasped.

"The eighties," Milly whispered and stared in awe at the bracelet.

"Were there dinosaurs in the eighties?" Mia asked, her brow furrowed at the seriousness of the question.

Mabel bit her lip. "No, Mia. There weren't."

"But Grandma and Grandpa were alive in the eighties, weren't they?" Milly asked.

Mabel nodded, unable to say anything without bursting into uncontrollable laughter.

"Let's go show Mummy and Daddy." Milly took

Mia's hand, and they ran ahead. Mabel followed, her shoulders shaking with a silent chuckle.

By the time she reached the kitchen, the girls were already showing off their presents.

"They're very pretty," Michael said, whilst trying to stir the gravy.

"Here, let me." Mabel took over the stirring so he could give them his full attention. She smiled warmly as she watched her nieces delight in their parents' attention. Mabel couldn't lose this. She had to do something to keep her family close. She would find a way to bring in more money and support them.

"Dinner won't be long," Michael said. He opened the oven and shook a baking tray. The smell of roast potatoes hit Mabel and her tummy rumbled. She hadn't eaten since the cream tea with Finn yesterday.

"How did your meeting with Finn go?" Michael asked. It was as though he had read her thoughts.

At the mention of a business meeting, Mabel smirked at her sister-in-law, who stuck her tongue out in response. "It was good. I've an idea of what he's looking for. I'm waiting for him to get back to me with a budget, and in the meantime, I'm looking out for furniture. I sent a few emails to some contacts this morning, but it'll be difficult because we want it to match." Mabel had tossed and turned most of the night, wondering how she could source everything. She couldn't lose the contract before she'd even signed it. There was also a small part of her brain, which kept replaying the moment her lips had touched Finn's cheek. Mabel quickly put those thoughts back in the box she'd locked them in.

"I've recently acquired a new client in Devon. They've purchased a hotel and are selling the existing furniture at auction next weekend." Michael handed Mabel his phone so she could read the email. They were selling off all the tables and chairs from the restaurant.

"Will you ask for a few photos so I can see if it would be any good? We're hoping to strip the pieces back to raw wood, so it needs to be in decent condition."

Michael nodded and tapped away on his phone, sending the email immediately. "I'll let you know when they get back to me."

"Thank you. Right, shall we set the table?" Mabel returned her attention to her nieces and recruited their help while Michael and Elowen dished up.

Mabel's parents usually hosted Sunday lunch, but with them away, Michael had taken over the role.

"Maybe we should have invited Finn," Elowen said.

Mabel choked on a roast potato. "Why would we invite him to Sunday dinner?" She wheezed and reached for a glass of water.

"To invite him into the community," Elowen said.

"I don't think we need to invite him into our home to do that," Michael replied.

"No, and I'm not sure I completely trust him yet," confessed Mabel. She'd been putting off telling Michael and Elowen about her worries.

"What do you mean? I thought you did?" Michael put down his cutlery and refilled his wineglass. Elowen had allowed them a bottle of non-alcoholic wine for the evening.

Mabel glanced at the girls to check they were distracted. She didn't want this going around the school tomorrow morning. "He's just had a restaurant in Mayfair fail. There were investors and all sorts."

"That doesn't mean he's untrustworthy. Lots of businesses fail," Elowen reasoned.

"There's more. What is it?" Michael studied her and Mabel shrunk under the attention.

"He mentioned there being investors in the pub. That's why I don't have a budget yet. He has to discuss it with them."

"Investors for a small pub in a Cornish village?" Michael massaged the bridge of his nose. "You're right, it doesn't make sense."

"I suppose if he lost money in the last place, he wouldn't have any to invest in a new venture. Is it an immediate red flag?" Elowen was the voice of reason, but Michael didn't look convinced.

"We need to be careful. What's your gut feeling?" asked Michael.

Mabel sipped her water and thought back to the day she'd spent with Finn. Despite the questions she had about his business practice, her gut feeling was that he was a decent person. The way he had spoken so openly about his mother had seemed genuine, and his passion for food wasn't something he could fake. "I'm not sure. He seems like a good person, but who knows what's going on? I think we have to take a chance and accept him at face value."

"Mabel's right. He's bought the pub now, there's no going back. If we can sway his decisions and involve the community, we have more chance of keeping the pub at the heart of the village," Elowen said.

"Keep your friends close and your enemies closer," muttered Michael.

"Who has enemies?" Milly piped up, putting an end to the conversation.

CHAPTER TWELVE

"Here's the furniture," Mabel said, turning her laptop to Finn. Michael's new client had emailed over pictures and Mabel had rushed straight to Fisherman's Rest to show Finn. It was exactly what they were looking for.

"Is that what your text was about?" he asked, peering at the screen. A dishevelled Finn had opened the door and ushered her in, explaining he'd just showered after his morning run.

Mabel nodded. She'd sent a quick message to Finn as she was leaving, letting him know she was on her way to show him something. In hindsight, she probably should have been more specific and given him more notice.

"It looks like furniture," he said, squinting as he zoomed in on the pictures. "You're the expert here. Do you think it's right for the pub?"

"I think so. It's difficult to say for sure without

seeing it in person, but from what I can see in the pictures, the quality looks good and I think we could make the country-style fit with the pub's new interior. They've even got a dresser which would fit perfectly in that alcove. You could use it for cutlery, condiments, and so on."

"You've really thought this through. If you think it's a good fit, let's go for it."

"Perfect. It fits with the budget you sent me. The only drawback is it needs collecting."

"Do you know any couriers?" He closed her laptop and pushed it back across the bar to her. Finn picked up his coffee and drained the contents.

"I do, but I know how much they'd charge. If you want to save money, we'd do better to hire a van and collect it ourselves."

Mabel watched as Finn mulled over her suggestion.

"I suppose it's an option, but isn't this an auction? We might not win the furniture and then we've paid for a van."

"It's Michael's client who's selling it and they've said we can have the furniture if we're interested. They asked if we could pick it up the day before the auction, which would be Friday."

"Okay. I'll sort out hiring a van. I've got a few meetings on Friday, so we'll have to go after lunch. Does that work for you?"

"It's a plan." Mabel clapped her hands.

"Do you want a hot chocolate?" Finn asked, taking Mabel by surprise.

"I'm never one to turn down a hot chocolate." She slipped her laptop into her bag and followed him to the kitchen.

"I've been testing recipes and think I've finally perfected it. You have to be honest with me about how it tastes." He put his coffee on the side and pulled out a selection of saucepans and whisks.

"I'm always honest when it comes to hot chocolate." Mabel rested against a worktop as Finn expertly sauntered around the kitchen. He disappeared into the walk-in fridge before reemerging with a handful of chocolate and whole milk.

"Do you like dark chocolate?" he asked, setting the ingredients on the worktop.

"I love all kinds of chocolate." Mabel moved closer so she could see what he was doing.

Finn rolled up his sleeves and Mabel's gaze fell on his tanned arms. She swallowed and watched as he unwrapped two bars of chocolate. He grated each bar until he had a pile of chocolate shavings. Then, using his hands, he mixed them. His touch was light and confident. Next, he filled a saucepan with milk and whisked until it reached boiling point. He sprinkled in the chocolate shavings and stirred as they melted, thickening the milk. The sweet scent filled the kitchen and Mabel took in a deep breath. Finn added a pinch of cinnamon and her mouth watered.

"Grab those mugs from over there." Finn pointed to the opposite side of the room. The mugs had pretty seascapes hand-painted on them.

"Are they Zoe's?" asked Mabel.

"Yeah. She brought them with her to our meeting last week." Finn poured the molten liquid into the mugs. Frothy bubbles bobbed on the surface from where he had whisked the mixture.

"Be careful, it'll be hot," Finn warned as Mabel went to pick up the mug. "Come on, let's sit outside. It's a nice day."

They wandered back through the pub to the doors, which led out to a decked area. It had seen better days, but there was a small gap between the shrubbery with a view down to the sea. The day was bright, but a chill lingered in the air. July would soon be upon them and chase away the last clouds. They sat on the edge of the decking, their legs dangling below them.

"How are you finding life in Port Isaac?" asked Mabel. She blew on her hot chocolate, eager to try it, but didn't want to scald her mouth.

"It's very different from London." Finn paused for a moment. He looked towards the sea, but Mabel suspected his thoughts were elsewhere. "I used to live in London in a flat above a takeaway. It was noisy at all hours of the day and the neon lights from the shop below would shine into my bedroom. I didn't mind so much as I was working all hours. It was a place to collapse into bed at the end of the day and it was mine. We moved a lot when I was young. My mother often couldn't afford the rent, so we downsized." A rush of air escaped him. "Sorry.

I'm making it sound all doom and gloom. Truly, it wasn't. I had a very happy childhood. My time working in London was great, but it always felt like something was missing. Being here in Port Isaac, it feels like I've found the missing piece. The sense of community here is lovely, the scenery stunning, and I could get used to the slower pace of life."

Mabel studied his face as he continued to look out towards the sea. His hair had grown since he'd arrived in Port Isaac and he looked more laid back. The worry lines on his forehead were slowly fading.

"I'm glad you're happy here." Mabel's voice shook as she spoke. "The community is special. We look out for our own." She held her head high. "They looked after me when I returned to Port Isaac. My heart was shattered, and I'd lost all hope for the future. The old landlord gave me some shifts at Fisherman's Rest and that was how I started to rebuild my life."

He gave her a sad smile at the mention of her broken heart. "You mentioned it was difficult turning your upcycling into a business, how did you begin?"

"When my grandmother died, I inherited a few pieces from her, but they were in an awful condition. I have a stool in my bedroom that was hers. As a child, I'd sit on it while she brushed my hair before bed. The legs were damaged, with gouges in the wood. I filled the holes and painted it my grandmother's favourite colour, then I recovered the stained cushion with one of her old dresses.

My mum told her neighbours, and the news spread, soon I had lots of people from the harbour asking me to do similar things with their loved one's belongings."

"That's lovely." He turned his smile on her and Mabel's heart stuttered. She fumbled with the mug in her hands and drank, wincing as the liquid burnt as she swallowed.

"That's really hot still," she gasped. "It tastes amazing, though. Thank you."

"Better than that instant rubbish?"

"Much better."

Mabel watched the sea as the tide retreated. Afternoon was setting in and the beach would soon be filled with children when school finished.

"Do you think you'll ever leave Port Isaac?" Finn's question came out of the blue.

"No, I won't. I tried it once and I have no desire to leave again."

Finn looked deep in thought as he considered her answer. Mabel sipped at her drink as she waited for him to form a response.

"I've never felt like anywhere was home," he confessed in a small voice.

"Port Isaac can feel like home if you embrace it." Mabel reached out and placed a hand on Finn's trembling shoulder. He tensed underneath her touch, so she pulled away.

"We'll see." He lifted his drink to his mouth.

Mabel cleared her throat and stood. "I should go."

"Of course. I'm sure you're busy."

Finn led the way back into the pub, and Mabel quietly followed. She'd overstepped an imaginary line.

"I'm sorry," Finn said as they reached the bar. "It's coming up to the anniversary of my mother's death." He stared at his feet, but Mabel could hear the sadness in his voice.

"Just drop me a text if you need anything this week. I'm always around." Mabel wound her way around the bar to the back entrance. As she reached the door, she paused. A letter on the side had caught her attention. Instantly, she recognised the logo. It was one of the big corporations that had been trying to buy the pub for the last ten years.

"Mabel?" Finn called, jogging into the hallway.

"What?" She jumped.

"I meant to ask if you know any local van rental places. I don't mind sorting it, but I'm not sure where to start."

"I'll text you a few recommendations." Mabel gave him a weak smile and let herself out before he could sense anything was wrong.

CHAPTER THIRTEEN

Mabel threw a cardigan around her shoulders and checked Ethel had water and food. Finn had texted to say he was leaving. They'd barely spoken since her last visit to the pub. She'd sent him the details of a local van rental and he'd replied to confirm the booking. Mabel hadn't ventured into the harbour this week in fear of bumping into him. She needed to know what the letter was about, but had to tread carefully. Had she been a fool to trust him so quickly?

A beep signalled Finn's arrival. The drive to the hotel was two hours, and Mabel was dreading it. Somehow, she needed to discover the answers to her questions without offending him.

"I'll be back later, Ethel," called Mabel.

Finn was waiting in a transit van at the end of her path. Mabel had to admit he looked rather attractive with his shirt sleeves rolled up and windswept hair.

"This is a beast," Mabel said as she climbed into the cabin.

He chuckled and handed her a travel cup. "I made you a hot chocolate for the journey."

"Thank you." Mabel took it from him. Her stomach somersaulted as her fingers brushed his. It was very sweet that he'd made a hot chocolate just for her. "Are you okay driving this?" It occurred to Mabel it was a little too late to ask such a question, but she felt she should say something.

Finn laughed and started the van. "I've driven transits before. I worked my way up in kitchens and when deliveries were delayed or cancelled, the person with a driving license was sent out to collect them. I'm more used to navigating the busy London roads, but I'm sure if I take it slow, then we'll be fine."

Mabel sank into the seat and sipped her hot chocolate as the Cornish scenery passed them by. It was a beautiful time of year when the hedgerows were blooming, although road visibility suffered for it. There were a few times Mabel winced as a car passed them by.

"Mabel, will you please relax? There was plenty of room," Finn groaned as Mabel hid her face as they passed a tractor.

"It didn't look like lots of room," she grumbled.

"Tell me, how many years have you been

driving for?"

"I had a handful of driving lessons. I'm not completely clueless."

Finn let out a noise between a huff and a chuckle, and Mabel glared.

"Trust me, okay?" he said, and Mabel's stomach flipped. Trusting him was causing her sleepless nights at the moment. She grunted and turned her attention back to the window.

Finn turned up the radio to drown out the silence as they drove. It wasn't long before they left the winding country lanes and joined the motorway.

⤜⤛

"Wake up, sleepyhead," Finn cooed.

"What's going on?" Mabel murmured, although it came out in a jumble of grunts and huffs as she dragged herself from the clutches of sleep.

"We're here," Finn said.

Mabel blinked a few times. They were parked by the side of a beautiful Art Deco building. She rolled her shoulders and leaned forward to get a better look at their surroundings. The car park was full and people were milling around.

"Looks like tomorrow's auction will be popular," Finn commented.

"Looks like it." Mabel jumped out of the van and stretched. She'd slept for most of the journey and was still groggy. Finn walked around to join her and they stared at the hotel as Mabel suppressed a yawn.

"You need a coffee," he said.

"I don't drink coffee. Come on. Let's get this over with." She was eager to go inside and see if the interior matched the vintage architecture.

"So you can snooze on the journey back?"

Mabel stuck her tongue out at Finn and walked ahead. She heard him chuckle before his footsteps followed. They were greeted at the door by a man around their age. He wore a suit and looked very put together. Mabel bit back a chuckle. He even looked like one of Michael's clients.

"Mr Taylor, I'm Mabel, Michael's sister," Mabel introduced herself.

"Mabel, lovely to meet you. Please call me Arnold," the man said, shaking her outstretched hand. "And you must be Finn Hart." He moved on to Finn.

"Nice to meet you, Arnold. Thank you for the opportunity to purchase the furniture outside of the auction." Finn had turned on his charm.

"Anything for Michael. Let me show you through. We've moved the furniture around to the back of the hotel. You can bring the van around and it should be easy to load."

Mabel followed, feeling like a child as they discussed the local economy. Her gaze swivelled from one room to another as they passed down a hallway. Each room contained the contents of a different area of the hotel. There was kitchen equipment piled high in what looked like it was once a library, while bed frames were stacked in the corner of the reception area. The hotel was stuck in an 80s time warp and all hints of the roaring twenties had been stripped away. Mabel longed to wander around and look at everything, but Finn and Arnold were strolling ahead and she was falling behind.

Arnold showed them into what looked like an old conservatory. Piles of furniture filled the room, and Mabel nibbled on her bottom lip. How would all this fit into the van?

Finn let out a low whistle. "There's a lot here."

"Take what you need, then we can discuss a price. Anything you don't take will go into the auction tomorrow. If you'll excuse me, I have a lot to get on with. I'll be around the first floor, so come get me when you're done." With a jaunty wave, Arnold disappeared back the way they came, leaving Finn and Mabel staring at the monumental task ahead.

"What do you think?" Finn asked.

"We're not going to fit all of this into the van, are we?"

Finn shook his head.

"I need to go through it all and make sure we pick the best pieces."

Finn glanced at his watch. "This is going to be a big job. I had hoped someone might be around to help us load the van. Looks like it's just me and you."

"It might have escaped your notice, but moving furniture around is literally my job."

"Good point. Come on, show me what to look for and hopefully, we can go through this pile quickly."

Mabel explained to Finn that they were looking for pieces with as few nicks and scratches as possible as it would save her time sanding. She told him to wobble all the legs as any repairs would only add time and costs to the project. Finn looked utterly overwhelmed, but nodded and wandered away to begin his inspections.

Finn swiped the back of his hand across his forehead to wipe the sweat. His top stuck to him and Mabel averted her eyes from how it clung to his torso. She didn't need a mirror to know she was red and blotchy from the heat and carrying heavy furniture. It had taken them two hours to inspect the furniture and load the van. Finn insisted on playing Tetris to maximise the space. Mabel had grumbled under her breath but had to admit they'd squeezed in more by doing it his way. A few tables and chairs remained, most of which were unstable or had deep gouges in the wood.

"I can't wait to get the air con on," Mabel said as she fanned herself.

"It'll be lovely. Shall we find Arnold and pay him so we can be on our way?"

Mabel nodded and followed Finn to the first floor. She'd considered heading back to the van while Finn dealt with the payment, but this way she got to see more of the hotel and poke her head into rooms filled with treasures from a past life.

They found Arnold in one of the guest bedrooms, removing a painting from the wall. Mabel left them to talk while she wandered around the room. It looked to have once been a suite with a large bay window looking out towards the beach at the bottom of the cliff. In its heyday, Mabel could imagine the hotel buzzing with life, with families from London visiting for some summer sun. Today the pale pink wallpaper was peeling from the walls, stains littered the patterned carpet, and the paint around the window was flaking off.

"You ready?" Finn asked, and Mabel jumped.

"That was quick."

"Cash in hand." Finn ushered her towards the door and Mabel nodded as though it was nothing, when in reality it was another strike against Finn's trustworthiness. "Let's get the air con on," Finn said, stopping at the bottom of the stairs for her to join him.

"Yes, please. It's so muggy today." She fanned herself.

The van was filled to the rafters with furniture, which would slow the journey home. Mabel was looking forward to getting home and reheating the lasagna Betty had dropped off earlier in the day.

Finn climbed into the driver's seat as Mabel was repositioning the air vents so they would blow on her once the engine switched on. The van spluttered to life and then cut out.

"What was that?" Mabel asked. She gripped the

sides of her seat.

Finn's panicked stare met hers. "I'll try again," he said and turned the key. The same thing happened. The van spluttered but didn't switch on.

"Do you have the number for the rental place?" Mabel asked.

Finn tried the van again, but nothing happened. "I'll call them. There are picnic benches in the shade over there. Why don't you wait there and I'll let you know how I get on?"

CHAPTER FOURTEEN

"What do you mean, they're sending someone out to us *tomorrow*?" Mabel spoke slowly, hoping she had misunderstood and Finn would correct her.

"They're closed for the day. The guy said they can't do anything until tomorrow." He shrugged.

Mabel groaned. "What shall we do? I can ask Michael to come and get us. Or maybe we could get a taxi." She'd need to check her bank balance before she booked a taxi.

"Don't worry Michael. It's almost six. You can't ask him to come out. Then we'd need to travel back in the morning. We passed an inn on the way. Let's ask if they've got a room for the night. I'll pay, it's work, so I can put it on my expenses."

Mabel's shoulders sagged in relief. She was

almost certain she couldn't afford a taxi back to Port Isaac, so she would have to accept Finn's offer of a room for the night.

"Are you sure?" she asked, although she was already standing.

"Very. Come on, we can do some sleuthing while we're here and inspect their local pub." He held his arm out and Mabel linked hers through his.

They wandered down the steep hill to the village below, popping in to tell Arnold about the van. He'd offered one of the empty rooms at the hotel, but Finn had declined.

"I didn't fancy sleeping on the stained carpets," he'd told Mabel as he recounted the conversation.

"Nor do I. Look, the inn is there." Mabel pointed across the road to a quaint pub. It was set back in a row of Tudor cottages, with a bench on either side of the door. A row of men occupied the benches, all with brimming glasses of ale and jolly smiles.

"Evening," Finn greeted them as they passed. He held the door open for Mabel.

It looked as though the sleepy village's residents were all inside the pub. Despite the bright sun outside, it was gloomy, with all the windows shrouded with dusty net curtains. A radio played from behind the bar but was barely audible over the sound of chatter. Tables were bursting with occupants and the bar was propping up many drinkers.

"There's a table in the corner. Quick, get it and I'll book us rooms and order dinner," Finn whispered. He was so close his lips almost brushed the top of her ear and it took a moment for Mabel to understand. "Quick, Mabel, before someone else notices it." He gave her a nudge on the small of her back and Mabel scurried away, not wanting to focus on the shiver that coursed through her at his touch.

As she waited for Finn to return, Mabel took in her surroundings. The pub looked like it had been decorated in the nineties and hadn't been updated. A mishmash of garishly coloured patterned carpets covered the floor. The once-white walls had yellowed, and the tabletops showed signs of use. It was all very dingy and yet the place was heaving with customers. Mabel watched people drinking, eating, and interacting. What was luring them to this place?

"They only had one room left, so we're going to have to share," Finn said and sat opposite her. The chair wobbled, and he gripped the table to steady himself.

"It's only for one night. Do you want to swap seats?" Mabel offered. She was keen not to linger on the thought of sharing a room with Finn.

"No, I'll be fine." He pushed a glass of wine towards her. "I hope that's okay. I'd already fought my way to the bar when I realised I hadn't asked you what you wanted."

"This is perfect. I don't drink often, so it's a real treat." She savoured the taste of the red wine.

"Good. I made them open a new bottle from the cellar. Their house red was like vinegar." Finn screwed up his face.

"I hope you didn't offend them."

"Of course not. I've worked in the service industry my entire life. I appreciate what they do."

"Sorry. I had my fair share of awful customers when I worked at Fisherman's Rest."

"What was it like before it closed?"

"It was the heart of everything in Port Isaac, but in hindsight, we weren't very welcoming to outsiders. The local community didn't spend enough to keep the place running." Mabel shrugged.

"That's going to have to change."

"I know."

"I promise to keep the pub at the heart of the community."

"Thank you." They shared a smile and Mabel felt a familiar burst of attraction. "What did you order?" she asked.

"They had fish and chips on the menu, so I ordered it for us."

"Perfect. I forgot to eat lunch, so I'm starving."

Finn stared at her, his jaw slack. "You forgot to eat?"

Mabel nodded.

"I don't understand how people can forget to eat." Finn shook his head.

"That's because your entire life revolves around food. I've been bouncing from one thing to another today. Betty dropped around a lasagna for my dinner, so I was focused on that and forgot lunch. Actually, I was really looking forward to my dinner."

"I'm sorry. It's my fault you're stuck here. I'll make you a lasagna soon to make up for it."

"I'll hold you to that," warned Mabel.

"I promise." Finn held his glass out for her to clink.

The food arrived, and Mabel almost inhaled it, and Finn chuckled. He watched her as he slowly made his way through his meal.

"That was good." Mabel hummed her approval.

"It was. This little place is deceiving. Looks-wise, it doesn't seem much, but it's obviously the hub of the village and the food is amazing." Finn had cleared his plate.

"Do you think they have dessert?" Mabel scanned the boards above the bar, but they all listed drinks.

"I didn't spot any on the menu. Shall we find a table outside and I'll ask about dessert?" The pub had slowly emptied while they were eating and there were now a handful of free seats.

"Okay. I'll come and find you if there's nowhere to sit."

Mabel followed a hallway to the back of the building, which led her to the beer garden. It was a small grassed area, but twinkling fairy lights were strung around the trees, and each table had a citronella candle burning away to repel the insects. Only a few tables were occupied, so Mabel chose one beside a pretty flowering bush. Vibrant pink flowers were in bloom and Mabel snapped a picture and sent it to Elowen, along with a quick message to let her know she was staying the night in Devon. El's lewd response came through immediately and Mabel rolled her eyes and stuffed her phone back into her pocket.

"No dessert, I'm afraid, so I got you a hot chocolate." Finn placed a chunky mug on the table. "I wouldn't ask for one at breakfast. They weren't very happy with the request."

"Sorry. I suppose it's not really the weather for it."

"It's always the weather for chocolate," Finn said. Mabel glanced at him and saw he'd got the same as her.

They sipped their drinks and enjoyed the balmy evening. Around them, the beer garden emptied, but neither of them made a move to leave. There was no awkward silence between them as they enjoyed each other's company.

"We should think about heading in soon," Finn said. The sun had set below the horizon and everyone else had left.

They took their empty mugs inside and left them at the bar before ascending the creaky staircase.

Finn clutched a key in his hand. The yellowing plastic keyring had a number five on it. The patterned carpet continued up the stairs and onto the landing. Mabel didn't have high hopes for the bedrooms.

"Ready?" asked Finn. He'd paused outside door

number five.

"I'm a little bit scared if downstairs's interior is anything to go by."

Finn chuckled and unlocked the door. They stood in utter dismay as each surveyed the room.

Mabel looked from the moss-green carpet to the yellow feature wall and over to the floral bedspread. It was truly dated and shabby. She was reluctant to touch the bedding, in case it was also vintage.

"This is awful," Mabel said. The more she looked, the more she spotted. Like the dusty net curtains and the pale pink velvet lampshades.

"I know. I'm sorry, it was the only room they had left." Finn still stood in the doorway.

"It's okay. We'd probably be thrown out of anywhere too fancy since we don't have a change of clothes." Mabel peered towards the bathroom and wondered what she'd find.

"We can ask for more pillows and create a divide," Finn said, and Mabel froze.

"What?" she mumbled. Mabel looked back at the room and realisation dawned on her. There was one bed. A double bed.

"I'm sorry. I can sleep in the van." Finn put the key on the bedside table and went to leave.

"Wait. You can't sleep in the van. It'll be fine. It's only for one night." Mabel shrugged, hoping she looked nonplussed, despite the way her heart was galloping in her chest.

"I'll go and ask for more pillows." Finn

disappeared before Mabel could even nod.

The bathroom was as dated as expected, with an avocado suite and carpeted floors. Keeping her shoes on, Mabel switched the shower on and waited while it warmed up. It took a full five minutes before it was warm enough to jump in for a quick wash. Mabel didn't allow her eyes to wander too far. She'd already spotted mould in one of the corners. She slipped her still-wet feet into her shoes and wrapped herself in a threadbare towel. Mabel glanced at her clothes. She had no pyjamas, so she put them back on to sleep in.

Mabel jumped as she walked out of the bathroom and spotted Finn in one of the armchairs by the window.

"How was the shower?" he asked.

"Lukewarm, but it did the job."

Finn grimaced. "The landlord said he would look for extra pillows and drop them off."

Mabel nodded and sat in the armchair opposite.

"This is a bit awkward." Finn cleared his throat.

"It is. Although, it's quite nice to have company." As soon as the words escaped her, Mabel wanted to take them back. She didn't know where they had come from, but she certainly hadn't meant to be so honest with Finn.

"Would you like to come back to work at the pub when it opens?" Finn asked.

Mabel's mouth formed an 'O'.

"It would be nice to spend my evenings with

you," Finn continued, adding to Mabel's shock.

She opened and closed her mouth, willing her thoughts to pull together and form a sentence.

"I'd like that," Mabel eventually whispered, unable to meet Finn's gaze.

Mabel could hear the smile in Finn's voice as he spoke. "Good," he said.

"It can be lonely in the evenings," she admitted, her voice small. Mabel swallowed back the wave of sadness which threatened to overcome her.

"It can be. When I was training, I would pick all the shifts up because I didn't want to go home. Unlike you, it wasn't an empty home, but it might as well have been. My mother's dementia began when I was in my teens, but we acted as if nothing was wrong. She was terrified of losing me. As I got older, I needed help, and that was when she started having carers. At that point, she only recognised me on good days. Quite often she mistook me for my father." Finn paused and cleared his throat. "My father wasn't in my life, and for the short time he was in my mother's, he treated her terribly. It broke my heart when she thought I was him. I found myself spending more and more time in the kitchen and not wanting to go home."

"I'm sorry, Finn." She reached out to hold his hand.

"Thank you. Sorry, I've never told anyone that."

"You can tell me anything you want."

He wrapped his hand around hers. "I like you, Mabel."

Air filled Mabel's lungs, but she still gasped for more. She shuffled to the edge of the seat and Finn did the same until their knees were touching.

"I like you, too," she said.

Finn held her gaze, and a flush rushed through Mabel's body. Her pulse thrummed as she glanced between his eyes and his lips. The air was charged and Mabel felt she would shatter into a million pieces if either of them moved. It was exhilarating and terrifying. They edged closer but were interrupted by a knock at the door.

"I've got your pillows," came the gruff voice of the landlord.

"Coming," called Finn, jumping up and letting go of Mabel's hand.

While Finn was busy at the door, Mabel stood and shook herself off, needing to dispel the build-up of energy and emotions raging inside. She watched a young couple out of the window as they wandered along the street arm in arm. Mabel wondered what she and Finn might look like wandering down a street together, but her thoughts were interrupted as the door closed behind her.

Finn had piled the pillows next to the door. All eight of them.

"I'll let you sort them," he said, running a hand through his hair. "I'm going to jump in the shower." He walked away without making eye contact.

Mabel eyed the pillows. They were both adults. Wasn't a pillow wall between them a little silly? Instead of piling them on the bed, Mabel left them on the floor and willed herself to sleep.

CHAPTER FIFTEEN

"What happened to the pillows?" asked Finn.

Mabel jumped at his voice. Despite her attempts, she hadn't managed to fall asleep. The sound of the shower had infiltrated all her thoughts as her mind wandered over images of Finn showering on the other side of the door.

"It seemed silly. We're both adults, we can share a bed."

"I agree."

Mabel snuck a glance at Finn. He was dressed in a pair of tight-fitting boxers, and no top. His tanned chest was muscular. Mabel felt her emotions scrambling, unsure of how to feel as a half-naked Finn stood in front of her, about to climb into bed beside her.

"If it makes you feel any better, I can't think of anyone else I'd rather be stranded here with," Finn said as he slid into the bed.

She looked at him through her lashes. "I can't think of anyone else I'd rather be here with, either."

Finn's eyes shone in the dim light as their gazes met. Mabel's ears filled with the steady thrum of her heartbeat.

"We should sleep," she said, her voice barely audible. Her eyes flickered from Finn's to his lips.

"We should," he agreed.

With a blush, Mabel pulled the duvet up to her neck. "Goodnight, Finn," she muttered.

"Night, Mabel," he replied.

Finn pulled the duvet towards him, but in doing so, he grasped Mabel's leg and she let out a soft gasp. His soft fingers gripped her thigh, sending a shiver through her body.

"Sorry," he said, his voice wobbled, but he didn't remove his hand. Finn moved his thumb in soft circles against her skin.

"It's okay." Mabel's lips parted as his fingers caressed the top of her thigh.

"Night," Finn said with a wicked smile as he pulled his hand back and turned over to sleep.

It was a long night. Mabel spent most of it staring at the ceiling, listening to the steady hum of Finn's breathing beside her. She fought the urge to reach over and touch him. It was so long since she'd shared a bed with someone. She remembered the last time. The night before she discovered her ex was cheating on her. The night before her entire life had shattered around her. Those memories replayed over and over in Mabel's head. She was unsure whether sharing a bed with Finn had brought them on, or if it was their earlier confession to liking each other. Either way, her emotions were stirred up.

It was a relief when Finn's alarm woke Mabel from the light sleep she had eventually fallen into.

"Morning," Finn said, his voice gravelly with sleep.

"Morning," Mabel muttered, ignoring the thrill that had gone through her at waking up beside Finn.

"How did you sleep?" he asked, sitting up, so the duvet pooled at his waist. Mabel swallowed. She looked up at the Artex ceiling and tried to wipe the images of a shirtless Finn from her memory. It was a futile attempt.

"Not too bad," she lied.

"Do you mind if I jump in the bathroom first? I want to call the hire company as soon as they open."

"Go ahead." Mabel fought the urge to watch Finn climb out of bed and walk to the bathroom. Once the door was shut and locked behind him, Mabel buried her head in a pillow and groaned. She was attracted to Finn Hart, and despite her resolve not to fall for somebody again, he'd already snuck behind her defences and she liked him.

❦

Breakfast was a sorry state of affairs. There were stale boxes of cereal, lukewarm yoghurt decanted into bowls, and a greasy fry-up sweating under heated lamps. Mabel picked a banana from the fruit bowl and poured herself a glass of milk.

"Is that all you're having?" asked Finn. He'd left her in the room to get ready while he went to call the hire company.

"Have you seen what's on offer?" Mabel raised her brows.

Finn surveyed the breakfast table, and his expression twisted into disgust. "A coffee and a banana sounds like the perfect way to start the day."

"What do you think the pub's appeal is?" Mabel asked, keeping her voice low so nobody could hear her.

"I think most people who stayed last night are here for the auction today. Look, they all have the brochure."

They were joined by five other people, all alone, and had an auction brochure lying on the table.

"Okay, but what about last night? The place was heaving with locals."

"I would have thought you, out of everyone, would know why they were here. This place is the heart of the community."

"Oh." Mabel glanced around the dingy pub. It might not be as nice as Fisherman's Rest, but it served the same purpose. At that moment, Mabel felt nothing but appreciation for Finn. Without him breathing new life into Fisherman's Rest, it would fall into disrepair. "Thank you for saving Port Isaac's pub." She shot him a warm smile, and he returned it.

"I couldn't do it without you. The hire company should be here soon. They're hoping to get the van started, otherwise, we'll have to transfer the contents into a new one."

Mabel groaned at the idea. Her muscles already ached from yesterday. She longed for a scalding hot shower at home, and a change of clothes. Poor Ethel would be wondering where she was.

"Let's hope for the best," said Finn. "They should be here in an hour. The sea's at the bottom of the road. Shall we go for a walk?"

It was a warm summer's day, and they wandered down the country lane to the small bay. With cliffs on either side, the bay was sheltered. The golden sand was soft and specks glistened in the sunlight, and the calm sea ebbed and flowed at the shoreline. Mabel kicked off her shoes and sunk her toes into the sand.

"You seem so at home here," Finn commented.

"What do you mean?"

"I could never imagine you somewhere like London. A big city."

"It's not for me. Even at university, I didn't often venture off campus. I like the feeling of a community around me. My favourite place to be is by the sea."

"You have such a sense of self, Mabel. It's admirable." Finn watched her as she dipped a toe into a retreating wave. It was freezing, but exhilarating. She wished she had her swimming costume so she could dive in.

"It's not all good. Sometimes I feel trapped in Cornwall." Mabel had never voiced these feelings aloud, but something deep inside her knew Finn would understand.

"I was trapped in London," he admitted. "Maybe it's my Cornish blood. My father is from Cornwall."

Silence hung in the air while Finn composed himself, and Mabel waited for him to continue. He sat on the sand and Mabel joined him, watching as he filtered grains through his fingers.

"I've told you he didn't treat my mum well. Because of that, I've always needed to prove I'm different to him. He lives near the coast, so I've always focused on being a city person." Finn let out a sigh. "It's difficult being here because it makes me happy, but it goes against everything I've ever tried to be."

"The only person you can be is you. If something makes you happy, embrace it."

Finn picked up a shell and turned it over, his fingers tracing the delicate grooves. "I've spent so long proving who I'm not that I'm not sure what truly makes me happy."

"Oh, Finn. Why don't we find out together?" Mabel took the shell from him, her fingers brushing his.

"I'd like that."

"Why did you come to Cornwall, Finn?" asked Mabel.

He wiped the sand from his hands and crossed

his arms. "I'm lost in London," he admitted, his voice catching. "It feels like an empty shell of what it once was, haunted by memories of my mother. Not the good ones, the ones from her worst days."

Mabel mulled over his words before she spoke. "I think you've done the right thing coming here. Stop chasing after Finn Hart who's different to his father, and start being you. Just because you enjoy being in Cornwall doesn't mean you're the same as your dad."

"Thank you, Mabel. The last few years have been difficult. When my mother started to mistake me for my father, it made me second guess myself. Was it her dementia, or was I turning into him? In the month before my mother's death, it got worse. I found myself in a very bad place and I was losing my grip on life. Things were spiralling out of control, and I made mistakes at work. A few days later, my mother passed away. I never knew if her confusion was the illness or my behaviour. Was I acting like my father and that's why she mistook me for him? It's eaten away at me." Finn looked out to sea.

Mabel battled the urge to reach out and hug him. She didn't know him well enough to know if he'd want affection in that moment. "I'm sorry, Finn," she whispered. "For what it's worth, from the little I know you, I think you're a good man and I like being around you."

He gave her a weak smile and wrapped his hand around hers, their fingers intertwined. "I like being around you," he said, and Mabel's heart stuttered. "It makes me happy."

They shared a shy smile, which was interrupted by Finn's phone ringing.

"It's the hire company," he said and answered it, dropping her hand. Mabel's hand felt cold and empty without Finn's around it, but she pushed those feelings aside and focused on the day's task.

⟫⟫⟩ ⟨⟪⟪

After a few tries, the repairmen got the van started and offered to follow them back to Port Isaac in case it broke down again. Neither Finn nor Mabel brought up the moment they'd shared on the beach. The radio filled the space between them, and Mabel fought the urge to doze with the engine's gentle hum and the sun's heat through the windscreen lulling her to sleep.

"We've got to unload all the furniture," Finn said as they drove into Port Isaac.

"I forgot about that."

"Is there room in your barn?" Finn asked as though it had only dawned on him how limited her space was.

"There's a garage around the back of the barn where we can store it. I'll take each piece out to work on."

The repairmen helped unload the van, so between the four of them they made quick work of it and Mabel's aching muscles were grateful for the extra hands. The men then drove the van to the hire company to save Finn the journey.

"Will it take you long to refinish the pieces?" asked Finn as they wandered back along the path to Mabel's front gate.

"Hopefully not. I can't say for sure as you never know what you'll unearth." She fought back a yawn but was unsuccessful.

"I'll let you have a shower and a midday nap. Why don't you pop around tomorrow evening? I owe you a lasagna."

Mabel's stomach filled with butterflies, and she nodded while she fought to find her voice. "I'd like that."

"Good. See you at six?"

"See you then."

He leaned forward and pressed a chaste kiss to her cheek.

Mabel leaned against the gate as she watched him walk down the hill and towards the harbour. Finn Hart was stirring up emotions inside her that had lain dormant for almost a decade, and she didn't know how to feel about it. A warmth spread through her as he gave her a last wave before turning the corner.

CHAPTER SIXTEEN

"Elowen Appledore, reporting for work," El called as she wandered along the path to where Mabel was scrubbing a table and chairs with a bucket of soapy water.

"Thanks for this, El. There's so much to get through." Mabel had texted Elowen yesterday to let her know she was home safe. Her sister-in-law had immediately suggested a coffee date to hear about Mabel's impromptu night away with Dishy Finn. Mabel knew Elowen wanted to quiz her on what had happened, so she was grateful to have the excuse of being too busy.

"I should be thanking you. You've saved me from another boring morning of filling out job applications."

"I'm sorry, El. Finn's paying me a deposit in the next day or two, so I'll pay you for the hours you work today."

"I wouldn't normally accept payment, but the girls have each come home with letters for a school trip. Each one is fifty pounds."

They grumbled about the cost of the trip while Elowen pulled on a pair of rubber gloves and got to work scrubbing a table.

"How was your night away?" Elowen asked, swiftly changing the subject.

"Awful, but the company was lovely." Mabel recounted the trip and the night's stay at the pub.

"You shared a bed?" Elowen's shrill voice caused a few birds to flee their perches on the surrounding branches.

"Nothing happened."

"How disappointing."

"He was shirtless." Mabel chewed her bottom lip at the memory of Finn emerging from the bathroom.

Elowen stopped her scrubbing. "Is he as dishy as his reputation suggests?"

Mabel giggled but nodded. The laughing ended abruptly, and Mabel knew she had to confess her growing feelings. She wanted to hide them in a box and forget about them, but she couldn't. The only person she could talk to about it was Elowen. Del was too wild and would tell her to risk everything for the sake of love, but Mabel couldn't do that.

"What is it?" Elowen's expression changed

from one of mirth to concern.

"I like him," muttered Mabel. It was the first time she'd admitted it to someone other than herself and Finn, and her stomach rolled at the confession.

"Does he like you?"

"He says he likes me. We opened up to each other, and it felt like we shared a moment."

Elowen's concerned expression softened. "Only you can decide to risk your heart again, Mabel. I can't decide for you, but from what I've seen of Finn and everything you've told me, I don't think you'd find a better person to risk it with."

Mabel scrubbed harder at a spot of ink. Deep down, she'd known what Elowen would say, but still, she found it hard to digest. A part of her had hoped she'd warn her away from Finn and allow her to retreat into her shell.

"He's invited me around for dinner tonight," admitted Mabel. She'd dropped the sponge, giving up on the ink. It would have to be sanded out instead.

"Are you looking forward to it?"

Mabel considered the question. "Yes, I am. I'm looking forward to seeing him."

"That's a great start. Don't overthink it for now. Concentrate on the excitement."

It sounded like good advice, so Mabel nodded and lost herself in the monotonous task of scrubbing each tabletop.

They scrubbed for hours until the furniture was clean and ready for Mabel to start sanding tomorrow. It was a big job, but it was one she was looking forward to getting stuck into. Knowing the pieces were going into Fisherman's Rest for the benefit of Port Isaac only spurred her on. Once she started, the tables would be quite straightforward to sand. The chair's spindly legs would be time-consuming. Mabel was eager to make a start, but her aching body slowed her down. Once they'd finished cleaning the furniture, Elowen and Mabel agreed it was enough work for one day. Elowen insisted on running home for a shower and getting sandwiches for their lunch. That had left Mabel with a spare hour to shower and clean and tidy before her sister-in-law returned. It wasn't that Mabel was untidy; it was just that her standards weren't as high as Elowen's.

"I've got egg sandwiches from Betty's," Elowen announced as she let herself back into the cottage without knocking. "Shall we have them outside?"

They wandered through to Mabel's back garden, where a small wrought-iron table and chairs were under a honeysuckle arch. The buds were bursting to flower, and with the warmer weather forecast, the arch would soon bloom with sweet-smelling flowers which bees would flock to. Mabel's little garden was a sun trap during the summer months and she looked forward to lounging in the warm rays with a good book and an iced chocolate milkshake. If you strained your ears, you could make out the sound of the sea.

"I love your garden. It's so wild and free," Elowen said. She'd spread a napkin on the table before putting down her sandwich, which Betty had carefully wrapped in foil.

Mabel hid a chuckle at Elowen's remark. "It's a peaceful place, and it's brimming with life," she said as she opened her sandwich on the table. Mabel had long since learned that Elowen's comments weren't meant in a nasty way. She genuinely liked Mabel's garden for its wildness, but her hangups would never allow her to have the same.

"What are you wearing tonight?" Elowen asked.

"I haven't thought about it."

"We'll look through your wardrobe once we've eaten," Elowen said in such a way that Mabel knew she wouldn't take no for an answer.

Elowen had brought a peppermint tea bag with her, so after making a drink, they went to look through Mabel's wardrobe.

"Do you have an outfit in mind?" asked Elowen.

"No. I don't want it to look like I've made too much of an effort."

"Let's see." Elowen put her mug on the bedside table and dived into Mabel's meagre selection. "This is beautiful." She got out a brightly coloured dress which Mabel had forgotten she owned. "Try it on," instructed Elowen.

Mabel took the dress into the bathroom and

slid it over her head. The soft material clung to her body and ended mid-calf. It was a pale pink with hand-painted flowers in reds, greens, and golds.

"It's perfect," Elowen said as soon as she saw Mabel.

"Do you like it? Zoe gave me it for my birthday. It's hand-dyed and painted by her. The dress is vintage. She bought it from The Cornish Vintage Dress Shop." Zoe had painted poppies over the dress with their green stalks standing out against the red and pink hues. The painting was in a watercolour style and blended perfectly with the fabric. Mabel had declared it a work of art when she'd opened the gift.

"It's gorgeous. You could wear a casual pair of sandals, or white trainers if you insist on walking home. Do you want me to do your hair? I've got half an hour before I need to leave to pick the girls up."

"Yes, please. Could you put it in a low bun for me?"

Elowen worked her magic on Mabel's hair and twisted her blonde locks into a casual low bun in the nape of her neck. It was understated, but pretty.

"It's so nice to have this time with you, Mabel. I'm always so serious around the girls, and life is so stressful right now. Michael and I never have fun." Elowen sighed and perched on the edge of the bed.

"You can always pop around to me for an escape," Mabel said, sitting beside her.

"Thank you. You're the sister I always wanted," Elowen whispered.

"Don't make me cry, El. I can't turn up to Finn's with puffy eyes."

Elowen laughed through her tears. "Sorry. Ignore me. There's so much going on right now and your support means a lot." She threw her arms around a stunned Mabel. Elowen rarely showed emotion. Mabel could count on one hand the times she'd seen Elowen cry.

"We'll be okay, El," Mabel promised, and for the first time in weeks, she felt as though they really would be.

CHAPTER SEVENTEEN

Mabel was entirely overdressed to walk to Fisherman's Rest. It was early evening and shops were closing as tourists headed home for the day. Mabel smiled at those she recognised but didn't linger, not wanting to be pulled into a conversation.

"Where are you off to, Mabel?" It was Gwen.

Mabel cringed internally and spun on her heel to greet the woman. "Hi, Gwen." There was no point lying. Gwen would see her enter the pub. "I've got a meeting with Finn. We picked up the furniture for the pub, so I need to finalise his plans for the interior," she rambled.

"Rather overdressed for a business meeting." Gwen raised her brow as she took in Mabel's appearance.

"It was a gift from Zoe," Mabel said, avoiding Gwen's inference.

"A lovely date night outfit."

Mabel decided it would be easier not to disagree with Gwen. "I ought to go. Finn's expecting me. See you soon, Gwen." Mabel waved and walked away before Gwen could answer.

"Enjoy your date," Gwen shouted after her, and Mabel's stomach twisted into knots. Everyone had heard, which meant by tomorrow morning the whole harbour would know she had a date with Finn Hart. Mabel's breaths came in fast, short gasps, and the evening closed in around her.

"Are you okay?" a voice called. It was Finn, standing at the pub's entrance.

Mabel nodded and hurried over to him. She didn't need to turn around to know everyone was watching them. "Quick, go inside." She nearly shoved him through the doorway in her rush to flee.

Mabel's hands grasped Finn's shoulders as they stumbled into the pub. His hands came to her waist to steady her, and he shut the door behind them. A blush rose on her cheeks as she worked to slow her breathing.

"You can let go now," she said, her eyes meeting his.

"Huh?"

"Your hands."

"Right." He gulped, then let go, stepping back until he hit the wall.

"I bumped into Gwen," Mabel explained.

"Ah." He ran a hand through his hair.

"Are you okay?" asked Mabel. He'd only managed a few words since she'd barrelled into him.

"Yes. Sorry." He shook his head and pushed off the wall. "You took me by surprise. You look amazing. Come on through." Finn led her through to the bar.

"I didn't expect it to look so different in here." Mabel slowed to take everything in. The carpets had been ripped up and the natural wood floors were exposed, the flaking paint around the windows had been stripped and the bar was half sanded, the thick varnish had been removed to reveal the beautiful natural wood underneath. "You can't leave that without a varnish," Mabel said, slipping into work mode. The wood would be damaged in no time with the inevitable spillages.

"I know. Nick is going to re-varnish it once we've stripped it. There were so many layers already on it that it was easier to strip it back."

"It'll look lovely once it's finished."

"How's the furniture coming along?"

"Elowen and I spent today cleaning everything so I can start sanding tomorrow."

"Do you need any help?"

"It's my job, Finn," she reassured him. "I'll be fine." She smiled to show she was grateful for his concern, even if it wasn't needed.

"Since it's such a mess in here, I've set up a table on the decking outside." He opened the door and held it for her to walk through.

Mabel stepped onto the decking and let out a soft gasp. The foliage had been cut back to make the most of the area. There was a gap in the hedge with steps onto the beach, providing a beautiful view down to the sea. Potted plants were scattered along the perimeter. Several wrought iron tables and chairs were dotted around, and fairy lights twisted around the overhead pergola. It felt like a sheltered haven at the edge of the world, with the sea stretching out for miles ahead.

One table had a crisp white tablecloth, cutlery set out, and a candle burning. A delicate jasmine smell wafted up with the flames.

"It's beautiful," Mabel said, keeping her voice soft, as though any loud noise would shatter the moment.

"The perfect secluded spot for dates in Port Isaac?" Finn stood close enough to touch, but Mabel kept her hands firmly at her sides. His gaze sizzled through her and she used her hand to fan herself.

"Are we test-driving it?" she whispered.

"I can't think of anyone I'd rather test drive the area with." He took a step towards her so his chest brushed hers. Finn placed a finger under her chin to tilt her head upwards. "You look beautiful," he said, his eyes never leaving hers. His lips were a breath away. Finn's hands fell to her hips, and hers came to rest on his shoulders. In the distance, the sea crashed and a handful of seagulls squawked above, but Mabel and Finn remained oblivious. Neither could look away from the other as their chests rose and fell. A loud beeping from Finn's pocket made them jump and leap apart.

"Sorry, it's the timer for dinner," he explained, turning it off. It was too late, though. The moment was over.

"Come on, let's check on it." Mabel threaded her fingers through his and led him to the kitchen.

It was hot and stuffy in there with the oven whirring, but the smells were mouth-wateringly delicious. "What's for dinner?" asked Mabel. She leaned against the doorframe while Finn busied himself checking the oven.

"I promised you a lasagna, didn't I?" He took out a glass dish. The cheese on the top bubbled as he put it on the counter. "It's a Cornish take on an Italian speciality."

"What's Cornish about it?"

Finn put a saucepan of boiling water on the hob and added spring greens. "I've tried to keep it as local as possible, excluding a few things I had to go further afield for. The carrots and leeks are grown locally. The mince is from the farm down the road. Then the cheese and milk used for the sauce are from the local dairy farm. I met with them about supplying the pub and they let me try everything. It was hands down the best business meeting I've ever attended. Where was I? Oh, yes. Then the pasta is made by one of the local ladies. She's from Italy and married a Cornish fisherman."

"Lucia? She's the mum of my niece's best friend."

"She makes amazing pasta, and sources all of her ingredients locally."

All this talk of food was making Mabel's stomach rumble.

"I'll finish off the spring greens and then dish up. There are bottles of wine and glasses in the storage room next door. Why don't you fetch them and I'll meet you outside?"

Mabel nodded and went to choose a bottle of red.

It was still a couple of hours until sunset, but the lighting was changing and there was a gentle golden hue above the glistening sea.

Dinner was as delicious as it had smelt. Finn had drizzled the spring greens in garlic butter and served them on the side. The flavours were rich and indulgent and Mabel knew they would have people flocking to Port Isaac for Finn's food. As they ate, the conversation flowed and Mabel couldn't remember laughing so much in one evening. Everything with Finn felt natural.

Time slipped through their fingers as the sun slowly set. It was a magnificent sunset with hues of orange and pink lighting up the sky as the sun slowly dipped below the horizon.

"Shall we go for a walk on the beach?" suggested Mabel. The sun had disappeared, and the moon lit the beach, reflecting off the glassy sea.

"That sounds lovely." Finn held his hand out for Mabel. She slipped off her sandals and followed him barefoot onto the sand. It was cool and soft beneath her feet as she sunk into it. Finn's firm grasp kept her from stumbling.

"Let's dip our feet in." Finn led her towards the water's edge, which lapped at the beach.

Mabel let out a little squeak as the water washed over her feet, up to her ankles. It was colder than she'd expected. Finn chuckled at her reaction and let go of her hand as he took another step forward.

"Fancy a swim?" he asked.

"I don't have my costume."

"We could skinny dip."

Mabel couldn't make out his features, but she could hear the smile in his voice. "After you," she teased.

As he turned to her, Mabel could make out his silhouette. She shrieked as he cupped a handful of water and flicked it her way. The cold water splashed against her legs, and she ran back to the beach.

"It's freezing," she complained as Finn followed her.

"It is. How do you swim in that?"

"I like it in the morning. It's an exhilarating way to start the day."

"Can I join you?"

"Of course. Maybe not tomorrow morning, but the day after?"

"I'll be there."

He stood in front of her, and Mabel reached out and held his hand. It was cold and damp from the sea. Finn's other hand cupped her cheek. She jumped at the cold water, but his touch burned through it. This time, there were no interruptions as his lips met hers. Her arms wound around his neck, and her fingers tangled in his hair. Finn's arms dropped to her waist, and he pulled her to him. His taut body against hers sent a shiver along Mabel's spine. She lost herself in the kiss until Finn pulled back and tucked a strand of hair behind her ear. Mabel's stomach was filled with butterflies. Their kiss had left her feeling as though she were floating.

CHAPTER EIGHTEEN

Mabel woke with a small smile playing at the corners of her lips. She sat up in bed and stretched. The sun looked high in the sky and she guessed it was much later than she normally woke. Last night, after their kiss on the beach, Finn drove her home and kissed her one final time on her doorstep. A dazed Mabel had changed into her pyjamas and stumbled into bed to lie there and dream about how wonderful his lips had felt against hers. It had been a magical night of romance and laughter. Mabel had never experienced anything like it before, and she suspected she would never experience anything like it again.

Mabel's happy mood continued as she readied herself for the day. Despite the late wake-up, she had a lot of furniture to sand down, so she threw on a pair of old shorts and a vest and had a quick breakfast of toast and chocolate milk. Her phone had buzzed nonstop all morning with texts from Elowen. Each one was asking how her date with Finn had been. Mabel glanced at the time. It was past school drop off, so she called Elowen rather than spend the morning going back and forth over messages.

"Tell me you've only just got home from a night with Finn," Elowen answered the phone.

"El!" screeched Mabel.

"Sorry. How was it?"

Mabel picked at the edge of one of her scatter cushions. "It was lovely, El. He set out a table on the decking. It was so romantic with fairy lights and candles. Dinner was delicious, and we talked and laughed for hours." Mabel's voice had become dreamy as she relived the evening.

"Did you kiss him?"

"Yes." Mabel blushed, even though there was nobody around to see.

"It sounds wonderful." Elowen let out a wistful sigh. "Are you seeing him again?"

"We're going swimming tomorrow morning."

"Have fun. We'll see you on Sunday for lunch?"

Mabel promised she'd be there and said goodbye to her sister-in-law.

Not wanting to spend a lovely day inside, Mabel opted to sand outside the barn. Mrs Lavender's car wasn't in her driveway, so she would have no complaints about the noise.

With the hot, heavy mask on, Mabel sanded table after table. It was hard and physically exhausting, but there was something so satisfying about peeling back the layers to reveal the beautiful wood. The oak grain was a swirl of patterns. It always amazed Mabel how nature had created something so understated, but beautiful.

By lunchtime, she'd sanded down a handful of tables. The tops were the easy part. She could use her mouse sander for those. It was the legs that were slowing her. In many places, they had to be sanded by hand to reach the fiddly areas. Mabel's fingers still held the ghost of vibrations from the sander and her hair stuck to the back of her neck where it had fallen loose from its bun. She huffed and stood up straight, stretching her sore back.

"You look busy," a voice called, and she jumped.

She watched as Finn strolled towards her with two takeaway cups from Fisherman's Brew. Mabel whipped off her mask and sucked in a lungful of fresh air. "Hello," she said, feeling shy around him after last night.

"Sorry, I didn't mean to interrupt." He looked good today in green linen shorts and a white t-shirt.

"No, it's fine. I could do with a break." She wiped her dusty hands on the back of her shorts and ushered him around to the garden. "I'd invite you inside, but I don't want to get dirt everywhere."

"It's fine. I stopped at Betty's and she told me this is your favourite summer drink." He pushed one of the takeaway cups across the table towards her.

"Mmm," hummed Mabel as she took a sip. "An iced chocolate."

"Do you ever drink water?" Finn chuckled.

"There's water in this."

"You know what I mean."

"I do, and yes, I drink water. I've gone through two bottles already today. It's so hot." She fanned herself.

"Do you need help? I've never done it before, but I'm sure I could do something."

"Thanks, Finn, but I'm fine. I'm used to this." She shrugged and sipped her drink, tilting her head back to bask in the sun. It was a glorious day, and she'd missed most of it under the shade of the trees.

He didn't say anything, so Mabel cracked open an eye and saw he was staring. "What?" she asked, blushing.

"Don't get me wrong, you looked amazing in last night's dress, but I love seeing you like this. You're in your element and you're glowing."

Mabel smiled. His words had left her speechless.

He cleared his throat. "Sorry, that slipped out."

"I liked it," she whispered.

"Good." He grinned. "I haven't got long. Nick's popped to his yard to pick up a few things. Then he needs me at the pub to make decisions. I did something this morning, and I wanted to tell you about it." His expression hardened.

"What is it?" asked Mabel. She reached across

the table and took his hand in hers.

"I've found my dad." He picked at the plastic top of the takeaway cup while Mabel processed what he'd said.

"Is that a good thing?" She tried to read his expression but couldn't.

"I'm not sure. Since we spoke about it, I've been thinking about him."

"How did you find him?"

"I know where he works. There's a picture of him on the websites and there's no mistaking it. It's him. He looks like an older version of me." Finn sucked in a shaky breath.

"Take some time, Finn. You don't have to act on this information until you're sure what you want to do."

"I know. It's strange because I've always known he lived around here, but now I know where he works, it feels more real. He's a chef, Mabel." The words hung in the air as Finn scrubbed a hand across his face and Mabel processed the information.

"Oh, Finn," she whispered. Mabel didn't know what to say, so she stood and pulled him into her arms. He clung to her.

"Sorry. I didn't mean to dump my emotions on you." He sniffed and stepped out of her embrace.

"Don't be sorry. I'm here if you need to talk, okay?"

He nodded. "Anyway, I should get off. Are we still on for our morning swim tomorrow?"

"Of course. See you there at six."

"AM?" He looked horrified.

Mable nodded.

"I'll roll out of bed at five to." He pressed a quick kiss to her lips before leaving.

Mabel got a cereal bar from the barn. She kept a stash in there for her lunches on busy days. It was a beautiful day, and she watched as a butterfly danced across the air and landed on one of her fuchsia pink roses. There was a calmness in the air, but it felt at odds with her after Finn's revelation. She'd been brought up in a loving family and community, so she found it difficult to relate to his pain. It saddened her to think of him all alone.

CHAPTER NINETEEN

Mabel packed the bag for her swim like any other morning. Only today, her heart was galloping, and she'd struggled to choose which swimming costume to wear. Eventually, she'd settled on her favourite red one and threw a jumper and shorts over it. The weather was overcast and cold, but that wouldn't stop her from having an early morning dip.

Finn texted as she left the cottage to say he was awake and would meet her on the beach. Mabel couldn't hide her smile as she wandered down to the harbour. A handful of people milled around, preparing for the day ahead. Some waved to her, but on the whole, most people were too preoccupied going about their morning tasks to worry about where Mabel was off to. Besides, there was nothing out of the ordinary about her morning trip to the beach. Nobody else knew she was meeting Finn. The excitement glistening in her eyes or the deep blush on her cheeks would give her away, but nobody's gaze lingered long enough to see.

As always, the beach was empty. Tracks in the sand from where the fishermen had launched their boats were the only signs they'd been there before sunrise. Mabel put her bag in its usual spot and got her towel ready.

"Morning," a groggy Finn called.

Mabel looked up as he walked down the steps from the pub's decking. His hair looked as though he'd just rolled out of bed. He wore navy swim shorts and a tatty old t-shirt.

"Morning," she called back.

"It's chilly," he complained. Finn put his towel beside hers and stretched as if he were about to go for a run.

"You'll warm up once you start swimming," Mabel stumbled over her words as Finn pulled off his top. His toned chest was tanned and his swim shorts sat low on his hips. Mabel flushed as she took him in.

"Mabel?" he prompted as he neared her.

"Sorry. Still half asleep," she lied.

"How do you usually do this?"

She cleared her throat. "Do what?"

"Swim. Are you sure you're okay?" Finn stepped closer, which set Mabel's pulse racing. His chest almost brushed against hers.

"I, er…I walk into the sea and swim?"

"On three?" he said, stretching a hand towards her. She glanced at his hand, wanting to take it and feel his strong grip on her, but she couldn't.

"Race you," she called and took off towards the sea.

Finn was hot on her heels and by the time she'd reached the surf, he'd caught up with her. His arms wrapped around her waist, and he pulled her into the sea with him. Mabel's laughter drowned out her objections as the cold water crept up her body. The sea was icy, but it couldn't extinguish the burning sensation that coursed through her.

"This is awful. How do you enjoy it?" asked Finn. He was gasping as his body adjusted to the temperature. He'd let go of her waist and ripples of cold water lapped around her middle.

"You need to move. How's your swimming?" Mabel kept walking into the water until it was over her shoulders and she kicked her feet and arms to move. The monotony of keeping afloat was what she needed to distract her from the shirtless Finn.

"I'm a strong swimmer."

"Good. Let's swim out to the harbour wall and back."

"Is it safe?"

Mabel rolled her eyes and swam, leaving Finn to hastily follow.

⋙⋘

By the time they reached the shore, Mabel had warmed up and felt invigorated. Meanwhile, Finn looked as though he was hating every moment.

"How was that?" Mabel asked as they walked across the beach to their towels.

"Horrible. It was so cold. Do you really enjoy it?"

"I wouldn't do it if I didn't enjoy it."

Finn got a towel and wrapped it around her before picking his own up. "Do you want to come in for a warm shower and a hot chocolate?"

"I'd love to." It was too early in the day for her to start sanding, so she had nothing to rush home to.

Finn showed her into the pub and upstairs to the flat. It was sparse and didn't look like he'd done anything to make it home. A handful of furniture remained from the previous owners, but beyond that, there was nothing to suggest Finn lived there.

"Have you not had time to decorate? Or buy anything?" Mabel asked as Finn led her into the living room.

He looked around as though he was seeing the place for the first time. "I've been so focused on the pub that I've not thought about it."

"There'll be plenty of time to make this home."

He dragged a hand through his wet hair and shifted his weight from one foot to another. "Let me get you a towel. You can use the main bathroom and I'll jump in the ensuite."

Mabel nodded, but Finn had already left. She

wandered around the room while she waited. There was a sagging sofa which looked like it was once a deep maroon but was now faded. The only other piece of furniture was a pine coffee table. It was covered in a laptop and piles of letters, some opened, others still sealed.

"Here we go," Finn said. He handed her a plush white towel. "There's shampoo, conditioner, and shower gel in there."

Mabel's brow furrowed. "Should I be worried a woman in your life is about to walk in on me in the shower?"

Finn chuckled. "No. Experience from a lifetime of working in hospitality."

"Just checking." She reached up on her tiptoes and pecked him on the cheek before scurrying to the bathroom to warm up and wash away the salty sea.

⇝ ⇜

"That's better," Mabel said as she wandered back into the living room, her wet hair cascading down her back.

"Much. Do you want breakfast?" Finn's hair had almost dried, and he was tapping away on his laptop. The pile of letters had been tidied away.

"Only if you have time." Mabel rested on the doorframe.

"There's always time for breakfast. Let's go down to the pub's kitchen."

Mabel toasted bread while Finn whisked up two hot chocolates. The kitchen was sparsely stocked since the pub wasn't open yet.

"When are you planning on opening?" asked Mabel. She'd found a box of miniature jams in the pantry and was sifting through them to check the dates.

"Nick said he can have the place ready in a couple of weeks. His dad has finished a job and is going to join him. Then it depends on how long you need for the furniture. I don't want to rush you."

"Two weeks should be okay. There's enough in the budget for me to pay Elowen for a few hours of help."

"Two weeks it is." He beamed.

They ate outside and watched as the beach came to life. The fishing boats returned and children ran to greet their fathers before being ushered to school. Morning dog walkers meandered onto the beach. Dogs ran in and out of the waves, and others chased balls on the sand. It was a hive of activity and Mabel sank into her seat as she watched.

"You look beautiful," he said.

Mabel fought the urge to check she hadn't smeared jam across her face. He reached out and took her hand in his. They sat like that for a while as they watched life pass by on the beach.

"I should go," a reluctant Mabel said. The fishermen were readying the boats for their second outing.

Finn reluctantly agreed. "I have a meeting

soon, and Nick will be here any minute."

Mabel gathered their plates and mugs and followed Finn inside. She set everything on top of the bar and Finn gathered her in his arms, kissing her before she even had time to catch her breath.

They broke apart at the sound of the door opening. "Will I see you soon?" Finn asked.

"I'll text you." Mabel blew him a kiss as she slipped out the back door. She took the steps down to the beach and walked around the pub to avoid bumping into Nick.

CHAPTER TWENTY

Mabel groaned as her alarm echoed throughout the small bedroom. Ethel stood and stretched, making her disgruntled feelings known before curling back against the pillow.

"Sorry, Ethel. You stay in bed. I'll be home later," Mabel said. She was usually an early riser, but today Mabel's body ached from sanding, and her dry eyes craved another hour of sleep. Instead of nestling her head back into the soft pillow, she rose from the bed and readied herself to meet Zoe for breakfast.

Mabel speed-walked to the bus stop and arrived as the bus turned the corner. She chose a seat towards the back. Although the bus was mostly empty, it would fill up on the way to Padstow-on-

Sea. Last night, Zoe had texted her asking if she wanted to meet for breakfast. She'd booked to go with Jada, but a last-minute staffing issue meant she couldn't go. Never one to turn down an invitation, Mabel had said yes. They'd agreed to meet outside The Seaside Cauldron in Padstow-on-Sea. The table was booked for the first breakfast slot available.

The bus wound its way along the Cornish country lanes, and Mabel watched as the vista passed. She longed to get out and stretch her legs, but the journey would take at least another half an hour. There was a haze across the sea, but once it burnt off, it would be a bright, lovely day. At this time of the morning, the roads were quiet, with a handful of people heading out to work.

Zoe was waiting outside The Seaside Cauldron when Mabel arrived.

"I'm sorry it's so early," Zoe said, hugging her.

"It's fine. I'm an early riser."

"I've not eaten here before, but I know Jada has, and she said their food is divine."

"Would you ladies like to sit inside or out?" asked a waiter.

Zoe glanced at Mabel. "Outside?" she asked.

"Always outside."

They were led to a terrace area with views towards the sea. Amongst the haze, were boats readying themselves for the day. In the distance, the sun rose over Padstow Bay, shrouding it in a beautiful glow. It was a wonderful spot to watch the harbour come to life.

"How are you?" Mabel asked as they took their seats.

"Amazing. Finn's commission means we'll have enough for a deposit, so we've put an offer in on one of the old fisherman's cottages."

"I'm so happy for you." Mabel beamed across the table.

Zoe's excitement was infectious. "We'll need furniture once we're settled, so expect to hear from us."

"Of course. I can't wait."

Zoe told Mabel all about the cottage they were buying and explained how she wanted to decorate it. Amongst the excitement, a waiter came to take their order. They both chose scrambled eggs with salmon on sourdough toast.

"So," Zoe dragged out the word. "How are things between you and Dishy Finn?"

Mabel blushed. "I wish everyone would stop calling him that."

"It's fine. Nobody calls him it to his face."

"They're good. It's early days and we're enjoying each other's company."

"It's nice to see you happy, Mabel."

Breakfast was delicious. The restaurant had filled up around them and there was a buzz of conversation.

"I'm going to pop to the bathroom," Zoe excused herself.

Mabel leaned back in her chair and took in her surroundings. She could overhear the table next to them complaining about the way the eggs had been cooked. The poor waiter sounded like he was at his wit's end and had promised to bring the chef out to speak to them. Mabel wondered how Finn would deal with a situation like that. Would he do everything he could to appease the customer, or would he let his waiting staff handle it?

In less than a minute, a man in chef whites walked out onto the terrace and went to chat with the table. He introduced himself as Lowen Bennett. Mabel's heart hammered in her chest and her palms grew clammy. She took in every inch of the chef's appearance. His eyes shocked her the most. Mabel knew what it was like to lose herself in those eyes, but here they were, on someone else. It was Finn's father. He was Finn's double with a sprinkle of grey hairs. Lowen appeased the customers and laughed with them. It wasn't long before he had whisked their plates away and disappeared back to the kitchen.

"Are you okay? You look like you've seen a ghost." Zoe slipped back into her seat.

"Sorry. I forgot about a piece of furniture and realised the customer is collecting it tomorrow. I ought to head home to work on it." Mabel needed to get Zoe out of the restaurant as quickly as possible. If the chef brought the fresh dishes back out, then Zoe would recognise the resemblance.

"It's not like you to forget." Zoe gathered her phone and slipped it into her handbag.

"Sorry. I don't know if I'm coming or going

lately."

"I paid on the way back from the bathroom so we can leave."

"You didn't have to do that."

"My treat."

"I'll treat you and Jada to dinner at the pub once it's open," promised Mabel. "We can celebrate your new home."

"That sounds lovely. Thanks for joining me, Mabel."

They hugged before going their separate ways. Mabel wandered back to the bus stop in a daze. She knew it would hurt Finn if she told him about today, but could she keep it from him?

The bus was already there, and Mabel stumbled into the first empty seat. Her phone buzzed in her pocket. It was a text from Finn asking if he could see her later. Mabel sucked in a shaky breath as she stared at the screen. She wanted to see him, but her thoughts were jumbled and she didn't know what to do for the best. Ignoring his message, Mabel shoved her phone back in her pocket. The Cornish seascape rolled past outside the window, but Mabel was blind to it.

⇛⋯⋘

Mabel threw herself into sanding furniture for the rest of the day. It was a surprisingly effective way of working through her emotions. She felt calmer, but was yet to decide whether to tell Finn.

"You've done loads." Mabel jumped at the voice.

"Finn. What are you doing here?" The colour drained from her face and her hands shook as she put the sander down.

"You didn't reply to my message, so I thought I'd pop by and check everything is okay?" He tentatively stepped towards her.

"Sorry, I must have lost myself in the furniture." It was only a half lie.

"I can see that. Do you know it's seven o'clock?"

Mabel gasped. "Is it really? My neighbour must be out for the evening. I usually stop when she gets home." As she blinked and looked around, Mabel noticed the lighting had changed and the evening glow was setting in.

"Shall I help you put all of this back?" Finn gestured to the furniture scattered across the grass.

"Yes, please."

It was a relief to have something to keep her busy in his company. Finn chatted away about Nick's progress at the pub, which meant Mabel needed to contribute very little to the conversation.

"I should shower," Mabel said, looking at her dust-covered self.

"Have you eaten?"

Mabel thought about it for a moment. She hadn't eaten since breakfast, but didn't want to tell him. "I forgot to have lunch."

"Why don't I make us dinner while you shower?"

Mabel thought about the contents of her fridge and winced. She was about to test his talents. "You can try," she said, a challenge in her voice.

Finn groaned. "Is it that bad?"

"I'm afraid so. Go straight through. You already know where the kitchen is. Don't let Ethel fool you into thinking she hasn't been fed today."

Under the hot spray of the shower, Mabel weighed the pros and cons of telling Finn. She wondered if there was anything to gain. He already knew his father lived in the area and knew where he worked. It would only upset him. But Mabel knew it was wrong to keep something so big from him. No doubt it would churn up some difficult emotions and thoughts, but she had to tell him. It hurt her to know she was about to tell him something that would cause him pain. Mabel stepped out of the shower, knowing she had to speak to him. It was the right thing to do.

Leaving her hair to air dry, Mabel threw on a dress and went to find Finn. Now she had reached a decision she wanted to get it over with. The longer she took, the worse it would be.

"What are you cooking?" Mabel asked. Her kitchen smelt delicious. Ethel's nose twitched as she enjoyed the new smells.

"Pasta. You had eggs and flour, so I made my own. It needs to rest in the fridge for an hour, so I'll make a sauce and let it simmer." He was frying an onion in a pan on the hob and had added herbs from the fresh ones growing on Mabel's window ledge.

They were purely for decoration since she didn't know what each one was.

"I never would have thought to do that. Did you check the onion for mould?" She peered around him into the pan. Mabel didn't know how long the onion had been sitting at the bottom of her fridge.

"I did." He chuckled. Finn put down the spatula and turned to her, his face suddenly serious. "I'm sorry for dropping around unannounced." He reached for her hand and squeezed it. "It's the first anniversary of my mum's death and I didn't want to be on my own."

Mabel's chest ached, and she hugged him. "I'm sorry, Finn. You're welcome here whenever." His arms wrapped around her and he clung to her.

They stayed like that for a few minutes until the smell of burning onion filled the kitchen and Mabel's fire alarm rang through the cottage. Ethel's hair prickled, and she ran for the cat flap.

"It's fine. It'll add to the flavour," Mabel promised as she grabbed a tea towel to wave in front of the alarm.

"I can save it." His voice was steady again.

The piercing noise stopped and Mabel watched as Finn added a tin of chopped tomatoes to the pan. It hissed and spat, but he'd already leapt away as if he knew it would happen. A look of concentration crossed his face, but there was a sadness in his eyes. She couldn't tell him about his father now. Not today. Mabel felt a tightness in her chest from the weight of her secret.

CHAPTER TWENTY-ONE

"We've run out of gravy. Meet me at Port Groceries in about fifteen minutes?" asked Elowen.

"Okay. I'm about to leave, so I'll meet you there." Mabel locked the door to her cottage. She was on her way to Sunday lunch at Elowen and Michael's. It was another beautiful day, and it looked as though summer was finally here to stay. Port Isaac was busy with tourists. Tour guides showed eager day trippers around the winding streets. They'd no doubt stop for a cream tea at Fisherman's Brew before a dip in the sea. Laughter filled the streets and the anticipation and excitement for the day was tangible.

"Good morning, little Mabel," Mr Trelawney said as Mabel wandered into the quiet shop. She returned his warm greeting and wandered down the aisle to the gravy granules, unsure which one to get. The bell above the door chimed, and Mabel was relieved to see El.

"Is everything okay?" asked Mabel as they perused the gravy selection—all two tubs.

"I heard Finn paid you a little visit last night," El said, keeping her voice low.

"He popped by and we had dinner."

"Did you cook?"

"Of course not. He made pasta. From scratch." Mabel raised her brows. "He threw it together."

"Stop it. You're making my legs go weak."

Both women chuckled.

"Did he stay?" asked El.

"No." Mabel glanced around to check there was nobody in earshot. "It was the anniversary of his mum's death, so he didn't want to be on his own."

"Oh, that's so sad. You should have invited him to dinner with us today."

"El, I've not been truthful with him." Mabel told Elowen about Finn's estranged father, Lowen Bennett, and how she had seen him yesterday.

"And you didn't tell him?"

"Of course not. How could I drop it into conversation after he'd told me it was the anniversary of losing his mum?" Mabel groaned. It was all such a mess.

"No, I agree, but you have to tell him. Come on, we should get back. I've left Michael juggling dinner and the kids."

Elowen picked up a tub of gravy and carried it to the till. Mabel hovered as El paid. Her eyes scanned the shop and as they fell on a figure, the pounding of Mabel's heart thrashed in her ears and black spots filled her vision. Gwen was in the aisle next to where she'd just been with El. She would have heard everything.

"Mabel, are you okay?" El asked, grasping her arm.

"We need to go." Mabel ran to the door, knocking over a display of magazines.

"Mabel," El called after her, but she kept running, her breath coming in gasps, and dizziness threatened to steal away her vision.

Mabel ran through the crowded streets to the pub. She went around to the back and thumped on the door. Her pulse pounded as she waited for Finn to answer, but nobody came to the door.

"What's going on?" Elowen asked. She'd finally caught up.

"Gwen was in the aisle beside us. I have to speak to Finn."

Elowen gasped. "I'm so sorry. I never should have asked you about Finn in a public place."

"It's not your fault, El. I should know better." Mabel knocked again, but there was no answer. She stepped back and looked towards the flat, but the curtains were all drawn.

"Why don't you call him?"

"Okay." Mabel's hands shook as she scrolled through her phonebook to Finn's number. "You get back to Michael. I'll be fine."

"No. This is partly my fault. I'm not leaving your side until we've resolved this."

Mabel nodded.

"Hello?" Finn answered almost immediately.

"Finn, it's Mabel. Where are you?" It came out as one long jumble as Mabel fought to catch her breath.

"I'm in Exeter."

"What are you doing there?" Mabel leaned against the wall as the initial wave of panic calmed. She sent Elowen a thumbs-up.

"A last-minute meeting tomorrow morning. I thought I'd drive down early this morning to avoid traffic and spend the day in Exeter. I knew you were busy seeing Elowen and Michael."

"No. That's fine. I need to speak to you, though, Finn. Before you see anyone else in Port Isaac."

"What's going on?"

"Nothing. Don't speak to anyone before me, okay?"

"Mabel, you're worrying me."

"Don't worry. What time does your meeting finish tomorrow?"

"It should all be over by ten."

"Why don't I meet you somewhere for lunch before you return to the harbour?"

There was a pause. "Mabel, what on earth is going on?"

"Gwen overheard a conversation I had with Elowen, and I want you to hear it from me before you hear any gossip."

"Should I be worried?" he sounded like he already was.

Yes. No. Yes.

"No," she forced the word out. "It's something I want you to hear from me."

"There's a nice pub I drove past about half an hour outside Port Isaac. I'll text you the address. How will you get there?"

Mabel glanced around. She could get a taxi, but it would be expensive. Elowen was watching Mabel to gauge how well the conversation was going.

"El has to pop out so she can drop me off." Mabel mouthed a sorry at El, who shook her head as if to say not to worry.

They said their goodbyes and Mabel slumped against the door.

"Okay?" El asked.

"He's in Exeter until tomorrow, and I'm going to meet him at a pub on his way back so nobody can get to him before I do."

"I'll drive you there."

"No, I can't ask that of you, El. I'll get a taxi or see if there's a nearby bus stop."

"I'm taking you. We shouldn't have spoken in public, and if I hadn't pushed you for gossip, Gwen would never have overheard it. The least I can do is give you a lift. No arguments. Come on, we ought to get back to Michael. I'll even allow you to open a bottle of wine."

El linked her arm through Mabel's as they

walked to her house. "It's going to be okay," she promised. They passed crowds of tourists as they wound their way up the hill. People stood taking pictures of doorways and of the view below. Everyone looked so happy and carefree, and Mabel was envious.

"I hope so," she mumbled.

"You hardly went looking for his father. He should have warned you if he didn't want to risk you bumping into him."

"I guess. It's just, I know how much he's struggling with it and I hate to be the one to bring up all that pain for him."

"You have to talk to him tomorrow, Mabel. I know you, and I know you're falling for him, so you can't be afraid to have conversations like this. Make sure you know him before your feelings deepen."

Mabel didn't reply. She didn't know how to tell Elowen it was too late for caution.

CHAPTER TWENTY-TWO

"You look lovely," Elowen said as Mabel got into the car.

"Thank you. I've been sanding, so I had to get ready very quickly." Mabel had woken early to make a start on the furniture and she'd been sanding the spindly legs of the tables ever since. It was the only thing stopping her from worrying about the impending conversation with Finn. Mabel had dressed in a plain white t-shirt and a pair of pink and white gingham trousers, which frayed at her ankles. Her wet hair was left to dry in the summer's breeze.

"Are you nervous?"

"Very."

"You've done nothing wrong."

"Apart from spreading it around the harbour."

Mabel groaned. Gwen would have spent her morning in the Fisherman's Brew telling everyone who would listen about Finn's long-lost father.

Elowen opened her mouth to speak, but Mabel jumped in first. "Don't you dare apologise again, El. It was my fault completely. I should know better than to speak about private things in a public space." Elowen had spent most of Sunday lunch apologising.

"We'll fix it one way or another. Here's the pub." El pointed to a white building on the side of the road. It didn't look like anything special. Finn's fancy four-wheel drive was parked up, but there was no sign of him.

"He must be inside," Mabel commented as she scanned the building for any sign of him.

"Good luck. Text me tonight. I'm going on to an interview, but I can pick you up later if you need me." El reached across the car and pulled Mabel into an awkward hug.

"Good luck for your interview," Mabel said and climbed out of the car.

She took a deep breath and squared her shoulders before she walked into the pub. It was quiet inside, with one or two locals enjoying a drink at the bar. Finn was sitting at a table in the corner, lost in his phone. Mabel paused for a second to take him in. He wore jeans and a blue polo shirt. Finn frowned as he tapped away on his phone. The door behind Mabel slammed, and he looked up. His frown changed to a smile, and he stood to greet her.

"Hello," he said and pressed a kiss to her lips.

"Hi," she squeaked out. Every ounce of her confidence disappeared.

"You look terrified. Come and sit down." He took her hand and led her back to the table.

"I've done something stupid." She hid her face in her hands.

"I don't believe you could ever do anything stupid." His voice was calm, but Mabel recognised an undercurrent to it.

"Elowen and I had a conversation in Port Groceries and it was overheard."

Mabel looked up from her hands as she heard Finn let out a rush of air.

"Is that it? I've been tossing and turning all night, Mabel. I thought you had something truly terrible to tell me."

"It's what I told her. Oh, Finn." Mabel chewed on her lip as she rallied herself to tell him.

"Your order, sir," a waiter said, handing over a paper bag filled with food containers.

"Thank you," Finn choked out and took it. "I ordered for us and thought we could drive to the bay. It's only a few minutes away. Shall we go now? I suspect this isn't a conversation we want people to overhear." Finn glanced towards the people at the bar.

Mabel nodded and followed Finn out to his car. They drove in silence to the bay where Finn parked and led her down to the soft sand. It was a secluded spot which only locals knew of, and so it was empty.

Mabel kicked off her trainers and allowed her toes to sink into the warm sand.

"What is it you need to tell me?" asked Finn. He'd chosen a spot for them to sit and kicked off his shoes.

Mabel joined him and picked up a handful of sand, watching it filter through her fingers. "I went out for breakfast with Zoe on Saturday morning."

Finn looked confused. "You didn't tell me."

"I didn't because I saw someone at breakfast." She let her words hang in the air, hoping Finn would understand what she was trying to say.

"Who did you see?" His voice was low, and he spoke slowly.

"Your father was the chef at the restaurant we went to."

His eyes grew cold and distant, and the confused expression on his face froze before turning into something Mabel couldn't read.

"Did you go looking for him?" His voice was tight.

"No. I promise you, I had no idea he would be there. It was a huge shock when he came out to talk to a customer."

"You saw me on Saturday night but didn't tell me?" His voice shook. Mabel wanted to wrap her arms around him, but she couldn't.

"I was going to tell you, but then you said it was the anniversary of your mother's death, and I couldn't do it. I knew it would upset you, and I didn't want to be the person to cause you that pain."

He took a deep, shaky breath. "Why are you telling me this now?"

"I told Elowen about it yesterday, but we were in Port Groceries. When I told her, I thought we were alone, but then I spotted Gwen down the aisle next to us."

Finn rubbed a hand across his face. "The whole of Port Isaac will know by now. Do you think she'd go as far as to visit my dad?"

Mabel wanted to reassure him that everything would be okay and nobody would approach his father, but she couldn't promise him that. "I don't know," she admitted, her voice sounding small against the crashing waves.

Finn stared out to sea as he took a few deep breaths. Mabel shifted to sit on her hands to stop from reaching out to touch him. He looked so alone and vulnerable in that moment, and she longed to comfort him.

"What was he like?" his voice trembled.

"He was like you. At least he was in looks."

His eyes sought hers, and Mabel felt a rush of sadness as they met. "Was his cooking as good as mine?"

"It was only scrambled eggs and salmon. Even I could have made it with fresh produce." She smiled at him and the corners of his mouth turned up in response.

"It was only a matter of time before someone found out," Finn eventually said.

Mabel took a moment to examine his

expression before she replied. His jaw was set. "Are you sure?" she asked. A selfish part of her needed to know he forgave her. While it was neither of their faults, she hated being the person to tell him something she knew would hurt him.

"Gwen would have found out eventually." He shrugged. "Nothing has changed, just everyone knows the truth." He gave her a weak smile. "If it gets back to my father, then so be it."

"Do you mean that?"

"Yes. He's not been a part of my life, so I'm not about to let him ruin anything for me." His body visibly relaxed. "I'm sorry for pulling you into my messy life," he said, reaching for her.

"All lives are messy, Finn." She shuffled across the sand to close the small distance between them. Mabel knelt in the sand as she brought her hands up to hold Finn's face. She lowered her head to kiss him. His hands roamed her body as they lost themselves in the kiss. All walls between them had shattered and there was nothing to hold them back.

CHAPTER TWENTY-THREE

The words 'Why is there a cat on my head?' were the last thing Mabel expected to wake up to.

"What's going on?" she mumbled.

"There's a cat on my head. I don't know how else to phrase it," came the muffled response from Finn.

"You're on her pillow," Mabel grumbled, rubbing her eyes, which felt like they had grit in them. After their heart-to-heart on the beach, Finn had driven her back to the cottage, and they'd tumbled through the door in each other's embrace.

"She has her own pillow?"

"Of course." Mabel reached out and tickled Ethel under the chin. The little cat purred at the touch and rolled around on Finn's head.

"Maybe you should stay at mine next time."

"Is that an invite?" teased Mabel. She scooped Ethel up and put her on the floor beside the bed.

"Stay tonight?" he asked, propping himself up and leaning to kiss the tip of her nose.

"Okay. I'll come over after I've finished here." She giggled, and he pulled her into his embrace.

"Good. I'll cook us dinner."

⟫⟫⟫ ⟪⟪⟪

They were both late for work by the time Finn left. Mabel had a few more items to finish sanding. The furniture was looking beautiful now it was in its original state. She would need to put a protective layer on it, but that would be simple compared to the days of sanding.

"Is it safe to come in?" Elowen called from the front door.

"Of course. Come in. I'm washing up the plates from breakfast, then we can make a start."

"I passed Finn on my way." She wiggled her eyebrows and Mabel chuckled.

"He stayed over."

"Everything went okay with your chat, then?"

"Yeah. I don't think he's truly processed it all yet, but he knows it probably would have come out sooner or later and he doesn't blame me."

"That's good. So, did he sleep over or did he *sleep* over?"

Mabel flicked soap suds at Elowen. "Come on, we have work to do. I'm so tired. I didn't sleep much last night." She bumped El's shoulder on the way past.

Elowen let out a squeal.

"Come on. I'm not paying you to stand around and gossip." Mabel couldn't risk losing herself in the memories of last night, or else she'd get nothing done.

It took them a few hours to finish sanding the furniture. They'd carried the big dresser out of the garage and between them sanded it. Both were covered in dust and their ears were ringing, but their smiles were huge.

"It's so satisfying to remove years of grime and varnish from a piece," Elowen said as she ran a hand across the natural wood.

"I know. Look at the grain on this dresser. It will look lovely with Zoe's new pieces displayed on it."

"Let's get this put away. I need to run home and shower before I collect the girls from school."

"I'd pay good money to see you pick them up looking like that." Elowen had an old Juicy Couture tracksuit on which was covered in dust. Her hair was coated in a layer of pale dust and mascara was streaked down her cheeks from tears of laughter. "Your yummy mummy friends wouldn't recognise you."

"I have to fit in, Mabel. If I didn't, then the girls would suffer for it."

"El, I know. I'm sorry. I didn't mean to make fun of you." Mabel hugged her sister-in-law. Despite Elowen's preened image, she'd had a turbulent childhood and did everything she could to give the girls the best start in life.

"I know. Are you still coming to my birthday party on Saturday?"

"Of course. I wouldn't miss it for the world."

"Bring Finn," Elowen called from across the front garden. She jumped into the car before Mabel could reply.

It took Mabel a little while to leave the cottage. She showered and packed an overnight bag, including her swimming costume. She couldn't wake up next to the sea without taking a dip. Ethel weaved around Mabel's feet as she packed, knowing something was going on.

"You'll have your pillow tonight," Mabel told her. She filled Ethel's bowls and fussed the cat.

By the time Mabel wandered into the harbour, the little shops and cafes were closing their doors for the day. She waved at Betty through the Fisherman's Brew's window but didn't stop to chat. Mabel knew people would soon start asking her about Finn's parentage, but she wanted to avoid it for as long as possible.

The pub was quiet. Nick had already finished for the day, and there was no sign of Finn downstairs.

"Hello?" Mabel called out.

"I'm just finishing a call. I'll be there in a moment. Go through to the bar and look at what Nick's done," Finn called from the top of the stairs.

Mabel left her bag at the bottom and went to see how the refurb was getting on. The bar area looked beautiful. Nick had done an amazing job sanding the thick, dark varnish, and it was now a beautiful oak which would match the tables and chairs. The original floorboards had been stripped back to make the most of them. It looked bright and fresh in the bar area. Mabel could picture the furniture in the space, dressed with Zoe's crockery, and bunches of flowers from the neighbouring flower farm whose crops changed with the seasons.

"Doesn't it look lovely?" Finn asked. He'd crept up behind her and wound his arms around her waist.

"I love it. The furniture will be ready soon. Elowen and I finished sanding today. I need to put a protective coat on it, then we can bring pieces down."

"It'll be a long process. We'll have to do a couple of bits at a time in my small van."

"We'll figure it out. Anyway, enough business talk. I believe you promised me dinner?"

Finn chuckled. "Did you forget to have lunch again?"

Mabel busied herself chopping garlic to go with their dinner. Finn was cooking crab. Now he was on good terms with the fishermen of Port Isaac, he had access to the best ingredients.

"What are we having with the crab?" Mabel asked.

"Garlic and lemon new potatoes."

"I can't wait. Elowen has invited you to her birthday party on Saturday. Would you like to come?" Mabel concentrated on the clove of garlic on the chopping board. She was cutting it into minuscule pieces.

"We want it big enough to taste." Finn took the knife from her hand and turned her to face him. "Would you like me to go?"

Mabel chewed on her lip. She hadn't allowed herself to think about him accepting the invitation. "I'd love you to come. It'll be Elowen, Michael, and my nieces."

"Ease me into meeting the family." There was a twinkle in his eyes.

"Exactly." Mabel felt a fizz of excitement. She hadn't realised how much she wanted Finn to be a part of her family. There were no doubts in her mind. He would instantly slot into the family dynamic.

"Should I get Elowen a present? Or maybe I should bring a dish?"

"Don't bring any food. Michael's doing a barbecue and he takes it very seriously. Elowen won't expect you to bring her a present. She'll be overjoyed to have you around. She'll be the envy of the school playground when news spreads that Dishy Finn went to her birthday party."

"Dishy Finn?" His eyebrows shot up.

Mabel clamped a hand over her mouth. She hadn't meant to let slip about his nickname. "It's what the mums call you in the school playground. A few dads too."

Finn chuckled, and Mabel thought she saw a small blush on his cheeks.

"And what do you call me?" he asked.

Mabel was feeling particularly brave when she replied. "My boyfriend?"

Finn's face lit up, and he pulled her to him. "I like it. Mabel Appledore. My girlfriend. I like it a lot." He tipped her chin to kiss her.

CHAPTER TWENTY-FOUR

"Morning, Del," Mabel answered the phone. It had been weeks since she'd last spoken to her friend, and so much in her life had changed.

"Mabes, I'm sorry it's taken me so long to call you back. Things have been hectic. I've officially signed the contract for my new job and I wanted to let you know I'll be home a month today."

"I can't wait to see you, Del. Have you got a place to stay?" Usually, Mabel would offer her sofa, or even the empty spot in her bed, but things had changed and that empty spot now had a slight Finn-shaped indent.

"The company's renting a flat for me in Padstow-on-Sea, as there aren't any available in Port Isaac. I'll be commuting a lot for the first couple of months. Their head office is in Exeter, and they want me to tour all their successful pubs across the country."

Mabel swallowed down her thoughts about a corporation taking over pubs. "Padstow-on-Sea is only down the road, so we'll see each other when you're not being paraded around the country."

"Mabes," warned Del.

"Sorry. I am completely indebted to this faceless corporation. They might be stealing the heart from communities, but at least they're bringing my best friend home to me."

"Remind me never to invite you as my plus one to any work events."

"Probably a good idea. Also, I have my own plus one these days."

There was silence from Del before a loud cheer resounded through the phone, so much so that Mabel had to hold it away from her ear. "Tell me everything," Del insisted.

"It's like something from a romance," Del said dreamily as Mabel finished telling her how she met Finn.

"I hope this one has a happy ending," Mabel whispered.

"I'm so proud of you for being vulnerable. I know how much you've protected your heart in recent years, but it's time you found some happiness."

"Do you think so?"

"I do. You put so much into other people's happiness, it's time you focus on your own. Besides, you've not always had terrible taste in men. Do you remember Tommy?"

"Del, I was five years old."

"He treated you lovely for the two months you were together," Del said and Mabel could hear the laughter she was holding in. "Do you remember the box of chocolates he bought you for Valentine's Day?"

"The discounted ones which had been in Mr Trelawney's shop for two years?"

"Hey, the thought was there. He was lovely." Del finally gave in to her laughter and Mabel soon joined in until tears slid down her cheeks.

⁂

By the time Mabel got off the phone with Del, she was running late. Finn was due to pick her up in under twenty minutes, and she still wasn't dressed. She put on a summery jumpsuit with wide legs and a lemon print across it. Her hair was wavy from air drying after her morning swim and she didn't bother putting any makeup on. Mabel scooped Elowen's birthday card and present into a rattan bag as Finn beeped from outside.

"Morning," he called as she got into the car.

"Good morning."

He leaned across the car to kiss her. "I missed

you," he said against her lips.

"You only dropped me at home two hours ago." She laughed and put on her seatbelt. "Are you ready to meet the craziest members of my family?"

"Michael seemed pretty normal."

"I meant my nieces."

The journey to Elowen and Michael's took longer than normal because of the tourists. Small lanes were littered with visitors taking pictures or standing admiring the view with an ice cream in hand. Finn squeezed his car onto the driveway and before they had time to get out, Milly and Mia came running out. They both threw themselves at Mabel once she got out of the car.

"Maple Syrup!" they both screamed and started talking over one another.

"Woah. One at a time," Mabel said, crouching down to them.

"We have your bracelet on," Mia said. She held out her arm to show Mabel the delicate gold chain on her wrist.

"Mummy said we could wear them because it's a special occasion," Milly chipped in.

"They look beautiful on you both and I love your dresses." Elowen had put both girls in matching white dresses with little daisies sewn onto them.

"Thank you," the girls chimed.

"I'd like to introduce you to my friend. Girls, this is Finn. Finn, this is Milly and Mia."

Finn held out a hand for both girls to shake.

With serious faces, they shook his hand.

"Do you know how to play fairies?" Mia asked.

"Erm."

"Of course he doesn't. He's a boy," quipped Milly.

"I can learn how to play fairies," Finn said. He already looked overwhelmed.

Mabel chuckled. "Come on. Let's go inside. I need to wish your mummy a happy birthday." She ushered the girls ahead of them and retrieved her bag from the car.

"Are they always like this?" Finn asked, glancing nervously towards the open front door.

"This is them relatively calm."

Michael and Elowen were in the back garden. Elowen was folding napkins while Michael was warming the coals on the barbecue. Everyone greeted each other, and Mabel gave Elowen her card and present.

"Did you bring a cake?" asked Milly, peering into Mabel's bag.

"Was I supposed to?"

"Daddy forgot to buy Mummy a cake." Milly shrugged, still looking in Mabel's bag as if hoping a cake would suddenly appear.

"It's okay. I don't need a cake," Elowen said, swotting away a fly.

"Everyone needs cake on their birthday," Mia said. She looked horrified.

"Do you have eggs, butter, flour, and sugar?" asked Finn. He'd been quiet until now, watching the events unfold around him.

Elowen thought for a moment. "Is it self-raising flour you need for a cake?"

"Yes. Or baking powder if you only have plain."

"We have self-raising and I'm sure everything else you listed."

"Brilliant. I'll make you a cake. It won't take me long." Finn rubbed his hands together and stood. He went to walk towards the kitchen, then paused. "If it's okay with you? Sorry, I'm used to being in charge of the kitchen."

"No, go ahead and make yourself at home." Elowen smiled sweetly at Finn and Mabel rolled her eyes.

"Can we help?" chorused the girls.

"I'm not sure," Elowen said.

"Of course you can," Finn said. "Do you know the first rule of baking a cake?"

Both girls shook their heads.

"We need clean hands. Can you show me to the bathroom?"

"I might divorce your brother and shack up with Finn." Elowen fanned herself as Finn disappeared inside.

"I can hear you," Michael called over.

Mabel laughed. "You'd never leave him," she said.

"True." Elowen stepped closer so she couldn't be overheard. "He seems like a good one, Mabel."

"I know. Right, I should go in and help him."

The girls had washed their hands and were

putting on their aprons. Milly's was pink and frilly, while Mia's was yellow with an equal number of frills.

"What about your apron, Finn?" Milly asked.

"I don't have one."

"You can wear Mummy's one," Mia said, collecting a purple frilly apron from the hook.

Finn looked dubious, but graciously took it from Mia and put it on. "No pictures," he said to Mabel as she took her phone out.

"Fine." Mabel giggled and put her phone on the worktop. "How can I help?"

"You can't help Maple Syrup. You don't have an apron," Milly said.

Mia looked deep in thought as she looked Mabel up and down. "Your outfit is too nice to get food on it."

"Mabel can supervise," Finn said. Despite his bravado, he already looked out of his depth. "She can start by showing us where all the ingredients are."

"We can show you." Mia took his hand and dragged him over to the fridge.

Mabel sat on one of the breakfast bar stools and watched as the girls helped Finn gather the ingredients. They'd found a tub of cocoa powder at the back of the pantry that was still in date and had decided to make a chocolate sponge. Finn set out all the ingredients and weighed them into little bowls so the girls could mix it themselves. Milly and Mia had dragged over their wooden chairs to stand and help. Finn looked on edge, constantly making sure they wouldn't fall. Mabel was enjoying watching the girls interact with him. Clearly, he didn't have much experience around children, but he was trying his best to include them in every step.

"Did you know Mabel painted that sideboard?" Milly asked, pointing to the other side of the room. She was stirring the flour and cocoa powder to ensure they were combined, while Mia helped Finn measure a teaspoon of vanilla essence.

Finn glanced up. "It's beautiful," he said, his gaze on Mabel.

"She painted it. It's called toilet joy," Mia informed Finn. Her face was a picture of concentration.

Mabel snorted and clasped a hand to her mouth as everyone looked at her. "It's toile de jouy," she explained. The serpentine sideboard had been a wedding present for Elowen and Michael. It was a beautiful piece of furniture, but the wood was damaged and Mabel knew Elowen wasn't a fan of raw wood. She'd painted it black and added a white toile de jouy pattern to the doors. Despite the years of little people running around and knocking into it, it still looked beautiful. It was Elowen's pride and joy, and she always bought fresh flowers to display on it. Today, there was a selection of lilies and sunflowers, and birthday cards scattered around.

The cake was finally ready for the oven, and Finn insisted on putting it in himself. "We don't want to ruin your mummy's party with a burnt finger, do we?" he said, opening the oven door and sliding the cake tins in. "I'll pop a timer on so we don't forget."

"Thank you, Finn," the girls said, hugging him.

"Thank you for helping me," he said, his voice thick with emotion.

"Why don't you both run upstairs to wash your hands again?" suggested Mabel.

The girls went off without a fuss. "Are you okay?" Mabel asked, slipping off the stool and going to Finn.

"Yeah. I'm not used to being a part of a family." He shrugged. "My mum didn't have any siblings. Birthdays were quiet. We'd bake each other a cake and watch a film." His eyes filled with tears. "The last cake my mum made me was a disaster. I didn't know how bad her dementia was until I took a bite of the cake and realised she'd forgotten to add flour."

Mabel nestled into Finn's embrace and rested her head against his chest. "I'm sorry," she said.

"She had moments of sensibleness throughout the day and we did laugh about it." He clung to her and they stood like that until the girls came running back.

"Come on. Let's get you a beer," Mabel said and held his hand as they wandered back outside.

It was a warm day, and the cool beer was welcome. Michael had almost finished the food on the barbecue and was looking increasingly nervous about a renowned chef eating his food. Elowen, on the other hand, was enjoying chatting with Finn. She was asking him about the pub and the menu he was creating for it.

"We have the official opening day set for the last day of July," he said. "I need to find some staff."

Elowen tore the edge off her napkin and shredded it into little pieces. "I have experience from waitressing while at university. It's not exactly relevant, but I did Business Management and Marketing at university and I've supported Michael from the day he set up the business." She stared down at her napkin.

Finn glanced at Mabel, who gave him a small nod. "I'm looking for someone to cover lunchtimes during the weekdays. Would that work around the girls?" he asked.

Elowen's head shot up. "Really? That would be the answer to all our problems."

"You'd be helping me out. I'm dreadful at recruiting. Why don't you pop into the pub on Monday and we can talk about interviews for the rest of the team? I'd pay you for your help." Elowen gasped and rounded the table to pull Finn into a hug.

"What's going on here?" asked Michael. He carried over a plate of cooked burgers.

"Finn's offered me a job at the pub. It's perfect. I can work around the girls' school hours so you don't have to take any time off work." Elowen let go of Finn and threw her arms around her husband. "It's the best birthday present," she declared.

The timer for the cake went off to save Finn from any further embarrassment.

"Thank you so much, Mabel," Elowen said once Finn had disappeared inside, the girls hot on his heels to see how their cake had turned out.

"I haven't done anything."

"Yes, you have. You've solved all of our money problems."

⤞⤝

Lunch was delicious and Michael had promised to share his marinade recipe with Finn. The cake had risen perfectly, and the girls had decided ice cream would be the best filling to sandwich the two layers together. It melted on the plates and everyone ended up with sticky ice cream around their mouth and over their fingers, but nobody minded.

"Thank you for inviting me," Finn said as they sat in the deckchairs watching Michael chase the girls around the garden. Elowen had gone inside to call her parents.

"Thank you for coming with me." Mabel reached out for his hand and he eagerly took hers in his.

"I've been thinking about my dad," he admitted. Finn kept his voice low even though there was no chance anyone would hear him over Milly and Mia's giggles as Michael tickled them.

"What have you been thinking about?"

"About how much he missed. All my birthdays and Christmases that he wasn't there for. There are so many memories I missed out on making with him."

"Oh, Finn." Mabel squeezed his hand.

"I want to try one last time to give him a place in my life. He wasn't a good partner to my mother, or a good dad to me, but people change, don't they?"

Mabel took a moment to respond. Finn stared ahead as the girls overpowered Michael and tickled him. A sad smile played on his lips. "Why don't you invite your dad to the pub's opening day? You could send him an invitation with a note."

"I like that," he said. Finn planted a quick kiss on her lips, but he wasn't quick enough.

"Eww," Milly called.

"Stop kissing Maple Syrup," Mia joined in.

"I'm afraid I'm going to have to agree with the girls on this one," Michael chimed in.

Mabel blushed, and Finn chuckled as he sat back in his chair.

"Can we make another cake?" Mia asked.

"I think it's time Finn goes home," Mabel said. Her overnight bag was stashed in the back of Finn's car.

CHAPTER TWENTY-FIVE

Time was running away from Mabel. For the last week, she'd been working on the pub's furniture from the moment the sun rose to the second it set. Every set of tables and chairs had to be finished. It was an arduous task, ensuring every nook and cranny was covered with a protective layer. Another commission had come in, and she was itching to start it. The large cabinet was to be turned into a drinks cupboard with a big Alice in Wonderland decoupage on the front, and the owner had given Mabel free rein to play with colours and texture. It would be a chance to let her imagination run wild.

"Are you ready for today?" Finn asked, handing her a hot chocolate in bed.

"It's going to be a long day." She rested her

head against the headboard and closed her eyes. They were transporting the furniture from her garage to the pub, and she'd finally see whether all her hard work matched the pub's interior. Nick had done a wonderful job decorating the place, and Zoe was coming in on Monday with her artwork and dinnerware. The little touches would pull it all together and shine a light on the community's talents. Finn had a few surprises, but he refused to tell Mabel what they were. He kept telling her to wait and see.

"I can't wait to see the furniture in place. You've worked so hard on it." Finn tickled Ethel under the chin. They'd learned to share the side of the bed.

"Are you excited about the pub's opening day?" It was a week today and preparations were in full swing. Elowen had taken on the role of organiser.

"I can't wait for everyone to see what we've done." His gaze darkened. "I'm scared, though. Everything relies on the community accepting the changes I've made. If they don't, then I don't just lose my business, but also my home."

Mabel's heart flew to her throat, and a cold sweat broke out across her body. "You can't leave, Finn."

"I don't want to."

"Good. If the pub doesn't work out, then we'll get through it. You're not alone anymore. Besides, the community will be grateful you've kept the pub out of the King's Head Corporation's hands."

"The who?" Finn asked. He'd spilt hot chocolate

down himself.

"It's the corporation that has been trying to buy the pub for the last few years." Mabel handed him a tissue. "They want to turn the pub into a corporate tourist trap. It would price out the locals and turn the harbour into a playground for London's rich and wealthy."

Finn audibly gulped.

"Don't look so worried. You've already won over the community." She took his hand and squeezed it. After a few moments, Finn leaned down to kiss her. When he pulled away, Mabel noticed the dark look still clouded his face.

⟫⟫⟩⟨⟨⟨

They began by putting the furniture out on the grass so it could easily be loaded into the van. After talking to Elowen, they'd hired a bigger van. It was peak tourist season and multiple trips into Port Isaac would take hours whilst navigating the big groups of visitors and tours. Michael was collecting a van from the hire company and would help them load and unload the furniture.

Mabel had found a couple of additional pieces of furniture as a surprise for Finn. There was a beautiful coat stand for the hallway. It would be perfect for winter when people's coats and boots were dripping wet. She'd also picked up a small regency sideboard which she'd stripped the varnish off, and hand-painted Port Isaac's famous crab and lobster logo on the front. Mabel rarely hand-painted her pieces as it took so much time, but she wanted to do something special for Finn and the pub.

"It's gorgeous. You really painted that yourself?" He pulled her to him and peppered kisses on her forehead.

"I wanted you to have something special to remember me."

"I'll never forget you, Mabel Appledore."

They were interrupted by the honk of a van as Michael arrived. "If you two are going to be all over each other, then I'm leaving the van here and walking home," he complained out of an open window.

"We'll be on our best behaviour. Promise," Mabel said, putting distance between her and Finn.

It soon became obvious they wouldn't fit all the furniture in the van for one trip as they had hoped. When they picked it up, they crammed furniture in every spare crevice, but now it had been refinished, they had to be more careful. Any little dents or knocks couldn't simply be sanded out.

By the time they had finished, Mabel's body ached. She was tired and hungry, but it had all been worth it. The beautiful oak tables and chairs were scattered throughout the pub. They'd moved the dresser to the back wall. It looked bare, but it would soon be adorned with Zoe's beautiful creations. Finn had insisted on putting Mabel's hand-painted piece by the door. He wanted to create a stand of local business cards so that people could easily pop by and find someone local for any job that needed doing, or any visitor looking for a local tour guide. It was all coming together and Finn's vision of showcasing local talent was breathing life into the place.

"Will you stay for dinner?" Finn asked Michael.

"I should get back to Elowen and the girls."

"Invite them around. I'll cook for us. It only seems right that we're the first ones to have a meal in the pub."

Michael left to fetch Elowen and the girls, while Finn disappeared into the kitchen. Mabel set out the big table in the middle of the room. They didn't have any placemats yet, so she used newspaper. She gathered a selection of mismatched cutlery from the kitchen and picked daisies from the decked area to put in a jam jar in the centre of the table. With the French doors open, the soft sound of the sea trickled in. Soon, it would be drowned out by the noise of her family, but for now, Mabel was enjoying it.

"Oh, this looks wonderful. Well done, Mabel!" Elowen exclaimed. "I put a box of candles behind the bar. Let me fetch them."

Mia and Milly came running in with a dishevelled Michael behind them. The girls' faces lit up as they took in the pub. They were too young to remember it when it was open before.

"I thought there were ghosts," Mia said, sidling up to Mabel.

"Not anymore. I told you, Finn scared the

ghosts away." Milly very much sounded like the in-charge older sister.

Mabel hid a smirk and caught Michael's eye. They both chuckled.

"You've done amazingly," he said, throwing an arm around her shoulders.

"That's big praise coming from you."

"You deserve it. Thank you, Mabel. For everything."

"Dinner's ready," Finn announced, carrying through empty plates.

"Did you make a cake?" asked Mia, peering behind him towards the kitchen.

"I'm afraid not. It's prawn linguine. Is that okay with you girls? I can rustle up a quick tomato pasta if not."

Michael stepped forward and took the plates from Finn. "They love prawn linguine. Thank you, Finn."

⇒⇒⇒ ⇐⇐⇐

Dinner was delicious, and as Mabel had predicted, the sound of the sea was soon silenced by her nieces' voices. They told everyone about the at-home spa day Elowen had thrown for them.

"Mummy even took us down to the beach so the fishes in the sea could nibble our feet. We saw it on television last week," Milly told them.

"Poor fishes," Finn laughed while everyone else

tried to keep a straight face.

"What are you two up to tomorrow?" asked Elowen. It was a Sunday, but Mabel wasn't going to her brother and sister-in-law's for dinner.

"We thought we'd have a lazy day on the beach," Mabel said, sharing a quick smile with Finn.

"Can we come?" Milly piped up.

"Please, Mummy," Mia pleaded.

"I thought we were going to have a day out to Padstow-on-Sea? You said you wanted to visit the jewellery shop Aunty Mabel bought your bracelets from."

At the mention of their day out, both girls instantly forgot about joining Mabel and Finn on the beach, and Mabel was very grateful for her sister-in-law's wonderful talent for diverting her children's attention.

As the girls yawned, Elowen and Michael said their goodbyes. The sun was low above the sea, and the air was warm and sticky. Mabel went to shower while Finn tidied away everything from dinner. She'd offered to help, but he refused.

Mabel put on a pair of shorts and a vest top before running a towel through her hair. She wandered from the bathroom to the living room to look out at the harbour. A few people wandered around, but the restaurants were busy and a gentle hum of conversation spilled out onto the cobbled streets. Turning her back to the outdoors, Mabel looked around the living room. It was as empty as it had been on her first visit. Finn had made very little effort to turn the space into a home.

"I'm going to jump in the shower," he said, poking his head around the door.

"Finn, once the pub is open, shall we go furniture shopping? If your budget is small, we can find second hand furniture that I can spruce up for you."

He cleared his throat. "I, um, hadn't thought about it. Maybe. Let's get through the opening day first." He disappeared as quickly as he had appeared.

Mabel wandered down to the bar and poured two glasses of red wine. Finn always became jumpy when she brought up the future. She took the glasses to a table and sipped her wine while she waited for him. It didn't take him long to join her.

"That's better," he said, strolling to her.

"Are you okay?" she asked.

"Yes. Why wouldn't I be?" He remained standing.

"You get funny when I talk about decorating the flat or when I bring up the future."

He sighed and sat. "I'm sorry. Settling down isn't something I'm used to. It's not that I don't want to be with you, Mabel."

"Promise?" she asked and stretched her hand across the table.

He grasped it and met her eyes. "I promise."

"Good. Shall we take these onto the beach?" Mabel wanted to leave behind the odd atmosphere and enjoy the rest of the evening.

They took their glasses onto the beach and

sat on the sand. A few people still milled around, enjoying the last hours of daylight.

"I posted an invite to my dad yesterday," Finn said, staring out to sea.

"Where did you send it to?"

"His work. I don't know his home address. There's a chance it won't make it to him, but I've tried."

"I hope it works out for you, Finn." Mabel shuffled closer so their arms and legs touched.

"Me too." He dropped a kiss to the top of her head.

CHAPTER TWENTY-SIX

"Is everything ready?" Mabel asked, walking in on a meeting between Finn and Elowen. It was the eve before the opening day and they'd been running around since sunrise.

"I think so," Elowen said, glancing at the list in front of her.

Mabel had spent much of the day making the pub look pretty. Zoe's pottery was stacked on the dresser for people to get when they needed it. She'd helped Zoe paint the crab and lobster logo on the plates. Beautiful mugs of all shapes and sizes were stowed behind the bar for when people ordered hot drinks. Zoe had even made vases for all the tables with little sailboats painted on them, each a different colour, and all with fragrant flowers in them. Local amateur artists had painted pictures for the walls. There were seascapes, sailboats, and wildlife adorning the pale walls.

Nick and Finn had spent much of the morning hanging bunting around the front of the pub, while Mabel weeded the plant pots and swept the front steps. Betty had been round to give the place a final clean from top to bottom. A new sous chef had started work during the week and Finn had been busy training him. Finn had offered Mabel some shifts in the bar, and she couldn't wait to spend her evenings there, watching the community come together again. But, more than that, she couldn't wait to spend her evenings with Finn.

After much persuading, Finn had secured a local band to play. They would sing traditional sea shanties. Word had spread through the harbour, and everyone was excited to hear them. Gwen had told everyone she met how much she was looking forward to the day. Surprisingly, nobody seemed to know about Finn's father. Mabel wasn't sure why Gwen hadn't spread that particularly juicy piece of gossip, but she wasn't about to ask questions.

Mabel straightened one of the beer mats, which were handwoven by one of the mothers Elowen was friends with. Little touches throughout the pub were by all the locals. It was those small things which were attracting the community back to Fisherman's Rest. Already, the Women's Institute had enquired about booking the function room. They'd always used the pub as a base until it closed. After, they had relocated to Betty's, but it was too small to house all the women and people often missed out on a seat. The Fisherman's Rest was becoming the beating heart of the community again, and it was clear how much it meant to the residents of Port Isaac.

"What more needs to be done today?" asked Mabel. She sat in the spare seat beside Finn. He took her hand as Elowen turned her list so they could read it. Mabel scanned it and let out a long breath. There was still so much to do.

"Some of this can be done tomorrow morning. We're not opening until midday," Finn reminded them.

"We need spare time for any last minute issues," Elowen said, her face stern and Mabel didn't dare argue with her logic.

"I'll make a start on washing up the champagne flutes," she said and pecked Finn on the lips before slinking off to the kitchen. They'd hired glasses, knowing they wouldn't usually need so many.

﹏﹏

It was gone midnight by the time Elowen went home. Mabel's feet throbbed and Finn looked as though he might fall asleep standing.

"Your sister-in-law is a force to be reckoned with," he growled as he locked the door. Mabel was sure it was more to keep Elowen out rather than any worries about their safety.

"How are you feeling about tomorrow?" asked Mabel as she got ready for bed. She now had a drawer of clothes at the pub, and Finn had the same at her cottage. They'd been splitting their time between their homes but hadn't spent a night apart for a while now.

"I'm excited for the pub's opening," he said and paused. Mabel didn't interrupt. She waited until he was comfortable enough to continue. "I'm also really nervous. What if my dad turns up? What if he doesn't turn up? I don't know which one I'd prefer." He sat down on the end of the bed and let out a big sigh.

"He might not have received the invitation," Mabel pointed out. If Lowen didn't turn up, it didn't necessarily mean he didn't want to see Finn.

"I know. If I'm honest, I regret inviting him."

Mabel felt the heavy weight of guilt wrap around her heart. It had been her suggestion to invite Finn's father to the opening day. She had hoped with so much going on, it might break the ice. "I'm sorry," she said and sat beside him.

"It's not your fault. At the time, it seemed like a great idea. Perhaps it'll be for the best if he doesn't turn up. So much in my life has been turned upside down lately. I'm not sure I'm ready for anything else."

A familiar bubble of nerves floated around in Mabel's stomach. "You keep saying this, Finn. What's wrong? You've settled here, haven't you? Even if the pub fails, you have me and my family. I'll support you in anything you do." Mabel ached to wrap her arms around him, but she didn't. She needed him to quell her worries and promise her he was planning on sticking around.

"I don't know what the future holds, Mabel," he muttered. "I can't say for certain that Port Isaac is where I'll settle." He sighed. "I came here on a whim, thinking I needed something for now. There was no future in my plans."

The blood in Mable's veins turned to ice as his words sunk in. He couldn't promise her he would stick around. She stood and walked to the window, staring out to sea but not seeing anything. Tears prickled, but she held them back, refusing to show him how much he'd hurt her. She'd taken a chance opening up to Finn, and here he was, proving why she shouldn't have risked her heart. He was everything she'd wanted in a partner but had never allowed herself to dream of. For a while now, Mabel knew she was falling for him, but she'd tried to put a lid on those feelings. Now, she knew for sure she loved him, but she also knew he was going to break her heart.

"I don't think I can stay here tonight," she muttered and gathered her few belongings.

He didn't say anything as she left.

⋙⋘

Mabel didn't go home. She walked to Michael and Elowen's, hoping El hadn't gone to sleep yet. Not wanting to wake the girls, she called her sister-in-law's mobile when she was outside.

"Mabel, what's wrong? Did I forget something?"

"I'm outside," Mabel said, but the words came out in a jumble as a sob ripped through her.

"I'm coming."

Less than a minute later, Elowen yanked open the front door and hugged Mabel.

"Michael's already asleep. Come on, let's get you a hot chocolate and we can have a chat."

They went through to the kitchen, where Elowen warmed a pan of milk on the stove and added more spoonfuls of hot chocolate powder than necessary.

"What happened? I only just left," she asked.

Mabel blew her nose on a tissue. "He's so flaky about the future, so I confronted him. I wanted him to reassure me that he'd stick around, but he did the opposite." Her voice wobbled as a fresh wave of tears overcame her.

"Oh, Mabel." Elowen poured the mixture into two mugs and led her to the deep velvet sofa in the snug. "Why do you think he's flaky?"

"I think he's scared to commit because his upbringing was so turbulent. He's used to people walking out on him." Mabel hadn't properly formed the thoughts until the moment she spoke them, but now it all made sense. "What if he doesn't want to commit to me or he's too scared to commit?"

"Is there a difference?"

"If he wants it, then we can work it out."

Elowen picked up the box of tissues from the side table and wiped away Mabel's tears. "Are you clinging to him because you're scared of the pain if you let him go?"

Mabel opened and closed her mouth, not knowing what to say. Elowen always knew the right questions to get to the point. It was something Mabel hadn't considered. Was she clinging to Finn because it was easier than the pain of letting him go?

"I don't know," she admitted.

"You need to work it out, Mabel. If you truly love him, and think your future is with him, then fight for him. Maybe he just needs someone to support him and show him commitment is possible. But you have to know if he's worth it. You have to put yourself first."

Mabel could only nod. Elowen's words had left her speechless and frantically searching her heart to decipher her feelings. It had taken a lot to pull down her walls and open up to him, but she'd managed it. She had seen a future with him and decided he was worth the risk.

Elowen squeezed her shoulder. "Talk to him, Mabel, but be open to what he says. He may say things you don't want to hear and you need to know what your deal breakers are. Whatever happens, I'll always be here, okay?"

"Thank you." Mabel gave her sister-in-law a watery smile and sipped her hot chocolate. It was never going to be easy opening her heart up again, but this was proving to be more painful than she had anticipated.

CHAPTER TWENTY-SEVEN

"Maple Syrup!" Before Mabel was fully awake and aware of her surroundings, two bundles of energy pounced on her.

"Girls," hissed Elowen through the open door. "I told you not to bother Mabel until she was awake."

"She's awake," protested Milly.

"Her eyes are open," added Mia, who pointed at Mabel's half-opened eyes and almost poked her eyeball.

"I'm in the process of waking up," mumbled Mabel.

"Sorry. They spotted your shoes in the hallway and ran upstairs before I could stop them." Elowen perched on the edge of the bed.

"That's okay. I should be up now, anyway. It's

going to be a busy day."

"Daddy's making pancakes. Do you want one?" asked Milly.

The smell of pancakes wafted up the stairs, and despite the somersaults her stomach was doing, they did smell tempting.

"Can I have chocolate spread on mine?" Mabel asked, glancing at Elowen, who rolled her eyes and chuckled.

"We still have a pot you brought over a few months ago. It's unopened in the cupboard. I'll let Michael know our three children want chocolate pancakes for breakfast," she said and disappeared downstairs.

"Come on, girls, let's have breakfast." Mabel got a jumper out of her bag to throw over her pyjamas. Her outfit for the day was at the bottom of the pile, all crumpled. She'd thrown everything in last night without a second thought.

"El, do you have an iron?" Mabel called as she followed the girls downstairs.

"Give it here. I'll steam it. Do you need anything else?"

"No, thank you."

Elowen whisked away the jumpsuit and Mabel followed the girls into the kitchen.

"Morning," Michael called. Mabel knew him well enough to read his expression. He wanted to ask her what was going on, but he knew better than to ask in front of tiny ears.

"Morning. Thank you for breakfast." Mabel sat

at the table with her nieces and poured them all a glass of juice.

"Chocolate pancakes all around," Michael announced and handed out plates. It didn't escape Mabel's notice that she had the biggest portion, with an extra serving of double chocolate ice cream. He shot her a smile and busied himself cutting up the girls' pancakes.

"I've left your jumpsuit in your room," El said, joining them. She wasn't having pancakes. Instead, she chose a piece of toast from the rack on the table and sliced a banana to go on top of it.

They ignored the elephant in the room as they ate. Elowen and Michael kept glancing her way while the girls chatted away about their week at holiday club.

"What time are you heading over?" Michael asked Elowen.

"I'll leave about an hour after Mabel does."

"On that note, I should get ready. Thank you for breakfast."

El followed her out into the hallway. "Do you need anything?" she asked.

"A whole lot of courage?"

"Will my make-up bag do? It's in the main bathroom."

"Thank you."

Mabel showered in the guest bathroom. Elowen kept the house well-stocked for impromptu visitors, so she retrieved the hairdryer and large round brush from the bedside table and dried her hair into soft waves. She brushed on some of Elowen's make-up to hide the signs of late night crying. El had hung her outfit in the guest room without a single crease on it. Mabel had found the jumpsuit online and immediately knew it was perfect for the opening day. It was bright white, with a vest top and wide-leg trousers, but what drew her to it were the vibrant red lobsters which decorated it. Mabel hardly recognised her reflection in the mirror. She was miles away from the woman who was usually covered in furniture dust, various shades of varnish, and cat hair. She searched for her phone to take a picture and send it to Del, but it was downstairs in the hallway where she'd left her handbag last night.

"You look lovely, Aunty Mabel," Milly said as Mabel walked down the stairs.

"Thank you, Milly. Are you dressing up for the party today?" asked Mabel. She scanned the hallway and spotted her handbag hanging on the coat rack.

"Mummy bought us new dresses at the weekend. She said her new job means we can have a treat sometimes."

"Good. You deserve a treat."

Mabel retrieved her phone from the bag and wandered back to the kitchen, where breakfast had already been cleared away. Elowen was upstairs in the shower and Michael had made himself a coffee.

"Are you okay?" he asked, studying her expression.

Mabel nodded. She'd seen how many missed

calls and texts she had from Finn. The texts were asking if she was okay. Did she get home okay? He was sorry about what he said. It had all come out wrong. Please could they talk before today's party?

"Mabel?" Michael squeezed her arm to get her attention.

"Sorry. I forgot my phone last night, so I was catching up on messages."

"Are you sure you're okay?"

"Yes. I should go. I need to talk to Finn."

"Okay. Remember, whatever happens, you always have us." Michael gave her a brief hug before seeing her out the door.

There was an atmosphere of sizzling excitement as Mabel wound her way through the harbour to the pub. The community was making the most of the day, and shops were setting out stalls hoping to increase their trade. Even Betty was setting out a table with cakes to entice people inside.

"Morning, love," she called as Mabel passed.

"Morning, Betty. How are you?" Mabel didn't want to stop and chat, but she couldn't be rude to Betty.

"I'm fine, dear. Although I have been meaning to ask you if you've seen Gwen lately. She's hardly been around, which is unlike her, and when she has, she's said no more than a few words. I know she's been spreading the words about the pub's opening day, but besides that, I can't get her to talk."

"That is odd. I'll check in on her soon. Let's get

through today first." Mabel planted a quick kiss on Betty's cheek and went on her way to the pub.

The front door was already open, so Mabel let herself in.

"You're here." Finn appeared in the hallway as she walked in. He looked dishevelled, his hair sticking out in all directions, and his eyes were swollen.

"I've only just seen you texted and tried to call me."

"Come through for a moment." He led her through the bar, where the day's preparations were already in full swing. Nick was polishing the bar while his girlfriend, Belle, polished glasses. Mabel could hear the radio playing faintly in the kitchen where the sous chef was at work.

Everyone greeted Mabel and said a quick hello before she followed Finn upstairs to his flat.

"I'm sorry about last night," he said once they were alone. "I've told you about the investors in the pub. I don't know what the future holds. If the pub doesn't make enough profit, then I'll lose it. There's a lot of pressure on the next few weeks for the pub to make enough money."

Mabel frowned but didn't interrupt to ask questions.

"It feels as though so much in my life is all over the place. I thought I'd processed the grief of losing my mother, but I'm slowly realising the heaviness in my heart is here to stay. I have a lot of adjusting to do, but the one thing I know for certain is I want you in my life. We'll make it work even if I can't stay at the pub."

"Do you think you might lose the pub?"

"Anything is possible." He shrugged nonchalantly, but Mabel recognised the pain in his eyes.

"You'll stay with me if you lose the pub?" She had to be sure he was committed.

"You're my home now, Mabel. We may have only been together for a short while, but I love you." His words hung in the air as Mabel gasped for breath. He cupped her face with his palm and closed the distance between them. "You don't have to say anything. I want you to know I love you and I'm sorry for what I said last night. None of it was about you. Everything but you are uncertainties in my life. When I moved here, I didn't expect it to be my forever home, because I didn't expect to meet you. Everything in my life is different now. You are my home."

Mabel's lips parted as she gazed up at him. She reached up on her tiptoes to kiss him.

The world spun around her, but Finn's lips kept her grounded. She clung to him as though her life depended on it.

CHAPTER TWENTY-EIGHT

Since their chat, Mabel had barely spent a moment alone with Finn. Their kiss had been interrupted by Nick, who called up the stairs to let them know the band had arrived. Mabel had taken over organising them, having experience with the last owners. They cleared a corner indoors and set up the speakers and microphones. Not long after, Elowen arrived and made sure everyone knew exactly what their role was.

"How did it go with Finn?" She led Mabel outside to the decked area where nobody was around to overhear them.

"It went well," Mabel whispered.

"I'm so happy for you." Elowen gave her a quick hug before sending her off to pour drinks for the helpers.

"This looks amazing," Zoe said, walking in with Jada.

"Doesn't it? Look at your beautiful vases on all the tables." Mabel joined them on the other side of the bar to greet them. The band was warming up in the background and old sea shanties filled the room.

"You're here. Fantastic. The function room is ready for you," Elowen said.

Zoe had agreed to be part of the children's activities, which were being put on in the function room. She'd made mugs for children to paint. Meanwhile, Betty had baked cupcakes to be decorated. A few other locals had offered various activities to keep the children entertained. There was even to be a sack race on the beach at two o'clock. Mabel's nieces had already signed Michael up for it.

"Do you need any help?" asked Mabel.

"No, I think we're fine. See you soon." Zoe threaded her arm through Jada's and went to set up.

Making the most of having a spare moment, Mabel dropped into the kitchen to see how Finn was getting on. They were operating a full menu today and with no idea how many people would turn up, there had been a huge amount of prep work needed.

"Hey, you." Finn's face lit up at the sight of Mabel. He beckoned her over.

"How're you doing in here?" She reached up on her tiptoes and pecked his lips.

"It's hard to know what will be popular. I don't

want to waste food."

"Whatever is left, we can eat tonight."

Finn chuckled. "A beach picnic?"

"That sounds wonderful." She loved seeing the community come together to celebrate, but she also couldn't wait until everyone went home and she had Finn to herself again.

"Five minutes until we officially open."

"Are you coming out to greet people?"

Finn nodded and wiped his hands on his apron before he took it off. "How do I look?"

Mabel smirked. "You look amazing and you know it." He was dressed in a pair of beige chinos and a white polo shirt, and his eyes sparkled.

"Come on. Let's officially open The Fisherman's Rest." He snaked an arm around her waist and they walked out together.

Elowen had put a ribbon across the front door and gathered the community on the other side. She handed Finn a big pair of scissors. "Do the honours and open the pub," she said.

"Only if you'll do it with me?" he asked Mabel.

"Of course." She took his hand, and they walked to the doorway.

They were greeted with hoots and cheers from the crowd. Mabel's heart swelled as Finn's hand wrapped around hers as they cut the ribbon.

"The Fisherman's Rest is officially open! Please, come in. Drinks are free for the next couple of hours. We're operating a full menu." They stood aside to let people in. Everyone greeted them as they passed.

Mabel's cheeks ached from smiling. This was the happiest she had been in a long time, despite last night's wobble.

"Maple Syrup!" Mia and Milly threw themselves at her as they walked through the door. They were dressed in pretty blue dresses with little sailboats on them. Their hair was in ponytails, with bows that matched their dresses.

"Hey, you two." Mabel hugged them back. "Did you hear there's pottery painting in the other room?"

"Will you paint with us?" Mia asked.

Mabel glanced at Finn, wondering if he needed any help.

"You go and enjoy yourself. I'll be cooking for the next little while," he said.

"See you soon." Mabel kissed him on the cheek and a few people whistled in the background.

⊰⊱

After helping the girls with their mugs, Mabel went from one group of people to the next. Everyone was enjoying the food and drinks on offer. The countdown to the two o'clock sack race was on, and Milly and Mia had ushered Michael onto the beach for some much-needed practice. The last food order had gone in and then the kitchen would be closed for the rest of the open day. A mixture of locals and tourists filled the tables. Everyone had complimented the interior and the beautiful crockery. Zoe had handed out so many business cards she'd run out and had to send Jada to her studio to get some more. It was a successful day all around.

"If everyone would like to make their way to the beach for the race," Elowen ordered.

"Do you think Michael stands a chance?" Finn asked, emerging from the kitchen. He looked exhausted but happy.

"Absolutely not, but he'll try for the girls. How was the lunch service?"

"Stressful but exhilarating. The sous chef is good. He's going to hang around the bar while we watch the race. Come on, we don't want to miss the start."

Finn held Mabel's hand the whole time they were on the beach. While they hadn't been keeping their relationship a secret, they also hadn't made a big deal out of it. With Gwen taking a break from spreading gossip, there was nobody around to keep Port Isaac up to date with local goings on. Mabel looked around at everyone on the beach, but there was no sign of Gwen. There was also no sign of Finn's father.

"Are you okay?" she asked him, checking to make sure nobody could overhear them.

"I'm fine. I've been so busy in the kitchen, I haven't had a moment to think about my father. He's not going to come, is he?"

"He might not have got the invitation."

"Thank you for trying to make me feel better. He hasn't been interested my entire life. Why would anything change now?"

Mabel squeezed his hand. Her response was drowned out by the cheers as the winner crossed the finish line.

"It's Michael." Finn let out an incredulous laugh.

"I can't believe it. Come on, let's congratulate him. We'll never hear the end of this."

Mia and Milly were beside themselves. They jumped up and down as Michael accepted his trophy from Elowen. He held it in the air and posed as the local newspaper snapped a picture.

"That'll be front page Monday morning and he'll frame it," Mabel pointed out.

"I'll get a copy to frame and put behind the bar." Finn nuzzled the top of her head.

"Yes, please. I want to be there for when he sees it."

"I hope you're always here, Mabel."

After many photographs of Michael and his trophy, everyone headed back to the pub for another drink.

"Did anyone come by?" Finn asked his sous chef as they joined him behind the bar.

"Just a man on his own." He shrugged and motioned to a corner with his head. Mabel turned to look, but there was nobody there.

"You can finish for the day. Pour yourself a drink and enjoy the celebrations." Finn shook his hand and went to serve the next person.

Mabel's interest was piqued by the mystery customer who had come in while they were all on the beach. She slipped out from behind the bar and wandered through to the empty function room. Only it wasn't empty. Finn's father stood looking out the far window.

"Can I help you?" Mabel asked, making him jump.

"Sorry. I was just—Nothing. I was just doing nothing. I should be going." He cleared his throat and put his empty glass down on one of the tables.

"Don't you at least want to say hello to him before you leave?"

Lowen froze halfway towards the door. "You know?"

"It was my idea to invite you."

"I shouldn't have come."

Mabel positioned herself to block the doorway. "What would be so awful about talking to him?"

"I can't." He shook his head.

"Isn't it the least he deserves?"

There were footsteps behind, and Mabel turned to see Finn. "The paper wants a picture of us both behind the bar."

"Finn," Mabel trailed off. She didn't know what to say, so she stepped aside.

The smile slid from his face as he saw who was inside the room.

"Lowen," Finn's voice was low.

"Finn," Lowen replied with a curt nod.

"Shall I leave you two to talk?" Mabel asked. For a moment, she thought neither of them had heard her, and nobody spoke. She went to walk away, but Finn reached for her.

"Stay," he said, and she heard the slight catch in his voice.

"I wanted to see what you'd done here," Lowen said, his voice gruff.

"I could make you some lunch?" Finn lit up at the idea.

Lowen cleared his throat. He looked between Finn and the doorway. "I've already eaten. I should go."

Finn's face fell, but he quickly collected himself and a frozen expression replaced it. "What about a drink?"

"I need to go."

"Please," Finn's voice cracked and Lowen's steps stopped.

"I can't be who you want me to be, Finn," Lowen said, his voice low and emotionless.

"Just be you."

A knot in Mabel's stomach twisted at Finn's small voice as he pleaded with Lowen.

"You've done really well for yourself. Your mum would be proud." Lowen cleared his throat.

"Are you proud?"

Tension filled the air as they waited for Lowen to speak.

"You're not mine to feel proud of. I'm sorry for what I put your mother through."

"What about what you put me through?" Finn's hands shook by his sides. Mabel reached out, and he grasped her hand so tightly it almost hurt.

"I've stayed away to avoid causing you any further pain. I don't know how to be a father, and I don't intend to learn at this late stage of my life. Please don't contact me again." With that, Lowen stalked out of the room. Finn stared after him. The frozen expression morphed into heartbreak. Instinctively, Mabel threw her arms around him and he hugged her back, clinging onto her.

"I'm sorry."

"It's my fault. I never should have sent the invite and got my hopes up."

Mabel knew there was nothing she could say to ease the pain, so she held him.

CHAPTER TWENTY-NINE

Since the open day, the pub had been heaving with locals and tourists. The community was grateful to have its hub back. Not to mention the amazing food Finn was serving. Mabel was finding it difficult not to visit every lunchtime. Already, Finn cooked for her most evenings. Since the pub was so busy, they'd spent most nights there. Mabel went back to her cottage every day to work on furniture and to check on Ethel. Finn had suggested she bring the cat with her, but Mabel knew she wouldn't like the new environment. She was much better left to her own devices. There was a spring in Mabel's step as she enjoyed her days breathing life back into furniture and spent her nights behind the bar at Fisherman's Rest. Finn was always busy, but with them working together, they occasionally snuck a quiet moment together. There hadn't been enough time to delve into how Finn was feeling after his encounter with his father.

"It's such a treat to have the day off," Finn said, winding a strand of her hair around his finger. They were lying in bed at her cottage. With the pub closed, they had stayed the night at hers. It felt like a little holiday.

"What shall we do?" asked Mabel.

"Shall we treat ourselves to lunch out? I'm a bit fed up with cooking."

"Let's go to Betty's."

"Fisherman's Brew?"

Mabel nodded.

"Sounds great," he said.

"Finn, how are you?" Mabel's words hung in the air. It was the first chance she'd had to ask him without someone overhearing the conversation, or one of them already being half asleep.

It took Finn a moment to reply. "I'm okay. It hurts to be rejected again, but I'm working through it."

"If you want to talk about it, then I'm here." Although their relationship was new, Mabel wanted Finn to feel he could open up to her.

"Thank you. We should get up soon. I'm covered in so much cat hair."

Mabel groaned. "Ethel, leave Finn alone."

"She's fine. I'm going to jump in the shower." He pecked her on the lips and disappeared into the bathroom.

Mabel lay in bed, listening to the sound of the shower. She knew Finn wasn't as okay as he said.

⋙ ⋘

They wandered into town holding hands. By now, everybody knew about their relationship. Finn had received a few hard stares from locals who had warned him not to break Mabel's heart. But on the whole, everyone was happy for them. The summer season was in full swing and the little streets of Port Isaac were bustling with people. They squeezed their way past the queue for ice cream and carried on towards Fisherman's Brew. In the background, the pub was closed. A few tourists stood outside reading the menu but disappointedly turned around.

"I hate seeing the pub losing out on custom," Finn said.

"So do I, but you can't work seven days a week, Finn. You already do a lunch and dinner service. It's too much to do that every day."

He sighed. "I know. We need more staff, but there's not the budget for it." He raked a hand through his hair. "Anyway, enough business talk. It's our day off." A smile chased away his stressed expression as he led her into the cafe.

It was busy inside, and Mabel couldn't sit at her usual table.

"I don't think there's a free table," Finn said,

scanning the room.

"Morning, loves," Betty called as she bustled past with a tray of food and drinks. "We're a bit busy at the moment, but why don't you jump on the table with Gwen? I'm sure she'd love the company."

Mabel hadn't spotted Gwen, but when she looked again, she saw the older woman sitting at her usual table. However, she wasn't engaged with the room and listening to conversations. Instead, she sat with her head low and her attention on the pot of tea in front of her.

"Is Gwen okay?" asked Mabel, unsure what to make of the unusually quiet woman.

"Hasn't said a word to me since she ordered her tea." Betty shot Mabel a concerned look before she hurried off to deliver the order.

"She hasn't said anything about what she overheard either," Mabel muttered once Betty was out of earshot.

"Do you think that's what's caused her to retreat into her shell?" asked Finn.

"I don't know. Gwen's lived in Port Isaac her entire life, but despite being the harbour's biggest gossip, not much is known about her."

"Come on. Let's see if we can get to the bottom of what's going on." Finn nudged Mabel towards Gwen.

The once vibrant and inquisitive woman didn't even look up when Mabel stopped by the table.

"Good morning, Gwen. You don't mind if we share your table, do you? It's so busy in here." Mabel had sat down before she finished speaking, not giving Gwen the chance to say no. Finn fell into his seat with a thump as Mabel yanked him down beside her. Gwen's expression was far away as she looked up at them, but it quickly shifted as her eye fell on them.

"I was hoping for a quiet drink." She sniffed, her gaze lingering on Finn before she looked back at her tea.

"We'll keep ourselves to ourselves," said Mabel, although she had no such intention. This behaviour was very unlike Gwen, and Mabel wanted to know what was wrong. "What are you ordering?" Mabel asked Finn. Out of the corner of her eye, she caught Gwen glancing towards him.

"What would you recommend?" he asked, turning the menu over.

"I like everything on the menu." Mabel chuckled.

"The avocado on toast is lovely," Gwen said. Her voice was small, and she turned to the table as she spoke.

"Thanks, Gwen. Avo on toast, it is." Finn beamed and leaned back in his chair.

"This isn't a fancy London brunch place, mind. You be nice to Betty about her food." Gwen's voice was stronger this time.

"I'm sure Betty's food is delicious," Finn said. His smile didn't waiver, despite Gwen's harsh words.

They were saved by Betty, who came over to take their order.

"Would you like anything else?" Betty asked Gwen.

"No. I'll be leaving once I finish this cup," Gwen replied.

Mabel shared a glance with Betty. It was unlike Gwen to turn down the opportunity to talk to someone from the village - especially someone like Finn Hart. Everyone wanted to know about the mystery chef who had returned the pub to the community. Finn was busy replying to emails on his phone and Mabel surreptitiously studied Gwen, whose face was turned to her pot of tea. Usually, Gwen's inquisitive eyes roamed over the cafe, searching for any tidbits of gossip.

Betty delivered their coffees and gave Mabel a nudge as she walked away.

"So, Gwen, how are you?" Mabel asked.

"I thought you were keeping yourself to yourself," Gwen reminded her as she poured the last of the tea out of the pot. Mabel sighed. This was not going to plan.

"Have you tried the new food at the pub?" Finn piped up. He'd closed his phone and put it back in his pocket.

Gwen jumped at his question but continued to stir sugar into her cup. "Not yet. No."

"Why don't you pop in this week? It's on the house. The only catch is, I need you to tell me what you think. I'd appreciate honesty, and I'd love to know if you think the food is what the residents of Port Isaac want." Finn finished with a small smile playing at the corner of his lips. Mabel was in awe. He'd known exactly the right thing to say.

"I don't think that's a good idea, but thank you." Gwen picked up her cup and drained the contents. "I should be off now. Goodbye."

"Wait, Gwen. Don't go. What's wrong?" Mabel reached out to touch Gwen's arm, but she flinched away.

"This has nothing to do with you, Mabel," Gwen said, and Mabel recoiled as she saw Gwen's eyes. They were filled with pain.

"Who is this to do with?" Finn asked, placing a reassuring hand on Mabel's shoulder.

"You." Gwen stared at him, and Mabel's stomach plummeted.

"Then don't take it out on Mabel. If you have a problem with me, talk to me."

Gwen's expression softened for a brief moment before her face became a blank canvas. She cleared her throat. "I don't have anything to say to you."

Mabel stepped in front of Gwen to stop her from leaving. "This is ridiculous. Everybody has noticed a change in you. Please, tell us what is wrong."

Gwen glanced around the cafe. Everyone was watching them and Mabel could hear the whispers spreading.

"Not here," Gwen said, her shoulders sagging.

"Let's go next door to the pub. It's closed today, so it'll just be us," Finn said.

"Shall I come?" asked Mabel, unsure if Gwen

would talk with her there.

Finn glanced at Gwen as if waiting for her permission. "You better do. I think he'll need you after he hears what I have to say," she said and walked past a shocked Mabel.

Betty bustled out of the kitchen door with their plates and came to a halt by a shocked Mabel and Finn.

"What's going on?" asked Betty.

"I'm not sure," Finn said.

"Gwen wants to talk to Finn," added Mabel.

"I'll make you fresh when you've had a chat," Betty said and went back to the kitchen with their plates.

"I was looking forward to that," grumbled Mabel as she followed Finn out of Fisherman's Brew.

"So was I. You don't have to come with me, Mabel. In fact, maybe it would be better if you didn't." He paused by the door. Gwen was standing on the other side, waiting for them.

"No. I want to be there for you. It's probably Gwen having a moan about your opening hours or the beer you've got on tap. Come on, let's get it over with so we can come back for lunch."

"Okay." Finn nodded, but he looked lost in his thoughts.

Mabel slipped her hand into his and walked out of the cafe with him. In silence, the three of them made their way to Fisherman's Rest. Finn unlocked the front door and led them into the bar area. Gwen took a seat at one a table near the doors which overlooked the beach.

"Does anyone want a drink? A coffee maybe?" Finn said, flicking on the lights.

"I think we might need something a little stronger than coffee. Why don't you bring over that bottle of brandy?" Gwen pointed to the spirits behind the bar.

Finn glanced at Mabel before he fetched the bottle and three glasses.

They joined Gwen at the table, and Finn poured three measures. Mabel sipped hers and winced as it burnt. Meanwhile, Gwen knocked back the measure and took the bottle to pour another.

"What's going on, Gwen?" asked Finn.

"My family were smugglers, you know?" Gwen mused, swirling the amber liquid around the glass.

"Don't tell me you brought us here for a history lesson," Finn quipped.

Mabel kept quiet as she sipped the fiery liquid. It was disgusting, but she suspected she'd need it to take the edge off of whatever Gwen was about to say.

"Perhaps." Gwen finished her second glass and poured a third. "It is relevant, though. You see, my family is your family, Finn."

Finn froze with his glass raised halfway to his mouth.

"Lowen is my brother." Gwen drank her third glass.

Mabel wanted to go to Finn, but she couldn't move. Her grip on the glass tightened as she tried to get her head around Gwen's revelation. It couldn't be true. Could it? She would have noticed a resemblance between them if Finn was related to Gwen.

"You can't be Lowen's sister. You're so much older," Finn finally croaked out.

"We have different mothers. Lowen was born much later in life. Our father wasn't present in either of our lives."

"That would make you my aunt?"

"Your very elderly aunt," confirmed Gwen.

Mabel watched as Finn and Gwen looked at each other. It was an odd conversation to be sitting on the side of. Mabel yearned to reach out and take Finn's hand to remind him she was there, but she didn't. He needed a moment to process everything.

"How long have you known?" Finn scrubbed a hand across his face as he broke the silence.

"I didn't know anything about you until you arrived in Port Isaac. You're the spitting image of my brother and father, so it was quite a shock. I pushed it to the back of my mind and convinced myself it was a coincidence. Then I overheard Mabel talking to Elowen, and she mentioned that Lowen Bennett was your father."

"Why didn't you say something sooner?" asked Finn, his voice wobbled.

"I was scared. You're not the only person around here with no family left. Unfortunately, Lowen takes after our father, and we haven't spoken for years. Before I overheard the conversation, I didn't know if you knew who your father was.

What if someone else had brought you up, and you thought they were your biological father? I couldn't risk it, but then I saw Lowen at the opening party, and I knew."

Silence settled as Gwen and Finn stared at each other. Mabel felt like a spare part in this family reunion.

"I think I should go and leave you two to chat without an audience," she said, wincing as the sound of her chair scraping backwards echoed around the bar.

"Okay." Finn nodded. "I'll speak to you later."

"Of course." Mabel dropped a kiss on the top of his head and waved to Gwen. "I won't mention anything to anyone," she promised.

CHAPTER THIRTY

Mabel gritted her teeth to stop a curse from slipping out. Yet again, the transfer hadn't adhered to the surface. With a huff, Mabel lined it up and rubbed it. She hoped that with a little more force, it would stick to the surface, which she'd spent a couple of hours prepping. Frustration bubbled in her stomach, but it wasn't all fuelled by the beautiful floral transfer. Communication with Finn had been nonexistent since Gwen's bombshell. He spent his days in the pub, cooking for hungry customers. Finn had even altered the opening hours, so they were open every day. He told Mabel it was to ensure the pub made enough money during the busy season to get through the long winter months. But she knew the truth. He was shutting himself away and focusing on his work to avoid confronting the emotions Gwen's revelation had stirred up. It wasn't healthy.

This time, Mabel held her breath as she peeled back the plastic backing. The pretty blush peonies and pale lavender stood out against the pale, raw oak. A local pub had seen what she'd done with the furniture for Fisherman's Rest and had asked her to upcycle a few pieces for their bedrooms. They had confided in her that they were saving with the hope of having her redo their bar furniture next summer. Work was steadily trickling in, and with the hours Mabel did at the pub, she was able to put aside a bit to replace the roof on her barn before winter.

A huff escaped Mabel's lips as she rocked back on her heels and stared at the finished piece. That was job one on her to-do list ticked off. Job two wouldn't be quite as easy. Mabel was determined to speak to Finn today and encourage him to open up. She'd planned a beach picnic for them. Obviously, she hadn't cooked anything. Instead, she'd asked Betty to prepare something, which she would pop by and collect. Finn had promised Mabel he'd arrange cover for the dinner shift and so everything was in motion.

Mabel washed and changed, putting her swimming costume under her summer dress. It was a beautiful day. The sun still shone high in the sky as Mabel meandered into Port Isaac. It was the busiest time for the little port, with families enjoying the bustling streets. Mabel squeezed by people and narrowly avoided a dropped ice cream cone. Port Isaac was thrumming with people, and it was lovely to see the sleepy village alive, although

Mabel did look forward to the dismal, grey days when the streets would be deserted and the cafes filled with locals. Those days would come, so for now, she enjoyed the vibrancy the tourists brought with them.

Fisherman's Brew was busy, but Betty spotted Mabel the instant she walked through the door and waved.

"I've got your picnic out back. Give me two minutes to take this coffee over to table three. We should be closing in five minutes, but I've had a table of six sit down. I tried to send them to the pub, but they said there were no tables left."

Mabel groaned. Finn wouldn't be able to leave the kitchen if it was that busy.

"Take your time, Betty. There's no rush." Mabel sat at the coffee counter and pulled out her phone. She had a text from Del. It wouldn't be long now until Mabel was reunited with her best friend.

"Here you go, love," Betty said, putting a wicker picnic basket on the counter.

"You didn't need to go to all this trouble," Mabel said, peering inside at the Tupperware boxes filled with different foods.

"Anything for you." Betty patted her hand before disappearing back into the kitchen.

Mabel called a thank you after her and took the picnic basket to find Finn.

The pub was filled to the brim with customers. As Mabel pushed through the front door, she heard the laughter and chatter from the bar area. Once she walked into the bar, she could hear the clinks of glasses and cutlery against dinnerware.

Elowen was behind the bar and sent her a wave as she spotted her.

"It's busy," Mabel said, slipping into a small space at the bar.

"I know. It's lovely to see it like this, though."

"I'm going to see if Finn is ready to leave. Let's have a catch-up soon." Mabel gave her a wave. Elowen's job at the pub was making a big difference to their financial situation, and it was clear the entire family was happier because of it.

"Finn?" called Mabel as she walked into the kitchen. The radio played in the background, but the music was drowned out by the sizzling sounds of cold food hitting hot pans, pots bubbling on the stove, and orders being called out. It was stiflingly hot in the kitchen, but Finn looked in his element as he plated steak and chips.

"Five minutes," he called to her and sent her a smile, which made Mabel's legs feel weak.

"I'll meet you on the beach," she said, unable to stand the heat any longer.

Mabel slipped through the crowds and down the few steps to the sand, where it was much quieter. Most day trippers had packed up to go home, while everyone else seemed to be in the pub.

The beach at Port Isaac was rugged, with the sea wall rising imposingly in the distance and the looming cliffs on either side. Still, the water glistened blue and the golden sand was soft beneath her feet. It was a haven from the busy streets.

Mabel chose a spot and laid out the food Betty had prepared. There were crackers, a selection of local cheeses, and a cream tea with thick raspberry jam and a pot of clotted cream. Mabel took out the flask of hot chocolate she'd packed and poured two mugs. Her mouth salivated at the sight of the food, but she waited until Finn joined her to tuck in.

"Sorry, it's been a busy day," Finn said as he slid onto the sand beside her. He'd changed out of his chef whites and into a t-shirt and shorts.

"Will they be okay without you?"

"They'll get by. I've trained them well, and it's as good a chance as any to see how they cope without me there steering the ship." He winked at her, before cutting a slice of the Cornish cheddar and laying it on top of a cracker. Mabel followed his lead and savoured the creamy cheese's sharp tangy aftertaste, combined with the salty crackers.

"This is good," Mabel hummed.

"Thank you for getting me out of the kitchen," Finn said, preparing another cracker. He handed it to Mabel and then made himself another.

"How are you?" Mabel was hesitant to ask, but she knew putting it off would do no good.

"I'm not sure. I hadn't ever considered whether Lowen had any other family. It's a shock to discover I have an aunt."

"Have you spoken to Gwen since?"

Finn shook his head. "No. She's popped into the pub twice, but I've hidden in the kitchen and made excuses."

"You should talk to her. Find out what she has to say."

"I don't know if I can. After my father's latest rejection, I feel as though I've closed the door on that side of my life. It hurts too much to keep opening it." He brushed the crumbs from his fingers and laid back on his elbows, watching the seagulls bob up and down on the calm waves.

Mabel traced a finger along his forearm as she carefully chose her next words. "She's not your father, Finn. Gwen won't hurt you like he has." Mabel had known Gwen for long enough. She was almost certain that if Gwen had known of Finn's existence, she would have done everything she could to be a part of his life.

"I'm not ready, Mabel. I didn't expect to find so many connections in Port Isaac." He rubbed his eyes and sat up. "Shall we tuck into this cream tea? The scones look gorgeous."

The scones were indeed gorgeous. They were made from Betty's family recipe and ripped apart with little effort. Under Mabel's watchful eye, Finn was careful to put jam on first, followed by cream.

As they finished the cream tea, Finn asked about Mabel's latest commission, but nothing more was said about him, and how he was feeling. Mabel noticed that when he thought she wasn't looking, the mask would slip and the pain on his face was evident. She wanted to wrap her arms around him, but she resisted. He wasn't ready yet, and she didn't want to push him too much. In time, she hoped he would come to her and open up.

CHAPTER THIRTY-ONE

Finn continued to hide away in the kitchen and was yet to open up to Mabel. Gwen had tried to talk to him, but he had ignored her. Mabel was watching him work to exhaustion to avoid confronting his feelings. Two weeks after the beach picnic, Mabel walked across the harbour to visit Gwen. She was careful not to bump into anyone, to avoid questions about why she was visiting the village's busybody.

Gwen's cottage, Chi an Mor, was on the cliff top overlooking the sea. It was named Cottage by the Sea because of its breathtaking vistas, but it wasn't really a cottage. The sprawling house had belonged to Gwen's in-laws, and Gwen and her husband had inherited it in the late eighties. It was a big place for Gwen to live alone, but she refused to leave because of the memories it held. The cottage had been extended over the years, but in a way which was in keeping with the age of the building. Lavender bloomed around the exterior, and the sweet smell mingled with the breeze as Mabel took a deep breath. She walked up the path with potted plants on either side. It was beautiful in summer, but Mabel knew the precarious spot on top of the cliff would be treacherous in winter.

With trembling hands, Mabel knocked using the heavy brass knocker. The sound echoed across the clifftop, but after a few moments, Mabel heard footsteps behind the door. Gwen greeted her in a sunhat and a long, frilly dress.

"Mabel, dear. Good morning. I'm out the back doing some gardening. Come in." Gwen stepped aside to let Mabel into the hallway. It was beautiful, with a white and black marble floor and dark green walls. To the left was a panelled wall with pegs for coats and a seat which ran the length of the hallway. Wellington boots and walking shoes were lined up on the floor. On the right was an archway leading through to a living room. It was country-chic with pale green William Morris floral wallpaper. Bookshelves lined the far wall in the same shade as the wallpaper, filled from floor to ceiling with books. Deep cream sofas were on either side of the room with pale green and peach scatter cushions. Throws that matched the wallpaper were neatly folded over the backs of the chairs. It was beautiful and Mabel was almost afraid to breathe in fear of disturbing something.

An oak Georgian desk faced the French doors. It was a remarkable piece of furniture and looked almost in perfect condition, given its age.

"That is why I don't like painted furniture," Gwen said, noting where her attention had slunk off to.

"I love it. Is it genuine?"

"Of course," Gwen scoffed. "As if my husband would have allowed any reproduction furniture in this house. He was an auctioneer, you know."

Mabel hadn't known. She'd never been inside Gwen's house, and it was even more stunning than she had imagined. Her eyes wandered to the stairs which led to the next floor. Without a doubt, Mabel knew this house was filled to the brim with beautiful furniture. However, that wasn't why she was here. A tour of Gwen's home would have to wait.

"I wanted to talk to you about Finn," Mabel said, tearing her attention away from the house's interior.

Gwen nodded. "Go through that door." She pointed to a stable door which led to the back garden. "I'll clean my hands and make a pot of tea."

Mabel did as she was told and wandered out to the garden. It was gorgeous, with manicured lawns which stretched to the cliff's edge. Rose bushes bloomed in different hues of pink, and the lavender continued around the perimeter of the house. A wicker outdoor table and chairs were set off to the right on a paved area. Mabel wandered over and took a seat. In the distance, she could see the sea far below, and if she squinted, she could make out Port Isaac.

It wasn't long before Gwen appeared with a tray of tea and biscuits. She poured the tea before taking the seat beside Mabel, who glanced dubiously at the cup. She'd have to force herself to drink it.

"It's nice to have a visitor," Gwen said, breaking a biscuit in half and nibbling it.

"I should pop by more often." Mabel had a sinking feeling of guilt. She'd judged the woman as a busybody without giving her the grace of getting to know her. Beneath Gwen's nosey exterior was a caring woman.

"That would be nice." Gwen patted her hand. "But it's not why you're here today, is it?" Typical Gwen, always cutting straight to the point.

Mabel sighed. "No. I shouldn't be here discussing Finn with you, but he won't talk to me, and I don't know what to do. All he does is work, and I can see it chipping away at him."

"He's an adult, Mabel. Neither of us can force him to do anything."

"I know." Mabel gazed towards Port Isaac. She could imagine Finn in Fisherman's Rest bustling around the kitchen preparing for the lunchtime service.

"He hasn't spoken to me since I told him. We shared a few words once you left, but not much was said. He's hurting and processing everything. That can't be rushed. I've tried to reach out to him, but he pushes me away. He needs to be left now. There's a lot of pain he needs to heal from."

Mabel nodded. "I know. I'm sorry for coming to you, Gwen. Nobody else knows and Finn won't talk about it. I feel as if I'm carrying a heavy weight around."

"Mabel, I mean this in the nicest way possible. It isn't your weight to carry. This is between myself and Finn. If Finn wants to talk to me, he knows where I live. You can't force him to talk, you can only be there for him. If that's something you can't do, you need to question your relationship."

Gwen sipped her tea and turned to the view as Mabel allowed the words to sink in. Her relationship with Finn was new, almost too new to cope with the situation, but did that mean they simply weren't suited to one another? No, that couldn't be it. Mabel had never felt so happy as when she was around Finn. It was a hurdle for them to get over. Gwen was right. Mabel needed to back off and allow Finn to find his own way through this revelation.

They didn't mention Finn again, but Mabel stayed for a couple of hours. Gwen recounted memories of summer days spent in the garden when Betty would join her and they'd drink gin and tonics and put the world to rights. For the first time in a while, Mabel's worries abandoned her and left her to enjoy the afternoon. At some point, Gwen had swapped the pot of tea for glasses of Champagne, and Mabel had happily sipped the fizzy beverage as she watched the sun slip lower in the sky.

"I should be getting off," she said, standing and stretching.

"Don't be a stranger."

Mabel hugged Gwen before she left. It was early evening and the pathway back to Port Isaac was quiet. Mabel only passed a handful of other walkers. She took the time to enjoy the scenery and slowly crossed through the harbour and back up the other side to her cottage.

Once home, Mabel threw open her doors and windows to allow the warm evening air to circulate. Ethel mewed in contentment as she trotted out to the path to bask in the last of the day's sun. Mabel flicked on the radio and made pasta for dinner. As she waited for the water to boil, she sent Finn a quick text to say she hoped he had a good dinner service.

Mabel closed her eyes and sipped her wine as she lost herself in an audiobook. She sunk her feet into the cool grass and sat back against the pile of cushions she'd brought outside. Ethel weaved in and out of her legs, purring at the attention, before curling up on the blanket beside Mabel. It was a beautiful evening, so Mabel had eaten her dinner outside and was yet to venture back indoors.

"Hello?" someone called. The voice was just audible over the narrator.

Mabel took out her earbuds as she turned to see who it was. Finn was standing in the doorway with a box in his hands.

"The front door was open. I did knock but there

was no answer, so I came through," he explained.

"I forgot I left the front door open. What are you doing here? It's lovely to see you." Mabel waved him over. She glanced at her phone and saw it was gone eight. Finn should be in the kitchen, in the middle of dinner service.

"We haven't spent much time together, so I thought I'd do something about that. I've also brought a slice of chocolate fudge cake. Elowen said you'd enjoy it." He opened the small box to reveal a slab of rich, chocolatey cake oozing with chocolate ganache.

"That looks amazing. You've been so busy with work lately." Mabel stopped herself from saying any more. Gwen was right, she had to allow Finn to come to terms with everything in his own time. "Let me get us some forks and I'll get you a glass."

They settled down on the blanket with the cake between them.

"This is amazing," Mabel said, savouring the bite.

"I should think so. It's from Betty. I was worried the pub opening would take business away from her, so to give back, I asked her to bake a few cakes a week for me to serve. I'm hoping customers will try them and then stop by Betty's for a bite another day."

Mabel smiled. "That sounds lovely. Thank you for thinking of everyone." She rested her head on his shoulder and relaxed in the moment. Birds tweeted from the branches above, and the gentle hum of conversation drifted up from the harbour. Her little garden was a haven for the two of them. "I visited Gwen today," Mabel said.

"How is she?" Finn asked, his voice tight.

"She's good. Her home is lovely."

Finn nodded but didn't speak.

He took their forks and put them to the side in the empty box. His soft hand cupped the side of her face. "I'm sorry for being so distant." His fingers caressed Mabel's cheek as his voice shook. "Just when I thought I was coming to terms with the fact I had nobody left, the rug was pulled from beneath me. I've never even imagined having an aunt, let alone one who lives up the road from me. I'm excited but terrified. What if she rejects me when she gets to know me? What if I'm like my father?"

Mabel placed her hand on top of Finn's, but she didn't say anything. He was finally opening up to her, and she didn't want to jeopardise it with her own silly, placating words.

"Then there's a part of me that's bitter. I went through so much caring for my mum. It was lonely and such a heavy burden. Every decision I made, I second-guessed it. I lived my life in fear of making the wrong decision for her. If Gwen had known about me, then my life would have been very different. Maybe I wouldn't have suffered through it all alone." He paused and swiped at his eyes. "On the face of it, I know I present as this confident chef who's got his life together, but that's not who I am underneath it all. There are dark, deep pits of pain within my soul. I'm not asking you to heal them for me, Mabel. I need you to be strong for me when I need time to work through things for myself. I wish I could tell you how long it'll take me, but I can't. Maybe I'll never truly heal from everything I've been through. But I want to."

"Oh, Finn," Mabel's voice quivered, and she wrapped her arms around him, pulling him tightly against her as his body shook with silent sobs.

"Sorry, I didn't mean for that to all spill out of me. I had hoped to calmly explain everything to you." He reached for his glass of wine.

"I'm glad you felt you could tell me," Mabel whispered, swiftly wiping her tears. "I know you've got a lot to work through, Finn. My trust issues mean I find it difficult when someone is holding a piece of themselves back, but I understand why you must. As long as we communicate, we can help each other through this." She held up her glass, and he clinked his against hers.

"To us," he said. They sipped their drinks before Finn placed them on the floor and kissed her.

CHAPTER THIRTY-TWO

After last night's conversation with Finn, Mabel felt lighter as she knocked on Michael and Elowen's door. The girls were excited to see her since Michael and Elowen hadn't told them who their babysitter was for the evening.

"Hi girls," Mabel said, carrying a large bag of arts and crafts through the door.

"What have you got there?" Milly asked, eyeing the bag with intrigue.

"Del is coming home tomorrow, so I thought you two could help me make a welcome home banner," Mabel said. She carried the bag through and set it on the dining table.

"That sounds like a wonderful idea," Elowen said. She'd followed them, hopping as she slid on a sparkly heel.

"Can we put lots of glitter on it?" Mia asked, already rooting through the bag of goodies.

"Only if you promise to hoover it up for Mabel," Michael said, strolling into the room.

"We promise," Mia and Milly said with angelic smiles. Mabel knew better than to take these children at face value. She would be in for a long night of hoovering once the girls were in bed. Michael's smirk told Mabel he was thinking the same as her.

"Where are you off to?" Mabel asked, unpacking the bag.

"Finn wanted to treat us to dinner, so we thought we'd take him up on the offer," Elowen said.

Mabel saw Michael and Elowen off at the door and got the girls into their arts and crafts aprons. Elowen was very particular about not ruining their clothes.

"You don't have an apron." Mia pointed at Mabel's oversized t-shirt that she'd thrown over cycling shorts.

"That's okay. It's a t-shirt I paint in."

"Are you sure?" Mia narrowed her eyes at Mabel as though she might catch her out in a lie.

Mabel bit back a chuckle as she promised. She needed to make more of an effort with the girls. Their parents were so serious all the time and they needed her to inject some wildness into their lives.

"Have I met Del?" Milly asked.

"No, she's been living in Australia for a long

time now."

"Then how are you friends?" Mia asked.

"We went to school together. Your daddy's friends with Del's brother. We used to go round to their house after school and play on their trampoline and their mummy would make us fairy cakes with chocolate icing."

"Yum," the girls' eyes had glazed over at the mention of sugar.

"Come on, let's make a start on this banner." Mabel redirected their attention before they could ask for cake.

Earlier in the day, Mabel had popped by Zoe's studio to get supplies, including a big piece of card for them to draw and write on. Mabel wrote 'Welcome home Adele' in big bubble writing so the girls could decorate each letter. She set them up with coloured pens, glittery gel pens, glue, and small pots of glitter.

"Is Finn your boyfriend?" Milly asked. She was concentrating on drawing a butterfly.

"Yes, he is. Why do you ask?"

"Grandma was asking Daddy about him when she called last night," Milly said.

Mabel raised her brows. "Was she now?"

"Yeah. Daddy had the phone on in the car and we heard. Grandma wanted to know if Finn's a nice man. Me and Mia told her he bakes good cakes. She didn't ask any more questions after that." Milly shrugged.

"We like Finn," Mia said. She was colouring in

one of the letters and frowned with concentration.

"Good." Mabel felt a little flutter of happiness at the thought of how much her family liked Finn.

"Is he our new uncle?" asked Milly. The girls put down their pens as they looked to their aunt for an answer.

Mabel cleared her throat. "Let's not get ahead of ourselves." A cold sweat broke out on the back of her neck.

"But he is your boyfriend?" Milly leaned closer.

Mabel nodded.

"And he lives in Port Isaac?"

Mabel nodded again. Mia had sat down to watch the conversation, and her head moved back and forth between her sister and aunt.

"Then why can't he be our uncle?"

"There's more to being an uncle than just being my boyfriend. Why don't we call Finn your friend for now, and we'll revisit this conversation in a year's time?" Mabel's shoulders sank as Milly's stern expression melted away.

"Okay." Milly was placated by that and went back to colouring in the banner, immediately tipping over a pot of glitter. Most of it ended up on the floor.

"Brilliant," Mabel grumbled and fetched the dustpan and brush from under the sink.

Despite the ridiculous amounts of glitter which had ended up on the floor, Mabel and the girls had fun making the banner. Once they'd gone to bed, Mabel had hoovered for what felt like hours until every speck was gone. She knew nothing less would meet Elowen's standards. Her arms ached from cleaning, and her face ached from smiling. By the time Elowen and Michael arrived home, Mabel had eaten all the snacks she'd brought and was watching her second romcom. The girls had gone to bed with little fuss after Mabel promised to see them again during the week.

"How was your evening?" Mabel asked as Elowen and Michael tiptoed into the living room, each shushing the other.

"It was lovely." Elowen sat on the sofa with a sigh and put an arm around Mabel. "Thank you so much for everything."

Mabel ignored the alcohol fumes her sister-in-law emitted and leaned into the hug. "It's nice seeing you two happy again."

"It's nice to feel happy again," admitted Michael. He'd sat on the opposite sofa, watching them with a smile. "Thank you, Mabel." With the pub's longer opening hours, Elowen had picked up some evening shifts and their finances were looking much healthier.

"You're very welcome. Now, get your tipsy wife tucked up in bed."

"I will. Do you want to stay in the spare room? I've drunk too much to drive you home, sorry."

"No, I'm going to stay at Finn's." Mabel gathered her bags and gave Elowen a last hug. "I'll see you later in the week. I promised I'd see the girls."

They said their goodbyes and hugged each

other.

The streets were dark and empty as Mabel wandered through them. She enjoyed those late-night walks when she had the entire harbour to herself. The light in the bar was still on when she reached the pub.

"Hello?" Mabel called. She went through the back door and left her bags by the stairs.

"I'm in the bar," Finn called back.

The pub was empty, but Finn was wiping down and putting bottles away. He looked utterly exhausted from all the long days.

"Do you have much left to do?" asked Mabel.

"I'm done. I was waiting for you and thought I'd do a little tidying."

"Michael and Elowen had a lovely evening. Thank you."

"They're a great couple. How were the girls?"

"They went mad over the glitter I brought with me. I've spent hours hoovering."

Finn chuckled and led her through to the back, flicking the switch to turn the lights off. He picked up her bags at the bottom of the stairs and Mabel followed him up to the flat. They still hadn't found the time to furnish the place. The walls were bare and there was a distinct lack of belongings in each room, but Mabel had to remind herself there'd be plenty of time once the season was over. They'd be able to have days off and spend them together.

"We're closed tomorrow," Finn said as he dropped her overnight bag off in the bedroom.

"Really? How come?" Mabel went straight to the kettle to make a hot chocolate.

"Our main oven needs servicing. I'm using it as an excuse to close for the day. Elowen will let the engineer in, so I have the whole day to spend with you."

Mabel groaned. Any other time, she would have been thrilled. "Del's flying home tomorrow and I was going to meet her at the airport."

Finn went to get the milk out of the fridge. "How are you getting there?" he asked.

"Taxi."

"I'll drive you. Unless you want time alone with Del."

"Really? Would you?" Mabel paused in the middle of spooning chocolate powder into the two mugs.

"Of course." He poured the milk in before carrying the mugs over to the microwave.

"I'd love that. Thank you. I can't wait for you to meet Del."

CHAPTER THIRTY-THREE

"What time does Del land?" Finn asked as he ushered Mabel into the car. They should have left half an hour ago, but she'd got sidetracked talking to Zoe on her way from the pub to the car. Zoe was fizzing with excitement. Things were progressing with their impending house purchase, and Mabel had wanted to ask her all about it. Finn had stood patiently, occasionally chipping into the conversation until he had to remind Mabel they needed to be somewhere.

"We have about an hour until she lands. She's just taken off, and it should only take us forty-five minutes to get to the airport. Plenty of time." Mabel smiled at him and checked the welcome home banner was neatly folded in her bag. Del had flown into London Gatwick and boarded another flight to

Cornwall.

"Are you excited?" Finn asked as they left the winding streets of Port Isaac. He'd reached over to hold Mabel's hand while his other gripped the steering wheel.

"Very. It's been so long since I saw Del. We talk as often as possible, but it's not the same."

"Didn't you ever want to fly out and visit her?"

"No. I'm not very good at leaving Port Isaac. I did it once and my whole life crumbled around me."

Finn squeezed her hand. "I'm sorry you went through that."

"So am I, but you've helped me learn to trust people again." The hurt which usually rolled over her when she thought of those days of heartbreak wasn't there. It had dulled and could no longer affect her in the same way.

Finn cleared his throat and took his hand back so he could turn. "I promise to never intentionally hurt you."

"Thank you."

⟫⟫⟩⟨⟨⟨

It was the first cloudy day in a while, which meant the roads were quieter than usual for August. Mabel unfolded her banner, and glitter floated to the ground in a sparkling puddle.

"Do we have to hold it up?" Finn asked, eyeing it with clear embarrassment.

"No. I was going to prop it up." The card was thick enough to stand up against their legs.

They watched as arrivals filtered through. Finn had no idea what Del looked like, so he kept pointing out people and asking Mabel if it was her.

"She's my opposite," Mabel said. "Del has short, black curly hair, is tall, and oozes confidence."

"You're confident."

"I'm slowly regaining my confidence."

Finn dipped his head to kiss her forehead.

"No kissing in front of me, please. I'm chronically single," Del said, her accent an odd combination of Cornish with an Australian twang.

"Del," cried Mabel. The welcome home banner fell as Mabel threw herself into her best friend's open arms.

"It's good to see you, Mabes." Del squeezed her and Mabel knew she was putting all the emotions of the last ten years into this one hug. A stray tear slid down Mabel's cheek, and she swiped it away before stepping back.

"I've missed you," Mabel said.

"I missed you, too, but I'm back now."

"Promise you won't jet off again anytime soon?"

"Promise."

Finn cleared his throat from behind.

"And who is this?" Del asked, turning to Finn.

"Del, this is Finn, my boyfriend. Finn, this is Del." Mabel stepped aside to let them greet each other.

"It's nice to meet you, Del," Finn said and stepped forward to kiss Del on the cheek.

"If you hurt her, you'll have me to deal with and I'm a hundred times worse than her brother, okay?" It was meant to be a whisper, but Mabel heard every word.

"Play nice. Come on, let's head back to the car." Mabel linked her arm through Del's and left Finn to follow.

They put Del's suitcases into the boot and climbed into the car.

"Where are we off to?" Finn asked. He'd carried the banner back to the car and his t-shirt was covered in pink and purple glitter.

"Padstow-on-Sea, please," Del called from the back of the car.

"Oh," Mabel muttered as Finn's grip tightened on the steering wheel. "I can ask Elowen to take us," Mabel whispered and put a hand on Finn's arm.

He rolled his shoulders. "No, it's fine. I can't stay away from there forever."

"Am I missing something?" asked Del. "I can call a taxi from Mabel's if you'd like."

"No, it's fine," Finn said. He'd already started the car and was pulling out of the car park. "There's someone I'd rather not see in Padstow-on-Sea, but I can't stay away."

"An ex?" Del asked.

Mabel chewed her lip, wondering if she should jump into the conversation and help Finn. She squeezed his arm and hoped it conveyed her message that she didn't mind if he said yes to Del's question.

"A dad," Finn said.

Silence engulfed the car.

"Sorry," mumbled Del.

"There's nothing for you to be sorry for. You weren't to know. Anyway, are you looking forward to starting your new job? I don't think Mabel has told me anything about what you do," Finn asked and threw an inquisitive look towards Mabel.

"I sort of fell into marketing while I was in Australia, so I've just accepted the role of marketing manager at a Devon-based corporation."

"I might have to pick your brains about marketing for the pub," Finn said.

"You should. Del has accepted a job with the King's Head Corporation, so she'll know all about marketing pubs in tourist traps like Port Isaac," Mabel added.

"The King's Head Corporation?" asked Finn. His voice was tight and his knuckles gripped the steering wheel.

"I know, they're awful, but we're going to turn a blind eye for now since they've brought Del home." Mabel chuckled, but her joke failed to raise a smile on Finn's stony face.

"It's temporary. Only until I get settled. In the meantime, I can gather marketing tips," Del added.

"We'll use them in the same way they use the small communities around here."

Finn pulled the car over into a lay-by.

"Are you okay?" Mabel asked, looking at him properly. He was pale and his skin had a clammy sheen to it.

"I think that coffee was off," he grumbled, letting himself out of the car.

"Can I do anything?" called Mabel.

"Stay here," he gasped, closing the car door behind him.

⤜⤛

By the time Finn returned to the car, he looked much better.

"Are you okay?" asked Mabel.

"Yes, sorry. Just got a little queasy and needed some fresh air." He switched the car on and rejoined the road. Mabel and Del chatted for the rest of the drive to Padstow-on-Sea. Finn drove them to the flat so they could unload Del's suitcases without having to trail through the crowds of tourists.

"I'll park the car and come back. Shall I drop into Jada's and pick up lunch?" Finn called from the car's window.

"Yes, please. I'll text you what to get." Mabel blew him a kiss and followed Del into the flat. "This is nice," she said as she walked into the open-plan living area. The flat was at the edge of the harbour, in the middle of all the shops and restaurants. Local builder, Nick, had been living there until he recently moved in with his girlfriend, Belle. He'd left behind a lot of furniture since there wasn't space in Belle's cottage.

"Isn't it? I'm going to get myself a car soon, then I can visit you whenever I'm not working."

"That will be nice. I still haven't learned how to drive." Mabel wandered over to the window to watch the tourists below.

Del was pulling things from her suitcases and organising them into different piles. "You downplayed your relationship with Finn," she said, glancing at her with a stern expression.

"We've had a few ups and downs already." Mabel shrugged.

"I'm glad you opened yourself up to love, Mabes. You deserve it, and he seems like a good guy."

"He is."

"What aren't you telling me?" Del dropped a handful of clothes and joined Mabel at the window.

"A lot is going on in his life and he's dealing with a lot of pain."

"Is this to do with his dad?"

Mabel nodded. It wasn't her place to tell Del about Finn's family situation, but it was so difficult to keep a secret from her oldest and closest friend, especially now she was standing in front of her.

"Is there stuff you can't talk to me about?" Del was perceptive.

"It's Finn's story to tell, not mine."

Del didn't say anything more. She hugged Mabel.

"I'm here for when you need a takeaway and

wine. We don't have to talk, we can throw on a terrible film and cry together."

"Thanks, Del."

Finn returned with paninis for everyone. There was a deep line in the middle of his forehead and he looked as white as a ghost. Mabel watched him pick at his panini before throwing it in the bin.

CHAPTER THIRTY-FOUR

Mabel winced as daylight shone through the open curtains. "Why did you do that?" she groaned and burrowed beneath the duvet.

"Our alarms went off half an hour ago." Finn chuckled and perched on the edge of the bed, slowly peeling back the cover.

Mabel squinted as her eyes adjusted. "I thought you were going for a run this morning?"

"I thought you were going for a swim this morning." Finn raised his brow and Mabel stuck out her tongue.

"Come back to bed," Mabel said, her voice husky with sleep.

"We have things to do," Finn said, but his gaze lingered on her. Despite oversleeping, it was still early morning, but there was always work to do at Fisherman's Rest.

With a sigh, Mabel sat up in bed, the duvet pooling around her waist. "Can I at least have a good morning kiss?"

Finn's lips captured hers, and he shifted his weight to lean into her. Mabel wrapped her arms around his neck. He pulled back when she tried to pull him down.

"We don't have time," he groaned.

Mabel pouted but got up and put her dressing gown on.

"What do you have planned for today?" asked Finn. He made the bed while Mabel got out some clothes.

"I'm going home for a bit. Gwen asked me to restore a Georgian side table. Her late dog chewed the legs, so it needs work." Mabel was to sand out the bite marks and varnish the legs to match the top. She was honoured that Gwen trusted her.

"Good luck." Finn smiled, but it didn't reach his eyes. While Mabel occasionally visited Gwen, he still hadn't spoken to her.

"I'll miss you," she said, reaching up on her tiptoes to kiss him. His hand gripped her waist as the other tangled in her hair. "We should have stayed in bed," she said against his lips.

"Tonight," promised Finn.

By lunchtime, the Georgian side table was looking much better. All the teeth marks had been sanded out, and the piece was ready to be stained. Mabel stretched and wandered out of the barn and into the sunshine. It had been too hot to work outside, so she'd been tucked away in the shade. Mabel went into the cottage and had a quick shower before she made lunch.

"Where did I put my phone?" she mumbled to herself as she sat down with her sandwich. She glanced around the room and heard it buzz from her bag by the door. There were ten missed calls from Del and lots of texts. Mabel wiped the crumbs from her hands before she scrolled through the messages.

Call me. Now.

Mabel, I don't care what you're doing. You need to call me.

Mabel!

CALL ME!!!

I'M ON MY WAY ROUND.

Mabel's fingers shook as fear flooded her. She hit Del's number. It only rang once before she answered.

"Finally. I've been trying to get hold of you for the last hour," Del's shrill voice echoed down the phone.

"What on earth is going on?" Mabel's hands shook.

"I learned something in my meeting that I need to tell you. I'll be with you in about half an hour."

"What's going on?" Mabel asked again.

"I can't tell you over the phone. I need to see you. Cancel all your plans for the rest of the day."

"Del, you're worrying me." Mabel sat down before her legs gave out beneath her. Del was usually the calm one out of them. Whatever had shaken her must have been bad. Del had been at her new job for a couple of weeks now, and whilst she didn't respect the company, she had enjoyed getting to know the local pubs.

"I'm only half an hour away."

"I have work tonight." Mabel checked the time. "It's one o'clock, so I'll have to head to the pub in a couple of hours to get ready for dinner service."

"Cancel work." Del's tone left no room for argument.

Mabel opened and closed her mouth, but didn't know what to say. "I'll call Elowen," she eventually gasped out.

"See you soon." Del hung up before Mabel could ask any more questions.

Mabel pushed away her sandwich. Her stomach was in knots. She called Elowen and told her something was wrong with Del and she wouldn't be able to make it in for her shift. El was understanding and promised to find someone to cover.

For the next half an hour, Mabel paced around her minute living room, waiting for Del to arrive. All sorts of thoughts were flying through Mabel's mind. She wondered if Del's job had been a scam, or maybe one of her parents was ill. By the time her car pulled up outside, Mabel was green with worry.

"Finally," she called as she yanked open the front door.

Del practically ran down the front path and closed the door behind her, locking it.

"Please, tell me what's going on?" Mabel begged. She was scared.

"How much do you know about Finn Hart?" asked Del.

Mabel froze. Ice flooded her veins. "What do you mean?"

"What do you know about him before he came to Cornwall?"

"He had a failed business in London. I know he lost his flat because of it. Then he found investors and bought Fisherman's Rest." Mabel swallowed, but she couldn't rid herself of the feeling of a lump stuck in her throat.

"The King's Head Corporation is the investor, Mabel. They're the majority share owners, which means any decisions they make can override Finn."

The room spun, and Mabel gasped for breath. Del led her to the sofa. Her legs moved beneath her, but Mabel didn't know how. With shaking hands, she picked up a cushion and hugged it to herself.

"The Corporation owns the pub, not Finn?" Her voice shook.

"It's a bit more complicated than that, but

effectively Finn doesn't have much sway over them. They're trying to force him out. I've seen the emails, and he's fighting to buy them out, but it doesn't seem like he's having much luck raising the funds."

Mabel went back over every conversation with Finn. He'd lied to her. Not just her. He'd lied to the entire community. She had introduced him to her friends and family and encouraged them to trust him. Yet again, Mabel had put her trust in the wrong man. Her heart lay shattered at her feet and the betrayal wound its thorny vines around the ruins.

As the shock wore off, the pain set in, and silent tears slid down Mabel's cheeks. Del wrapped her arms around her.

"Why do I always pick the wrong one?" Mabel sobbed.

"It's not your fault. Finn has lied to not just you, but the entire harbour. The company doesn't know half of what he's spent their money on. Everything is theirs. Every penny that's gone into the pub is the corporation's. He's working as both the manager and chef, but they've plans to put a new chef in. King's Head are doing everything they can to remove Finn and become the sole owners. They've used him as a front to purchase the place."

Mabel squeezed her eyes shut. Not only had he lied about the pub, but he'd led her on and allowed her to think they had a future together. Had he always known they would buy him out?

"I've been such an idiot, Del. So many times I've asked him about the future and he hasn't been able to commit to it."

"Come here." Del hugged a shaking Mabel and held her as she sobbed silently.

"Wait, Del, do you have a picture of your company's logo?" Mabel remembered the letter she'd spotted months ago. She already knew it was the corporation, but she needed confirmation.

Del took out her phone and opened up an email. Mabel gasped and clasped a hand to her mouth. It was the same logo.

"I've been such an idiot. There was a letter at the flat with the logo on it. I spotted it months ago." Mabel dug her nails into the palm of her hand. "I'd meant to look into it and ask Finn questions, but then I got distracted by the way he made me feel. The signs were there, but I was too enthralled by him to recognise them for what they were." A sob built in Mabel's chest. "He's used me," she muttered.

"This isn't your fault. Nobody will blame you. He's hoodwinked the entire community."

"Do you remember how ill he came over when we picked you up from the airport?" Mabel was piecing together Finn's erratic behaviour.

Del nodded. "He must have realised I'd uncover his lies sooner rather than later."

"I need to see him and talk to him. I want answers."

"Is that a good idea? Do you think you should sleep on it?" Del asked, but she held up her hands as Mabel shot her a glare. "Okay, do what you feel is right."

"Can you give me a lift into the harbour on your way home?"

"Of course. Do you want me to stay over tonight?"

"No. I'll be fine on my own." Mabel didn't want anyone to see her when the shock wore off and the pain set in. "Just give me a moment."

Mabel locked herself in the bathroom and leaned against the door, taking a few deep breaths. Nothing could calm her, but she needed a moment to collect herself. She wouldn't cry in front of Finn. Determination filled her, and she squared her shoulders. With her hair tied back into a bun, she splashed her face with water to rid the tear tracks covering her cheeks. It was time to confront Finn. She needed to know if any of it had been real or if his feelings towards her had been a part of the facade he'd created.

"I'm ready," Mabel said, her voice flat as she walked ahead of Del to the car.

CHAPTER THIRTY-FIVE

Del dropped Mabel outside the pub's front door.

"Good luck," she called. "Call me if you need anything."

Mabel nodded and waved Del off. Groups of customers walked up the steps. She took a deep breath of sea air and pushed past the dawdling tourists.

"Mabel, what are you doing here? I thought you weren't coming," Elowen said from behind the bar.

"Change of plan," Mabel replied. "I need to speak to Finn."

Elowen opened the hatch to allow her to slip behind the bar. "What's wrong?" she asked.

"He's lied to us all, El." It took all of Mabel's strength to stop her voice from cracking.

"No." El's face fell.

"Can you send everyone home? I need the truth and it can't wait."

"Of course. I'll tell them we've got no water in the kitchen and to come back tomorrow for a refund. Do you want me to stay?"

Mabel shook her head. "Go home to your family. I'll deal with it." Mabel kissed her on the cheek and walked to the kitchen.

As she walked away, Mabel heard the disappointed groans from customers as El broke the news. Mabel lingered in the hallway as she heard El charming the customers. She offered refunds and boxed-up meals for people to take home. El explained it was against health and safety for the pub to stay open and they'd be shut down if they were caught. The locals were keen not to lose their pub again, so ushered everyone out.

With the sound of people leaving, Mabel braced herself for the coming conversation. It was the sous chef's day off, so Finn would be alone in the kitchen. She squared her shoulders and stood tall, readying herself for what might be the most heartbreaking conversation of her life. It was hot inside the kitchen and Finn stood at the hob, cooking a piece of meat.

"Everyone's leaving," Mabel said, her voice small against the whirring of ovens and the spit of pans.

Finn whirled around at her voice, confusion knitted across his brow. "What do you mean?"

"We sent them home." She shrugged as though

it was nothing.

"Mabel?" Finn turned the heat off on the hob and stepped towards her, but Mabel held her hands out to stop him from coming any closer.

"You lied to me," her voice quivered, so she took a deep breath. "You lied to the community. To my friends. To my family. Even to your own family." Mabel saw the flash of pain at the mention of his family.

"What are you talking about?"

Mabel let out a harsh scoff. "Just be honest for once in your life, Finn Hart. Or are you not capable of it?"

"Honest about what?" Sweat beaded on his forehead, but Mabel knew it had little to do with the temperature in the kitchen. Finn was used to working in hot, stressful environments.

"King's Head Corporation are your investors." The words hung in the air and Mabel watched as Finn's face drained of colour.

"I'm sorry," he whispered, his eyes wide.

"I thought I could trust you. You lied to me, Finn. In the worst way possible."

"I tried to tell you, Mabel."

"How on earth did you try to tell me?"

"I told you I had investors."

"But you missed the part where those investors were a soulless corporation wanting to take over our pub and turn it into a money-making machine at the expense of the community."

"Can we talk? Properly?"

Mabel silently nodded.

Finn led her through to the bar where tables lay covered in plates, and chairs were at odd angles where everyone had left so abruptly. He poured them each a drink, and they found an empty table.

He sighed and tugged a hand through his hair. "I really am sorry, Mabel. I was desperate. Grief had turned me into someone I didn't recognise, and I needed to get out of London. While searching for my dad, I came across the Fisherman's Rest for sale. There was something about it that called to me, so I contacted a broker to help me find investors." He paused and drained his drink. "They were only supposed to be investors. By this point, I was desperate and when my broker told me he had a good deal, I accepted." Finn wandered back to the bar to pour another drink. "I didn't even read the contract. I just signed it," he admitted as he leaned against the bar.

Mabel tipped back her glass and winced as the amber liquid burnt her throat. "You didn't even read it?"

"No. I took a chance on it and then my whole world changed when I met you. For the first time, I was excited about the future. I could see us running the pub together, and you upcycling furniture in your spare time. You're everything I've ever dreamed of. Then the corporation started putting pressure on me. They've got more control than I ever realised was possible. I've been trying to arrange a meeting with them and raise the funds to buy them out. I was going to tell you, Mabel, but I wanted to make everything right beforehand."

Tears streamed down Mabel's cheeks and she used the back of her hand to wipe them away. "You promised you'd never hurt me." Mabel's legs shook as emotions crashed over her.

"I promised to never intentionally hurt you."

Mabel felt cold. Even his promise to her had been calculated, ready to throw back in her face when he needed to. "I should never have trusted you," Mabel gasped. Fresh waves of pain engulfed her heart, and she felt as though the world around her had faded in colour. Life would never look the same after tonight. She'd vowed to stay strong, but as the tears welled in her eyes, Mabel couldn't stop them from falling.

"Mabel, no," he said and walked back to the table, kneeling in front of her chair. Finn gathered her hands. "Please, Mabel. I only want you to be happy. I didn't mean to hurt you."

"You were always going to hurt me, Finn. The moment you lied to me, you sealed our fate."

"It doesn't have to end like this. I can make it right. I'll buy the pub. It can be ours." He'd closed the gap between them and grasped her hands in his.

Mabel took a step back. "No. We can't." Her voice was strong as she stepped away from his touch.

"I love you, Mabel," he said, his voice a plea.

"No, you don't. If you truly loved me, you wouldn't have kept lying. I had to find out from my best friend. Do you know how humiliating that was? Soon, the harbour will know of your lies and I'll look like a gullible idiot that didn't ask any questions. Or worse, they'll think I was in on it with you. There is no happy ending here. Goodbye, Finn." Mabel went to leave, but Finn called after her.

"Don't leave." His voice was thick with emotion.

"I have to," she whispered. With a final glance back at his crestfallen face, Mabel walked out of the pub and into the evening.

It was busy outside. Most of the pub's customers were still milling around, wondering what to do with themselves. People looked her way, but Mabel didn't linger.

With a steady stream of tears streaked across her cheeks, Mabel knocked at Elowen and Michael's.

It didn't take long for Elowen to answer the door. "What's going on?" she asked, taking in Mabel's appearance.

"He lied," sobbed Mabel.

Elowen gathered her in her arms and ushered her indoors. "Michael's putting the girls to bed. Let's go through to the kitchen." El led her to the small sofa in the snug. "Can I get you anything?"

"A tissue would be nice," Mabel sniffed.

Once Mabel had wiped her eyes and blown her nose, she steeled herself to tell Elowen. Her sister-in-law listened in silence as Mabel told her everything. Elowen's expression became increasingly annoyed, but she didn't interrupt. Instead, she reached out and took Mabel's hand and gave it an encouraging squeeze.

"Oh, Mabel," Elowen said as she finished. "I'm sorry he's done this to you." Elowen didn't try to justify Finn's actions, and Mabel was grateful. Trust was a deal breaker for her, and he had shattered it.

"Everyone will think I knew."

"Don't think about that now. It's a problem for tomorrow."

"I don't think I can stay here, El." Mabel knew her heart would break every time she looked at Finn.

"This is your home, Mabel. You can't leave because of him. Where would you go?"

"I don't know," sobbed Mabel.

CHAPTER THIRTY-SIX

Mabel got up before anyone else in the house. She went through the bottom drawer in the guest room and took out an old swimming costume. It was one she left at Elowen and Michael's for impromptu trips to the beach, or water fights in the garden with the girls. She took a towel from the bathroom and tiptoed downstairs, scribbling a note for Elowen when she woke. Mabel had intended to go home last night, but Elowen and Michael had insisted she stay. She slid out the front door and closed it as quietly as she could behind her. A huge yawn ripped across Mabel's face as she wandered the quiet streets. She'd hardly slept last night and had tossed and turned, unable to rid her mind of Finn. Her eyes were swollen and stung in the morning air. Each step felt heavy.

The birds were only just rising as Mabel stepped into the cold sea. Despite the shiver which ran through her, Mabel was exhilarated by the chilly water lapping at her shins. She dived into the waves and swam until her muscles ached. Mabel lay on her back and floated in the waves, looking up at the sky. There wasn't a cloud in sight, and it would be another beautiful day. Yet Mabel couldn't rustle up an ounce of excitement for it. She could hear the harbour coming to life, so Mabel got out of the water and wrapped a towel around herself. No doubt, news of the pub's untimely closure would have circulated, and she didn't want to bump into anyone and have to answer their questions.

Before she left the beach, Mabel couldn't help but glance towards the pub. With a jolt, she recognised Finn's silhouette at the back door.

⋙⋘

The day passed like any other. Both Elowen and Michael had texted to see how she was doing. Last night, Mabel had made Michael promise he wouldn't talk to Finn. It was her mess, and she would deal with it. He'd argued that Elowen had been dragged into it, and therefore, it was his problem, too. Thankfully, Mabel's sister-in-law had sided with her and told Michael she could also stand up for herself.

Mabel had spent most of the day working on

furniture with an audiobook playing to stop her mind from wandering down unsavoury avenues. While she waited for Del to pop around, Mabel called her mother.

"Hi, darling," her mother answered on the second ring.

"Mum. It's good to hear your voice," Mabel's voice trembled.

"What's wrong?"

Mabel told her mother about Finn's lies. She had to stop a few times to blow her nose and dab her eyes.

"Mabel, dear. I wish we were home to make you hot chocolate and to hug you," her mother said. The thought alone sent a fresh wave of emotions crashing over Mabel. She really needed a cuddle from her mother.

"I don't know what to do, Mum."

"Why don't you come and stay with us for a while? We've got to pack up your grandad's home and we could do with the help."

"Maybe." Mabel wanted to run away from the harbour, but would that be the coward's way out? If Finn was here to stay, she'd have to see him when she returned.

"Let us know, Mabel. We can pick you up from the train station and keep you busy for a couple of weeks."

"Thanks, Mum."

They chatted for a while longer, avoiding any topics that might dredge up references to Finn or the pub.

At half-seven, Del came around with a takeaway and a bottle of wine.

"How are you?" Del asked as she dished up their fish and chips.

Mabel poured the wine as she considered the question. "I've not allowed myself to feel anything today," she admitted.

"That's not healthy," Del scolded her.

"I know. It will hurt like crazy when I finally drop my walls." She sighed and drained the glass of wine.

"It's inevitable. Don't put it off too long, Mabes, or those walls will never come down again."

Mabel nodded but didn't say anything. She didn't intend to drop her walls again, so if keeping them up protected her, that was exactly what she would do.

"Shall we eat outside?" Del suggested, glancing out the backdoor to the beautiful evening.

Mabel's stomach twisted as she thought of the evening Finn had come over and they'd sat outside as he opened up to her. "No, let's go sit on the sofa. Much more comfortable."

Del gave Mabel a strange look but led the way to the living room. They settled on the sofa with dinner on their laps, and wine on the coffee table. Ethel padded into the room and settled on the back of the chair between them, her beady eyes focused on the battered fish on the plates. Mabel ate, but she didn't taste the food. She was sure it was lovely, but she wasn't hungry. The only reason she finished it was to stop Del lecturing her.

"I spoke to my mum earlier. She suggested I stay with them in Kent for a while."

"That sounds like a good idea."

"Would I be running away?" Mabel swirled the liquid around her wineglass.

"Does it matter? If running away is what you need to process this, then do it. Think of yourself for once, Mabes."

⇶ ⬿

It was late by the time Del left, but Mabel was restless and couldn't settle. She slipped on her trainers and walked into the harbour. The sun had set, but the sky was still light. Mabel wandered down onto the beach and sat by the water's edge. The damp sand seeped through her shorts, but she didn't mind. She trailed her finger through the sand as she took in deep breaths of sea air.

"Mabel?" someone called.

Mabel tensed as she recognised the voice.

"What do you want, Finn?" she asked, refusing to turn to look at him.

"Are you okay?" He was behind her.

"What does it matter?" she spat back at him.

"This is all such a mess. I'm sorry, Mabel."

Mabel sighed and stared out at the sea. The waves were rough as they crashed against the seawall, and the moored fishing boats bobbed up and down. "There's nothing left for us to say to each other," she whispered, keeping a tight hold of her emotions.

"Isn't there?"

He was sitting beside her now, and Mabel finally turned to look at him. This was the man who loved her. But he was also the man who had lied to her and broken her heart. "No, I don't believe there is."

"I'm going away for a bit. I've got someone to cover my shifts at the pub."

Mabel swallowed hard. It was a relief to hear Finn was leaving. At least she would have the space she needed to process his betrayal and heal from it, but she couldn't deny the fresh wave of pain at the thought of him not being around anymore.

"Mabel, I regret hurting you. King's Head Corporation are fighting me for ownership of the pub. They're disputing my ability to repay their investment. If I lose the pub, I've asked them to keep it the way it is with the community at the heart of it, but I don't know how much sway I have anymore." He paused for a moment. "I'm sorry, Mabel. I've made such a mess of everything. Hand on heart, I promise you, I intended to find a way to buy the pub. I wanted it to be ours."

Mabel's chest tightened at Finn's words. He had wanted the pub to be theirs. Before she could lose herself in a new spiral of heartache, she strengthened her walls and blocked the words from her consciousness. "It's too late for apologies, Finn.

You betrayed my trust. You can't undo that."

"No, I know. I'm not asking for your forgiveness. Not yet."

"What does that mean?" Mabel ground her teeth. "Not yet?"

"It means I don't give up on love that easily. I have to leave and sort my life out. It's no excuse, but I don't think I'm coping very well with the grief of losing my mum, and everything with my dad has only added to it." His voice wobbled and Mabel fought the urge to reach out to him. "I don't want to blame my actions on my mother's death, because they were all my decisions and I messed up."

Mabel didn't know what more to say. There was little point in her reminding him how much he had hurt her. He already knew it. Despite his words, she could see the hollowness in his eyes.

"I'm going to make this right, Mabel. I'll be back soon." He pressed a kiss to the top of her head. "I love you," he said and left.

Mabel heard his footsteps retreating but didn't turn to watch him go. She felt as though the weight of the sea was on her chest as she gasped for breaths.

"I love you, too," she whispered towards the sea. Her voice was so low that the crashing of the waves swallowed her words. Mabel angrily swiped at a stray tear and stood, brushing the sand from her. Finn was leaving, and it was time she allowed herself to fall out of love with him.

CHAPTER THIRTY-SEVEN

It was a few days before Mabel felt ready to venture into Port Isaac again. Elowen had popped around, and Michael had even stopped by last night with the girls. They'd brought leftovers and had dinner in Mabel's cramped living room. The girls had loved it, but poor Ethel had hidden in the bedroom. Nobody had mentioned Finn, but Mabel had been itching to ask if he was still around.

That morning, Mabel's customer had collected the latest piece of furniture she'd been working on. It was a small dressing table which had belonged to the woman's grandmother. The eighties-style table didn't fit the style of the woman's home, so she had reached out to Mabel to see what she could do. Mabel had painted the piece a beautiful pale blue to match the woman's bedroom and replaced the horrible plastic handles with brass ones. It looked modern and suited the woman's home, but retained the memories.

Mabel had helped to load the dressing table into the car and waved the woman off. She had poured her emotions into that piece, so it was a relief when the woman drove off with it. For now, she had nothing else to work on. A nearby hotel had sent her a contract to refinish their bedroom furniture, but they wouldn't be ready to start until the end of September. With no more excuses left, Mabel set off into the harbour for a chocolate milkshake at Fisherman's Brew.

Stares swivelled her way as she walked, but Mabel ignored them. She even pretended she hadn't heard a few people calling her name. The last thing she wanted was to talk about Finn. Mabel knew news of his duplicity had spread, but nobody had told her how it had been received.

It wasn't too busy in Fisherman's Brew. With the nice weather, everyone was choosing to take their food away to enjoy it on the beach.

"Mabel!" Betty's voice was filled with surprise as she spotted her step through the door.

"Hello, Betty." Mabel smiled timidly at the woman.

"Oh, it's so good to see you." Betty put down an empty tray on the nearest table and pulled Mabel into her embrace.

"I'll cry if you're too nice to me." Mabel sniffled

as she returned the hug.

"Let the poor girl go before you squeeze the life out of her," Gwen called from her usual table.

Mabel was pleasantly surprised to see Gwen. She gave her a small wave as Betty stepped aside and went to greet some customers.

"Come and join me," Gwen called her over.

Mabel slid into the seat opposite Gwen. She pushed away the memories of sitting in Fisherman's Brew with Finn.

"How are you?" Gwen asked once Betty bustled off to make Mabel's order.

"Not good," Mabel said. She knew it was pointless lying to Gwen.

"I'm sorry he lied to you."

"It's not your fault, Gwen."

"He's my flesh and blood. It feels like my fault. I could throttle my brother." Gwen took a moment to calm herself, and Mabel raised her brows. She'd never seen Gwen so angry. "If he had been there for Finn and his mother, none of this would have happened. Finn needed support through everything. Instead, he was left to fend for himself and it backfired for him."

Mabel felt guilt settle in the pit of her stomach.

"Mabel, you did nothing wrong," Gwen said. "It wasn't your place to support him through it all. He should have had the support of family during those days, but we failed him." Gwen let out a heavy sigh.

"Things should have been different for him, but he needs to take responsibility for his actions.

He's an adult, Gwen." Mabel's tone was cold.

Betty put down a triple chocolate milkshake in front of Mabel with extra cream and two flakes. "The girl's right," Betty said to Gwen. She nodded to one of the waitresses and took the empty seat beside Mabel. "We've all been through tough situations in our lives. How we recover from them shapes us into the people we are. Finn still has to learn that lesson."

Mabel scooped up some whipped cream on the end of the chocolate flake and bit it off as she watched Gwen digest Betty's words. It was difficult since Betty didn't know about Finn's relation to Gwen.

"Can I tell you a secret, Betty? We've been friends for enough years that I know I can trust you," Gwen said, leaning across the table.

"A secret? Gwen, darling, I doubt there's anything you know that you haven't already told me. You tend to share gossip before it's even left the lips of the person telling it." Betty chuckled, but she leaned closer to hear what Gwen had to say.

Mabel snorted and covered it with a cough. Gwen's eyes shone, but she kept a stern expression. "Finn is my nephew."

Betty's face fell as she processed the words. She turned to Mabel, who nodded.

"Why is it a secret?" Betty asked once she'd got her head around it.

"Finn and I only discovered it recently. My brother is his father."

Betty nodded. She obviously knew Lowen well

enough for no further explanation to be necessary.

"Poor boy," Betty said after hearing how alone Finn had cared for his late mother.

"Betty," Mabel groaned.

"Sorry, love. It doesn't undo what he did to you, but he must have been struggling. Losing a parent is a pain unlike any other. Especially if they're all you have left."

Mabel scooped more whipped cream onto her flake, shoved it into her mouth, and slumped in her chair. Perhaps coming out had been a terrible idea.

"How's work?" Gwen asked, effortlessly changing the subject.

"It's good. I had another happy customer this morning. I've got a contract starting in a couple of weeks, but nothing for now."

"I should get off. Pop in for lunch one day this week, Mabel. It'll be nice to have company. If you're at a loose end with furniture, I can dig something out for you to work on."

"I'd love to. Thanks, Gwen." Mabel smiled. The thought of looking around the furniture in Gwen's house sparked a small glimmer of happiness. Something Mabel hadn't felt over the last few days.

Gwen left, but Betty hovered to make sure Mabel was really okay.

"I promised your mother I'd look out for you while she was away," Betty said. She squeezed Mabel's shoulder before wandering to a table to take their order.

Mabel blinked back the tears as she thought of

her mother. She'd give anything for one of her hugs right now.

Once alone, Mabel sipped her chocolate milkshake until a family of four came in and she gave up her table to them. With a wave to Betty, Mabel left Fisherman's Brew and decided to pop to Zoe's studio to see if she was around. If she went home now, she'd only sit in front of daytime television, feeling sorry for herself.

As Mabel rounded the corner, she stopped dead as she came face to face with a big van. She watched as boxes were unloaded under the watchful eye of a middle-aged man who stood with his arms crossed and his eyes narrowed.

"Mabel." Elowen emerged from the back of the van.

"El, what's going on?" Mabel helped her jump down.

"It's a mess, Mabel. The temporary manager Finn employed walked out after a few hours, and now the corporation has installed their own manager."

"That's not right." Mabel glanced back towards the man to see him watching them. "How long is he staying for, with all this stuff?"

"I don't think they're anticipating Finn returning."

Mabel's jaw slackened.

"He seems awful. I should get back to it." Elowen looked back to the van but didn't move.

"I'm sorry, El."

"It's not your fault. I think Mr Grumpy over there is the real face of the corporation. I hope Finn can raise the money and buy them out."

Mabel's face fell.

"Sorry, Mabel. It doesn't excuse his actions, but I am glad he set the pub up with the community's input. We have to do everything we can to keep it this way. Anyway, I should get back to it. His pen collection won't unload itself, and he certainly isn't going to do it." El kissed Mabel on the cheek and disappeared back into the lorry.

Mabel let out a slow breath through her nose.

"Why did I venture into town?" Mabel groaned. Daytime television was beginning to look quite attractive. Instead, she continued on to Zoe's studio. The lights were on, so she knocked.

"Oh, it's you," Zoe said as she opened the door.

"Sorry, were you expecting someone else?" Mabel was taken aback by Zoe's greeting.

"You don't know what's going on, do you?" Zoe's expression softened, and she stepped aside to allow Mabel in.

"No. What is it?" Mabel looked around the studio. It was a jumble of art supplies and half-packed boxes.

"You better sit down." Zoe pushed a stool towards her while she sat on a packing box.

"Zoe, you're worrying me. What is it?" Mabel studied Zoe. Her eyes were red-rimmed, her hair unwashed, and her nails bitten. "Is it Jada?"

"None of my invoices have been paid," Zoe said.

Mabel's jaw dropped. "None? Have you checked your bank details on your invoices? Maybe there's a typo or an 'O' in place of a zero?"

"No, Mabel. None of my invoices have been paid by Finn, the pub, or the corporation."

"Have you checked them for mistakes…" Mabel trailed off. She knew it was pointless. "Oh, Zoe." A crushing guilt consumed Mabel as she took in the woman's dejected body language.

"We should have been exchanging contracts today, but we've had to pull out."

"No, you can't do that. Have the money they paid me." Mabel knew her invoices had been paid. The money was sitting in her account now.

"He must have paid you before the corporation pulled the funding. I don't know if anyone else has been paid."

"Anyone else?" The words came out very slowly as Mabel willed them not to mean what she thought they might.

"They've pulled their investment, so Finn has no money to pay us. I spoke to him this morning. A few payments have been processed, but the rest were waiting for the corporation's approval and it doesn't look like that will happen now."

"Zoe, I'm so sorry. I never would have got you involved if I'd have known how this would turn out."

"It's not your fault, Mabel." Zoe reached out and hugged her and they clung to one another.

CHAPTER THIRTY-EIGHT

Visiting Gwen's house was similar to a day out at a National Trust property, and it was just the distraction Mabel needed. After spending last night worrying about Zoe and Jada's situation, Mabel had got up early and walked over to Gwen's. She'd spent the last hour sauntering around the rooms and admiring the furniture. There were lots of impressive Georgian pieces, all in near pristine condition. Gwen had shown Mabel into the dining room, where a mahogany serpentine sideboard was pushed up against one of the walls, with a towering vase of pastel-coloured flowers atop it. Mabel was particularly drawn to the piece with its spindly legs and brass handles.

"My late husband bought me that for our

fifth wedding anniversary," Gwen said, running her fingers along the top.

"The year of wood." Mabel smiled.

"He was a good man." Gwen cleared her throat and turned to put her back towards the sideboard. "Shall we have tea in the garden? It seems a shame to be indoors on such a lovely day. It won't be long until the rain clouds draw in until next season."

Mabel grimaced at the thought of another cup of tea. She didn't have the heart to tell Gwen she didn't like it. Instead, she nodded and wandered out to the garden. Mabel now had a usual seat, which she slid into. The warm breeze blew across her, and she tipped her head up to the sun as she listened to Gwen humming in the kitchen. Mabel always offered to make the tea, but Gwen would never accept. Mabel revelled in the feeling of the sun and the warmth on her skin. Her eyes were tired, and her mind wouldn't quieten. She wanted to ask Elowen if she had been paid, but was scared to learn the answer. It was possible that the local food suppliers hadn't been paid, or the builder Finn had employed. Although it wasn't her fault entirely, Mabel felt the blame lying at her feet.

"You look lost in your thoughts," Gwen said as she placed the tea tray down. There were homemade scones today with ramekins of jam and clotted cream.

As she slathered jam and cream onto a scone, Mabel told Gwen about how Zoe hadn't been paid and her worry about whether anyone else had.

"Have you spoken to your friend who works for the corporation?" asked Gwen, topping up the hot water in the teapot.

"No. I should, but I'm scared." Mabel huffed. She'd stared at her phone most of yesterday evening, trying to find the courage to call Del. In the end, she'd run a bath and put on an audiobook to escape.

Gwen nodded and sipped her tea before she steered the conversation onto her small vegetable plot around the side of the house. Mabel helped her to harvest the broad beans, and Gwen sent her home with a handful.

On her walk back to the harbour, Mabel felt much more positive. There was still an ache in her chest for Finn. Sometimes, when she was half asleep, she could feel the ghost of his fingers trailing across her skin, or the soft brush of his lips against her collarbone. When she woke, the emptiness inside of her was all-consuming, until her memories returned and she remembered why he was no longer beside her.

With the broad beans stuffed inside her bag, Mabel popped into Port Groceries to pick up a few things to make dinner with. She didn't know what, but she'd browse the shelves until inspiration hit.

The bell above the door chimed as Mabel entered. Instead of his usual warm welcome, Mr Trelawney clucked his tongue and disappeared into the backroom. Mabel's brow rose, but she ignored it and set about finding something for dinner. She browsed the vegetables but soon decided the beans were enough. As she glanced down the next aisle, she saw a couple of women huddled together talking. Now and then they would glance towards her. Mabel thought she recognised them as parents from the girls' school.

Feeling as though all eyes were on her, Mabel picked up a block of butter and a piece of fish. At the end of the day, the fisherman would sell any leftover fish to Mr Trelawney. Mabel took the items to the counter and got out her purse while she waited to be served. After a few minutes, Mabel peered into the backroom. It was unlike Mr Trelawney not to come running out the second there was a customer.

"I don't know how you can show your face here," one of the mums said as they joined her at the till.

"Excuse me?" spluttered Mabel.

"After everything you've put this community through," the other woman added, shaking her head as she looked Mabel up and down.

"Poor Elowen was in pieces when she dropped the girls off this morning," the first woman said.

"What's happened?" Mabel asked. Fear gripped her at the thought of anything happening to her family.

"She's been utterly humiliated."

Unable to bear their cryptic replies and snide looks, Mabel put her shopping back on the shelf and left. She heard Mr Trelawney emerge from the backroom as the door shut behind her.

"Thank you, ladies," he said.

Another wave of sadness rolled over Mabel, but she didn't have time for it to engulf her. She had to speak to Elowen.

It was Michael who opened the front door, and Mabel instantly knew something was wrong. He was ashen, and his eyes were red. "Michael," Mabel began, but didn't know what more to say.

He looked over his shoulder before he spoke. "Elowen's been sacked."

"Sacked?" Mabel could hardly believe her ears. She'd expected Elowen to quit, but she hadn't expected her to be fired. "What on earth happened?"

"You better come in." Michael led her through to the kitchen where Elowen sat in the snug, topping up her glass of wine. The usually well-turned-out Elowen had been replaced by her scruffy doppelgänger. She wore an oversized tracksuit, her hair was tied up in a scruffy bun, and streaks of mascara ran down her face.

"El, what happened?" Mabel asked, slipping into the seat beside her.

"I'll go and check on the girls. They're watching a movie in bed," Michael said. He shot a nervous glance towards Elowen before he left. Usually, the girls would get home from school and start on their homework.

"He sacked me, Mabel. That vile troll of a manager sacked me." Elowen reached for the box of chocolates and plucked one without looking to see which one it was. She popped it into her mouth and closed her eyes as she chewed.

"Why did he sack you?" Mabel was finding it difficult to understand what had happened. The women in the shop had alluded to it all being Mabel's fault, but she didn't understand.

"They want a fresh start for the pub. They've fired everyone and are looking to recruit outsiders to train them within the company. In Finn's absence, they've completely taken over. It's as though they already own the place."

Mabel sucked in a deep breath as she steeled herself to ask the question that was gnawing away at her. "El, have you been paid?"

"Not for all of my hours. Finn has paid me for some."

"What have I done?" Mabel held her head in her hands as the room spun. This was all her fault. She'd made the mistake of trusting Finn in those early days, despite everyone else's reservations. Mabel had pushed everyone to trust him and to get on board with his vision. Now people were out of pocket and could lose their homes, all because of her. It wasn't just the pub they'd lost this time, people would lose their income and their homes.

"Mabel, you can't blame yourself for this."

"Michael didn't want to trust him, but I forced everyone to. I'm useless at judging people and it's finally caught up with me."

"Don't do this to yourself." Elowen held the box of chocolates out for Mabel to take one, but she refused.

"Look at you, El. This isn't you, and it's all my

fault."

"I quite like this new look. Maybe it's time I reinvented myself."

"Don't you dare!" Mabel stepped back to look at Elowen. She'd never forgive herself if her actions led to Elowen changing who she was. "Elowen, you're perfect the way you are. You'll have a few days feeling sorry for yourself, then you'll get up, brush yourself down, and get back out there. I'm sure Betty can offer you a few shifts. Maybe try the new seafood restaurant in Padstow-on-Sea? You'll find a new job and you'll blossom again. This is a hiccup in your story."

"Thank you, Mabel." Elowen hugged her tightly. "This is a hiccup in your story, too."

Mabel pulled back. "You'll be okay. I should slip out before the girls realise I'm here."

"Call me tomorrow?" Elowen asked.

"Of course. See you soon."

With a last hug, Mabel left and began the slow walk back to her cottage. It was closing time for all the shops, which was the worst time Mabel could have chosen to walk through the harbour. "You've got some cheek. Showing your face after all you've done," Demelza, the sweet shop owner, said. She was taking in the sign outside her shop.

"Good evening, Demelza," Mabel said through gritted teeth.

"You trusted Finn Hart. You convinced us all to trust him. Now look at us. We're stuck with a corporate pub. They've sacked all the locals and haven't paid them." The woman's disdain for Mabel was clear. "If you hadn't driven him out of the harbour, then none of this would have happened."

Mabel's jaw dropped. Was the community siding with Finn even after all he had put them through?

"He lied to all of us," Mabel said. It took all of her strength to keep her voice calm.

Demelza scoffed. "He lied to you to get you into his bed and you lapped it up."

Mabel was frozen to the spot as Demelza gave her one last scathing look before disappearing into her shop. Hot, angry tears pooled in Mabel's eyes. Feeling everyone's gaze on her, Mabel trudged up the hill towards her cottage, knowing that she couldn't stay in Port Isaac for another day.

Mabel got home as Del was pulling up outside.

"Are you okay?" Del asked.

"No. Let's go inside before people start throwing rotten fruit at me."

"What's happened?" Del followed her into the cottage and went straight to the kitchen to put the kettle on.

"Everyone blames me for everything that's happened. I have to leave, Del. I'm going to book a train to Kent and spend some time with my parents."

Del reached out to stop her from picking up her laptop. "Before you do that, I need to tell you something. I spoke to Finn," Del said. She left the words hanging in the air as Mabel digested them.

"Why?"

"Someone had to tell him the company was pulling the investment, and I wanted it to come from me. Did you know he was trained by Lachlan McLeod? He's staying at his castle in the Scottish Highlands, cooking at his restaurant."

"Del," Mabel warned

"Sorry. Not relevant. I asked him why you were the only person he paid." Del stopped to sip her drink.

"And?" Mabel asked impatiently.

"He used his inheritance to pay you. Every other payment needed the corporation's approval."

The knot in Mabel's stomach twisted, and an uneasy queasiness overcame her. "Inheritance?" she mumbled. Mabel dug her nails into her palm. Finn had paid her enough to live on for at least six months. A year if she watched every penny.

Del took Mabel's hand. "His mum left him money. She had stipulated that it couldn't be spent on his business. It wasn't his business, and he was paying you for the furniture, and your upcycling skills, so he got around the conditions."

Mabel grasped Del's hand and used it to anchor herself as emotions washed over her. "He can't do that," she murmured.

"He already did."

"Why me? Nobody else has been paid, but he used his money for me."

"He paid some of Elowen's wages, too, but he ran out of money. Finn did it so you didn't learn about the corporation's involvement. Don't narrow your eyes at me, Mabel. I truly think he meant well. He's in a really bad place at the moment. His mother's death affected him more than he'd realised, and the rejection from his father only added to it. You were all he had, and he didn't want to risk losing you."

"Don't," Mabel said and tugged her hand from Del's. She stared at her best friend in disbelief. How could she take Finn's side?

"I'm not telling you to forgive him. I'm just saying I can see why he did it. His intentions were good. He was in talks with investors about buying out the corporation. I've seen the emails he sent. He had a meeting booked for this week with the chief finance officer to discuss how much it would cost to buy out their investment."

Mabel swallowed against the lump in her throat, but it wouldn't move. "That doesn't undo his lies. He'll never be able to make this right. King's Head has been trying to get their hands on the pub for years and he's handed it to them on a platter. They'll never let him buy it."

"I know. He's doing everything he can, and he's trying to get everyone paid."

"It's the least he could do."

Del took the hint and didn't say anymore. Ethel joined them and curled up on Mabel's lap as she absentmindedly raked her fingers through the cat's fur.

"Everyone blames me, Del," Mabel admitted. She told her about last night's trip to Port Groceries, and her walk into the harbour that morning.

"That's not fair. You knew as much as they did."

"They're also blaming me for Finn leaving. This is too much, Del. I have to get away for a while." Mabel scooped up her laptop and booked the next train to London, which wasn't until the following morning.

"What about Ethel?" Del asked as the cat jumped onto the sofa and curled up.

"I'll ask El—No, I won't. I can't ask anything from her after I've ruined their happiness." Mabel chewed her thumb as she thought about who she could ask.

"You know I'd have her if it wasn't for my allergies," Del said.

"It's fine. I'll ask Gwen. She's more of a dog person, but I'm sure she won't mind popping by and feeding Ethel for me."

CHAPTER THIRTY-NINE

The train journey was awful. Memories of her time with Finn had plagued her thoughts as she stared out of the window, willing her tears not to fall. She could still feel the ghost of his touch on her waist, and the softness of his lips against hers. Mabel's jaw ached from clenching her teeth for the last few hours, and her head pounded. She'd changed in London and got the train into Kent, where her mother had insisted on collecting her. It was a small station, and Mabel's mother was waiting on the platform. She looked very similar to Mabel, with long blonde hair thrown up in a messy bun, and the same green eyes. Mary even wore an outfit that Mabel had gifted her. The sea green Capri trousers were from a small boutique in Padstow-on-Sea, and the frilly white blouse was from an online Cornish shop.

"My little Mabel," Mary said and hugged her.

Mabel sunk into her mother's embrace.

They stood like that until the train pulled away. "Shall we head back? Your father and grandfather have popped to the pub to give us some space." Mary led her towards the car.

"Thanks, Mum," Mabel sniffled. She felt stronger after her mother's hug and was ready to recount the last few months.

"Head straight up and sort yourself out. I'll put the kettle on," instructed Mary as they pulled up.

Mabel did as she was told and took her bag up to the room she used to share with Michael when they visited during the school holidays. It was exactly how she remembered it, with chintzy pink covers over the bed, dusty stuffed toys lined up on a shelf, and the plush green carpet beneath her feet. Mabel cracked open a window to let some air in. It had been a while since the room was last used. The fresh air filled the room, but left a bitter taste in Mabel's mouth. It wasn't the salty sea air she was used to. She pushed back all thoughts of her home and went downstairs.

"I sent your father to the shops when you called, so we have some of your favourites in," Mary said. "Shall we sit in the garden?"

Mabel nodded. Her mother had made hot chocolates and set out scones, jam, and clotted cream.

The garden was how Mabel remembered it. The small manicured lawn was surrounded by blooming rose bushes which filled the air with their delicate scent. Mabel's grandmother had always taken great pride in her garden and had been filled with dread when Mabel and Michael would visit in the holidays. They'd kicked up more than a few tufts of grass playing football on the lawn. Eventually, balls had been banned from the garden after a particularly nasty tackle saw Michael tumbling into a thorny rose bush. He was fine after a trip to the local minor injuries unit, but her grandmother's nerves had been frazzled.

"The garden was overgrown when we arrived, but we've done our best to get it back to how your grandmother loved it," Mary said.

"I think you've done a wonderful job."

"There's so many happy memories here, it'll be sad to leave for the final time."

Mabel nodded and picked up a scone. As she spread the jam over the crumbly surface, memories of Finn caught up with her. Her stomach churned, and she put the uneaten scone back on her plate.

"Mabel, dear, what happened? It's not like you to leave Port Isaac. I know Finn broke your heart, but it's not worth you running away from home."

"Everyone hates me." Mabel swallowed back a sob.

"That's not true. You have your family and Betty."

"They all blame me. Elowen's lost her job because of me. Nobody has been paid. It's awful."

Mary's brow furrowed, and she set her mug down on the table. "They're upset and looking for people to blame. Once the shock wears off, people will realise it's not your fault."

Mabel nodded, unable to speak.

"You have got yourself into a pickle, haven't you? I don't agree with how Finn lied to you, but it sounds like he was in a difficult place. Don't frown at me. You've not had the heartbreak of losing a parent, so you don't know how much it can turn your life upside down. It sounds as though his mother was the only person he had left in the world. Combine that with losing his business and his home, I'm not surprised he made some bad decisions."

"Why didn't he tell me? If he had been honest from the beginning, I could have helped him."

"Mabel, darling, I love you and don't mean this in a nasty way, but you wouldn't have helped him. Port Isaac is your world. You wouldn't have given him a second look if you'd known who his investors were. You most likely would have rallied the community and chased him away."

Mabel's shoulders sagged. She picked up the scone she'd prepared and took a bite, barely registering the rich flavours.

"Don't bury this," her mother warned.

"What am I supposed to do?" muttered Mabel around a mouthful.

"Talk to him and see if you can find a way to

move past this."

"He lied to me, Mum. And he's working for the enemy."

"Mabel, you don't have to take on the harbour's problems. There's a whole world outside of Port Isaac. Don't limit yourself to living for the community. You deserve to be happy. I know you've been hurt before, but is this the same?"

It was an effort to swallow the mouthful as Mabel processed her mother's words. Was it the same? Finn hadn't cheated on her, but he had lied to her, or at the very least, deceived her. "I don't know if it's something I can get over," she admitted.

"It's as easy and as difficult as following your heart."

Mabel scoffed.

"The best place to start is to talk to him. No relationship is easy. They all take work and require compromises."

Silence enveloped them as Mabel chewed over her mother's words. What did her heart want? Mabel didn't have to think long to know that her heart still loved Finn.

"I need to pick your father and grandfather up from the pub. Do you want to come?" Her mother stood and stretched.

"No. I think I'll stay here for a while."

Mary dropped a kiss on the top of her head and left.

The soft scent of roses blew over to Mabel, and it was as though her grandmother was beside her.

"I don't know what to do." Mabel hadn't expected her mother to encourage her relationship with Finn. She'd been ready to rip apart his character and go to bed feeling like she'd made the right decision to end their relationship. Instead, her thoughts and emotions were scattered, and she didn't know where to begin to sift through them.

Mabel pulled out her phone and scrolled through pictures of her and Finn. Despite their short time together, they'd taken many photographs. A weight settled in Mabel's chest as she looked at her carefree smile. Her favourite picture was of her and Finn standing outside the Fisherman's Rest's front door with the freshly painted sign above them. They held each other as they beamed at the camera. Zoe had just finished painting the sign and called them out to see it, then insisted on taking a photograph of them beneath it. Mabel could still feel the ghost of the happiness from that day. She looked at Finn and took in his warm smile and gentle eyes. They'd got into a routine of finishing work and falling into bed, where they would lose themselves in each other's arms. Sleeping alone again left her feeling empty and dreading going to bed.

"I miss you," she whispered and closed the picture.

CHAPTER FORTY

Being back in Kent, surrounded by her childhood memories, was like a comfort blanket wrapped around Mabel's shoulders. She'd learned to accept the uncertainty inside of her. With her grandfather's impending move, there was lots to do packing up the house. Despite the busy days, every night when she climbed into bed, her chest still ached for Finn. Mabel wanted to follow her heart, but each time she tried, her head stopped her. Finn had sent a handful of texts, apologising and wishing her well. Mabel ignored them and eventually, he stopped. She'd silently sobbed into her pillow on the first night he didn't send one, but over the last few days, she'd come to terms with it.

"Morning, love," Mabel's father said as she padded down the stairs.

"Morning."

"Your mum's in the kitchen making breakfast.

I've got to nip out for some more boxes."

The kettle had just boiled when Mabel walked into the kitchen. Her grandfather was sitting at the dining table with a bowl of cereal and a coffee in front of him. He was frail and Mabel was filled with guilt for all the years she hadn't made the trip to Kent to visit him.

"Morning," she said and gave him a quick hug.

"Hot chocolate?" asked Mary, getting another mug out.

"Yes, please."

"I got some pastries from the bakery." Mary pointed to a paper bag in the middle of the table. "Help yourself. It's going to be a busy day."

There was just a week until the sale of the house was finalised, and they were still packing. Through it all, they'd had to declutter and donate items to charity as there wasn't enough space at Mabel's Parents'. Her grandfather had found it difficult, and they'd spent a long time reminiscing. Mabel had chosen some furniture to take home and refinish. One of the pieces Mabel had chosen was an Art Deco walnut cocktail cabinet. It would be a tight squeeze in her living room, but she had many fond memories of the piece. When they visited, her grandmother would make drinks for everyone from the cabinet. Little Mabel was in awe of the mirrored surfaces against the beautiful wood. Inside the cabinet was a full Art Deco cocktail set. Mabel would watch her grandmother whip up fancy cocktails for the adults. As a treat, Mabel and Michael would have mocktails. Her favourite tasted like a cherry Bakewell and was topped with a maraschino cherry. Michael didn't like the cherry, so she always ate his too.

"Mabel?" her mother called, pulling her from the memories.

"Sorry, what was that?" asked Mabel around a mouthful of croissant. They weren't as nice as Jada's, and Mabel felt a pang of homesickness.

"I think your phone is ringing," she repeated.

Mabel tuned in to the sound of her phone ringing from upstairs. "I'll see who it is." She took her hot chocolate and croissant with her.

As she picked up the phone, the blood drained from Mabel's face. Finn's name flashed up on the screen. She scrambled to put her mug down and clasped the phone in clammy hands.

"Hello?" answered Mabel, her voice muffled as she struggled to swallow her last mouthful of pastry.

"Mabel," Finn said. Goosebumps broke out on Mabel's arm at the sound of his voice.

"What do you want, Finn?" she asked, her voice soft but her words harsh. His voice made her stomach flutter and her heart thrum.

"I need to talk to you. Are you home?"

"No."

"Can we meet later?"

"I'm in Kent,"

"What are you doing there?"

"I needed some space. From you. From the

harbour. People blamed me, and I had to get away from it." Mable bit her lip to stop tears from spilling down her cheeks.

"I'm sorry. I never meant for you to get tangled up in this mess."

"Stop apologising. It doesn't change anything, and I'm sick of hearing those two words."

"Sor—" he stopped himself before he could finish. "I do need to talk to you."

"Fine, tell me what it is you have to say." Mabel would be home soon, but didn't want to tell him. She couldn't bear the thought of waiting an entire week to find out what he had to say to her.

"I've got the opportunity to buy out the investors."

There was silence on both ends of the call as Mabel processed the information. "Where have you got the money from?" It was a personal question, but she needed to know.

"Gwen."

Mabel's brow furrowed. His answer had only raised more questions.

"It's a long story and one I'd like to tell you when we're face-to-face," he said, as though he knew how she would react.

"What do you want me to say?" Mabel slid down onto the floor and pulled her knees to her chest.

"If you never want to see me again, I won't do it."

His words hung in the air as Mabel digested

them. He had the chance to buy out the corporation. The investor that he had told her about. He might have deceived her, but had he necessarily lied to her? Mabel chewed her lip. "I don't know," her voice wobbled.

"I want to do things the right way. There might not be a way back for us, but I'd like things to be amicable between us."

Mabel could taste blood. "Buy them out," she said. It was the least Mabel could do for the community after everything she had put them through.

"I'm going to make things right. Everyone will be paid and will get their jobs back," promised Finn.

"How?" It was a monumental task.

"My friend Lachlan has a lot of sway. A bad word from him can ruin a business. I know I should have been more careful when I signed the agreement for an investor, but I feel duped by them. They paid off my broker, and I trusted him. I'll make sure everything is put right. I promise."

Mabel ground her teeth. The corporation really was slippery.

"If I could go back and do things differently, then I would." He sounded so heartbroken that Mabel almost felt sorry for him.

"Me, too," she replied.

"Let's talk when you're home."

"Maybe. Goodbye, Finn." Mabel hung up and let her phone fall to the carpeted floor. Her heart still ached for him.

CHAPTER FORTY-ONE

"Are you ready, love?" Mary asked. She stood beside Mabel as they watched the removal men shut the van's doors.

"As ready as I'll ever be," Mabel replied.

They were heading back to Port Isaac today. Her grandfather's house was completing tomorrow and his belongings were packed into the back of a van for the drive to Cornwall.

"Are you ready to see him again?" her mother asked as they walked to the car.

"I don't think I could ever be ready. It's going to hurt because I still love him."

"This doesn't have to be the end, Mabel. Talk to him. From there, you can decide if you can trust him again."

Mabel nodded. "I'm scared, Mum. I can understand why he did the things he did." She paused to suck in a shaky breath. "I still love him, but he's broken my heart once. What if he does it again?"

"Nothing in life is certain. You won't know what to do until you talk to him."

Mabel nodded. Deep down, she knew her mum was right.

"I know the circumstances which brought you to us were horrible, but I'm glad you came. We couldn't have done it without you." Mary squeezed her shoulder before going to help Mabel's grandfather into the car.

"You ready, love?" Mabel's father called from the driver's side of the car.

"Yes, sorry. I was saying goodbye to the house." Mabel joined her mother in the back of the car and looked out of the window as they drove away.

〜〜〜〜〜

It was a long drive with many stops, but they eventually arrived in Cornwall. Mabel was surprised to find herself excited to be home. She undid her window as they drove by the sea and sucked in big lungfuls of air. A bubble of nerves was growing in her stomach at the thought of bumping into Finn. Hiding beneath the nerves was a fizz of excitement.

"Do you want us to drop you at home?" her

father asked as they neared the harbour.

"No. I'll help you unpack and get settled." Mabel was dreading going back to her cottage and being alone. Ethel wouldn't even be there since Gwen had insisted on having her to stay while Mabel was away.

They drove through the harbour and Mabel sank further into her seat, hoping nobody would spot her through the window.

She didn't mean to look at the pub as they passed it, but she couldn't stop her head from swivelling in its direction. With a jolt, she saw Finn sitting on the front steps on a phone call. He looked up as her eyes settled on him and their gazes met for a fraction of a second and Mabel's stomach flipped.

"Is that him?" asked Mary.

Mable nodded, unable to find the words.

"I can see why you fell for him." Her mother winked and Mabel couldn't help the giggle that escaped her.

"Mum!" Mabel gasped around uncontrollable laughter. It was the emotional release she needed.

They reached her parents' home and unloaded the car. Mabel went straight through to put the kettle on. Before it had even boiled, little footsteps echoed through the hallway. "Maple Syrup?" Mia and Milly called as they ran from room to room looking for her.

"I'm in the kitchen," she called back, bracing herself for the two little bundles throwing themselves at her.

Mabel caught the girls in her arms and giggled

as they squeezed her. She swallowed against the lump in her throat. Guilt had stopped her from calling Elowen or Michael, so she hadn't heard their voices for a while.

"We missed you," the girls said.

"I missed you, too. It's good to be home."

"Hi," Michael said from the doorway.

Mabel let the girls go. "Michael," her voice caught in her throat. "I'm sorry," she said.

"Don't be so silly, Maple Syrup. None of this was your fault." He hugged her and Mabel felt relief flood her. She'd worried her brother would never forgive her for what she'd put them through.

"El will be here in a minute. She's just finishing work."

"She's working again?"

"Betty needed an extra pair of hands."

"I'm glad she found something."

Mabel went back to the kettle and got out extra mugs. She dropped tea bags in some and chocolate powder in others.

"Mabel, I need to talk to you before you hear it from anyone else," Michael said. He sounded tense.

"Okay?" Mabel put the kettle down, suspecting this conversation shouldn't happen while she was pouring boiling water.

"I think you should sit down."

"Is it that bad?"

Michael pulled out a seat and motioned for her to sit on it. Mabel wrung her hands as she sat. Her chest tightened, and a sense of dread overcame her.

Michael sat opposite, his expression serious. "I'll start with the good news. Everyone has been paid."

Mabel breathed a sigh of relief. Why did she have to sit down for that? "Good. Hopefully, that means I'll get fewer glares from the locals."

"There's more." Michael paused. "Finn forced the company to pay everyone. It was part of his deal with the corporation to buy out their investment. He threatened them with bad publicity. Did you know he was friends with Lachlan McLeod?"

"I know," Mabel said. "Finn called and asked for my blessing."

"That was... nice of him?"

Mabel nodded.

"Anyway, the contracts have been signed and the pub should be open again by next week. He's asked me to be his accountant. Is that okay?"

"Of course. I would never ask you to turn down work." Mabel crossed her arms to hide her shaking hands. Slowly, Finn was creeping back into her life.

"Good. I think he means well. Gwen is the majority share owner. She has the final say on all decisions. They've agreed that if anything happens to Gwen, her shares will go to the community."

"I like that."

Their conversation was brought to an abrupt end when Elowen arrived, and everyone bustled into the kitchen. Michael took over making the drinks and left Mabel sitting and staring at the back wall.

"Are you okay, love?" Mabel's mother asked. She

placed a hand on Mabel's shoulder, causing her to jump.

"I'm fine." She plastered on a false smile and turned to face the room, pushing the conversation to the back of her mind. Once she was home, she would revisit it.

Elowen slowly wandered over. She looked more like the old El, dressed in a black t-shirt and trousers, with her shiny hair pulled back into a neat ponytail. The sprinkle of cocoa powder across her chest was the only sign she'd been working. "I've missed you," she said. Mabel wasn't sure who moved first, but they were hugging.

"I've missed you, too. Sorry for not getting in touch."

"So am I. Things have been hectic. Mabel, I need to ask you something." Elowen steered Mabel into the garden. "Finn has offered me the job of managing the pub when it reopens. The money is amazing, and he understands my hours need to be flexible around the girls' school." Elowen stopped and bit her lip. "I won't take the job if you don't want me to."

Mabel almost laughed. "El, don't be so silly. The job is perfect for you and it'll solve your money worries. You can't turn it down because a man broke my heart."

"Do you really mean that?"

Mabel crossed her fingers behind her back. "Of course. If Finn is back in Port Isaac, then it's something I'm going to have to get used to. This is my home, too, and I'm not going anywhere."

"Thank you, Mabel." Elowen pulled her into a bone-crushing hug.

CHAPTER FORTY-TWO

As the first light broke outside her window, Mabel gathered her swimming costume and strolled into the harbour. Her footsteps echoed through the empty streets, and she picked up her pace, eager to immerse herself in the water. She'd gone to bed early last night, the cottage feeling empty without Ethel, who she was picking up today. As she'd laid in bed, Mabel's thoughts had been filled with the glimpse she'd caught of Finn. She'd thought about texting him, but didn't know what to say. When she'd finally fallen asleep, Finn's eyes featured in all her dreams, and she woke longing for his arms around her.

The beach was empty, and she left her belongings in the usual spot. Nothing had changed since she last swam, but everything inside her felt different. Mabel held in a squeal as the cold water lapped at her feet. With a deep breath, she plunged beneath the waves and a calmness overcame her as she floated in the water. The water was icy and chilled her to the core, but she kept going. She needed the clarity that swimming brought her. The cold cleared her mind, and for the first time in weeks, the weight of her worries lifted from her shoulders.

Mabel wrapped herself in a towel and looked towards the pub. Finn was at the window, looking out towards her. Without waiting to dry off, Mabel gathered her belongings and walked home with her towel still around her.

"What are you doing here?" asked Mabel as she rounded the corner to her cottage and found Del leaning against her car.

"I thought I'd drop in on my way to work."

"It's good to see you," Mabel said. They'd shared a few messages during her time in Kent but hadn't spoken much. "I need a quick shower, but come in and make yourself at home."

Once clean, Mabel threw on some old shorts and a top and joined Del.

"I was going to make hot chocolates, but there's no milk in your fridge," Del said.

"Sorry, I only got home yesterday. I've not had the chance to get any shopping." Michael had offered to take her shopping when he dropped her home last night, but Mabel had been too worried to bump into somebody she knew.

"How are you?" Del patted the space beside her on the sofa.

"Confused," admitted Mabel as she took the seat. "After everything I did to protect myself, it still feels as though I'm rebuilding my life."

"You can't avoid love, Mabes."

Mabel sighed. "I know. I still really like him, Del. He hurt me, but I think he meant well."

"He still lied to you when he realised who his investors were," Del pointed out.

"He did, but he was honest in telling me he had investors." Mabel shrugged. These thoughts had been whizzing around her mind for weeks.

"It's not your fault, Mabes."

"I don't know whose fault it is, Del. Am I just looking for someone to pin the blame on?"

"What are you going to do?"

"I need to talk to him."

"Why don't you do it today? Get it over with, or else you'll find yourselves avoiding one another."

"I can't. I've told Gwen I'll pick up Ethel today."

"What if he's there?"

Mabel's jaw dropped. She hadn't considered he might be there. "He wouldn't be, would he?"

Del shrugged.

"Will you collect Ethel for me?" Mabel grasped Del's hands.

"I have to go to work. Actually, I need to leave now or else I'll get caught in the rush hour traffic. Shall we meet for a drink at the weekend?"

"Sure."

"Fisherman's Rest?" Del asked and raised her eyebrows.

"I'll get the bus to you," Mabel said as she walked Del out to her car.

⇶ ⇇

"You're collecting your cat. Not walking a runway," Mabel muttered as she discarded yet another dress. Gwen hadn't mentioned Finn when she'd spoken to her on the phone, which was surely a good sign. Mabel wanted to believe Gwen would ensure Finn wasn't around when she went to collect Ethel, but she knew the woman wouldn't be able to resist interfering.

Eventually, Mabel settled on jeans and a pretty, summery top with bluebells stitched onto it. She put on a pair of trainers for the walk across to Gwen's and readied herself to go into the harbour, unsure of how people would treat her.

"Morning, love," Mrs Lavender called as she reached the end of her path.

"Morning," Mabel called back but didn't stop. If she delayed the trip, she might never find the courage to go.

With each step, Mabel's nerves grew. She caught a handful of people watching her as she made her way through the winding streets.

"Mabel," Betty called from the bakery. She was collecting her morning order of bread.

343

"Hi, Betty." Mabel jogged over to hug her.

Kelly, the baker, was putting her shop's sign out. "It's good to see you back," she said warmly.

"Thank you." Mabel's eyes prickled with tears of relief. She only hoped Kelly's reaction would spread through the harbour.

"We won't stop you, but don't be a stranger," Betty said and waved her off.

Mabel found a few other locals smiling at her as she walked on. Her confidence was slowly growing as she reached the other side of the harbour.

"Mabel," someone called her name from behind.

Mabel spun on her heel and saw Mr Trelawney hurrying after her with his stick. She stopped until he caught up.

"Mabel, love. I wanted to apologise for how I acted the last time I saw you. I'm afraid I let my emotions get swept up in the local gossip. I'm very sorry." He gave her a warm smile, which Mabel couldn't help but return.

"Thank you. I appreciate the apology."

"Stop by soon. I've got more comics for the girls."

Mabel felt lighter as she continued her walk to Gwen's. She wasn't naïve enough to believe everyone would be happy to see her back, but the people who mattered were, and that was enough. Gwen's house was just visible in the distance and Mabel slowed her steps as she squinted to see if there was any sign of movement. There was no fancy car in the driveway and Mabel hoped that meant Finn wasn't around. She squared her shoulders as she strolled the last few steps and rang the bell.

Mabel's stomach dropped as Finn opened the door. It had only been three weeks since she last saw him, but it felt like a lifetime had passed. He looked the same, but his eyes were burdened with emotions. He was still handsome and the sight of him still made her stomach flood with butterflies.

"Mabel." Surprise coated the word.

"Finn," Mabel said.

"It's good to see you." His face softened, and Mabel squished down the flutter in her stomach.

"I'm here to collect my cat," she said, steering the conversation away from anything to do with the past.

"Oh, right." He glanced nervously behind him.

"What?"

"It's just, Gwen took her to the vet this morning."

"The vet?" Mabel screeched. "What's wrong with Ethel?"

"She's developed a small bald patch. Gwen thinks it's the washing powder as it's the side Ethel likes to curl up on."

"A bald patch?" Mabel's day was going from bad to worse.

"I thought she would have messaged you. They shouldn't be long. Gwen left about an hour ago. Her car wouldn't start, so she called me over to use mine and asked me to wait in for a parcel."

Mabel groaned. "I think I'm the parcel." She took a deep breath. "She's set us up."

Finn tugged a hand through his hair. "She has, hasn't she?"

"I'll come back later." Mabel turned to leave, but Finn reached out to stop her. His soft fingers wrapped around the top of her arm and a shiver rushed through her.

"Gwen can't be much longer. It's silly for you to walk home and come back later."

Mabel sighed. He was right. It would take up most of her day. They'd have to get used to seeing each other around, so ten minutes of small talk, while she waited for Ethel, was probably a good place to start.

"Okay, but no tea, please. Gwen always makes a pot, and I have to force it down and pretend I'm enjoying it."

Finn chuckled. "No tea. I don't think Gwen has any hot chocolate. Shall we skip the drink?"

Mabel nodded and followed him into the living room. They sat on opposite sofas, admiring the room's decor to avoid looking at each other.

"I'm sorry," Finn eventually whispered.

Mabel steeled herself for the barrage of emotions that came with those two words. "Don't, Finn."

"I need you to understand why I did what I did." He waited for her to say something, but when she didn't, he continued. "I was in a bad place when I came to Port Isaac, but I didn't want to admit it to myself. In the space of six months, I lost my mother, my business, and my home. Although, truthfully, I lost my mother years ago. She slipped away bit by bit until she wasn't my mother anymore. I still cared and loved her with all my heart, but it took its toll. Losing my restaurant and my home tipped me over the edge and I did what I had to survive. I had bad credit, so when an investor made me an offer, I didn't even read the contract. My broker told me it was a good deal considering my circumstances, and I signed it immediately." He paused, his eyes searching hers, but Mabel kept her walls up. She had to be strong. She couldn't let him know she loved him and probably always would. Her heart ached for everything he'd been through and she longed to reach out to him, but she couldn't forget the hurt he'd caused, even if her heart was screaming at her to move on from it. "I should have asked questions and read the document, but I had nothing to lose. All I wanted was to leave London and the memories it held, and this felt like my golden ticket. Then I met you. My whole life changed in those weeks we spent together. You felt like home and I couldn't imagine leaving you."

"Finn, I understand why you signed the contract, but what I don't understand is why you lied to me."

"A couple of weeks after I arrived in Port Isaac, the investors started to put pressure on me. They demanded to know where I was spending every penny and wanted me to use their own suppliers.

Still, I didn't think much of it. Then, you mentioned the King's Head Corporation, and I realised the name rang a bell. That night I looked through my documents and realised they were my investors. I knew the truth would shatter you, so I've been trying to agree on a price to buy them out and raise the funds. You might not believe this, Mabel, but I was going to tell you the truth. I wanted everything organised and to know I could buy the pub before I told you."

"You should have been honest with me from the start."

"I know. When I came to Port Isaac, I had nothing to lose, so I didn't think twice about who my investors were. The joke was on me because, as it turned out, I had everything to lose."

"Finn…" Mabel started, but trailed off, unsure what to say.

"I went up to Scotland when I left Port Isaac and spent some time with Lachlan. He owns a castle which he's turned into a hotel and restaurant, but it's in the middle of nowhere, so it's a good place to go when you're running away from everything. Lachlan listened to me, but he also told me some home truths. He made me realise how much I was struggling with grief. I don't want to blame my actions on my past, because I do accept responsibility for them, and I am sorry."

"Stop apologising," Mabel quipped. He'd stirred up her emotions, and she was battling to stop her walls from crumbling. She'd watched his lips move as he spoke, and her mind wandered to how they felt against hers.

"How did you end up back in Port Isaac?" she asked. It was the only part of the story that Mabel didn't know.

"Gwen phoned me. She was quite harsh, actually. Told me I was being a stupid pillock." A smile tugged at his lips. "She also told me how much she'd always wanted a family of her own, but it had never happened. If she had known I existed, then she would have been involved in my life, no matter what my father thought."

"I'm sorry." Unable to bear it any longer, Mabel moved to sit beside him. She took his hand in hers and squeezed.

"My life could have been very different. Gwen told me I had two options; grow old and bitter, or fight for a future that excites me. Lachlan offered to finance the purchase of the pub, but I felt icky about it. Friends and business don't mix well. I told Gwen, and she suggested she back me. At first, I said no, but I promised to think it over. After a few more chats, she wore me down and made me realise it was the perfect solution. We came up with a plan, which means Gwen has a majority interest. Eventually, it will revert to the community. With the help of Lachlan, the corporation agreed to sell to me. We've signed contracts and in a day or two, Gwen and I will own Fisherman's Rest."

"You have to do it all above board this time, Finn."

"I know. Everyone was so welcoming and happy to see me back that it only made me feel worse for what I'd done."

"So, you're here to stay?" Mabel threaded her fingers through his. Perhaps she was too quick to trust him last time, but this time around, he could earn her trust. She still loved him and she couldn't deny the pull she felt to him. If she pushed him away, then it would only be herself she was hurting.

"I am," he confirmed.

"Then maybe you should ask me out on a date."

"Would you say yes?" His eyes widened, and he turned his body to face her.

"You'll have to ask to find out. But, Finn, we take it slow this time. You have to earn my trust. If you lie to me again, then it's over."

"I promise. Mabel Appledore, will you go on a date with me?"

"Yes." She leaned forward and pecked him on the lips as the front door opened and the sound of a meowing cat filled the hallway.

EPILOGUE

"We're not using those awful, cheap decorations you got last year," Mabel said with her hands planted firmly on her hips.

"Why not? They're not *that* bad," Finn complained, looking up from the box of Christmas decorations he'd carried down from the loft.

"They made Milly cry."

"How was I supposed to know the light-up Santa would have a hole in the middle of its face?"

"We'll see what we can salvage, then we'll pop to Padstow-on-Sea tomorrow to buy more."

Finn rolled his eyes but knew better than to argue. He undid the box and took out a handful of decorations. His nose scrunched up as the smell of damp and mould filled the room. Mabel coughed and ushered him outside with it.

"You can't go opening that inside. Health and Safety will shut us down," Mabel complained. She closed the doors and left him on the terrace.

"Mabel, let me back in." He knocked on the door.

"No. Go home and shower first. You're a hazard."

"Mabel," he pleaded.

"What's going on?" Elowen asked. She hung her coat behind the bar and shook the snow from her hair. It rarely snowed by the sea, but a few stray flakes were floating in the air today.

"Finn's going to get us closed down with those disgusting decorations from last Christmas," Mabel explained.

"Oh, no. We can do better than that. I've got new ones arriving tomorrow." Elowen had settled into her role as pub manager and was always one step ahead. "Well, they're not new. Zoe picked up some second hand baubles and is hand painting them for us."

"You're the best."

"I hate to break up this little bonding moment between you, but do you think I could come back into my own pub?" Finn called through the glass. He'd wrapped his arms around himself but was still shivering.

"Mabel's right, you're a hazard. Here, take a spare key and run back to mine to shower. Michael'll be in his office, but I'll text him to warn him," Elowen said.

"I could go home," Finn said.

Elowen glanced up at the clock above the bar.

"Not enough time. Lunch service begins in two hours and you need to prep. Here's my key." She opened the door to him and handed him the key.

With a few choice words, Finn went to Elowen and Michael's for a shower.

"How are you finding living together?" Elowen asked.

Mabel was polishing the glasses for the lunchtime service. They had new champagne flutes, which Zoe had painted the crab and lobster logo on.

"It's really nice," Mabel admitted. For the last year, they'd lived between homes, until last month, when traipsing back and forth with suitcases of clothes finally got to Mabel. Her suitcase had burst open on the walk down and the harsh November breeze had swept her clothes in all directions. With Mabel still busy upcycling furniture, it made sense for them to move into her cottage, so she kept the barn. Finn had rented out the flat above the pub and things were working well.

"I'm happy for you." Elowen smiled.

"Thanks, El."

"I spoke to Mary this morning about Christmas and she said you and Finn wanted to host dinner at the pub?"

"Yes, we thought it would be nice. Gwen and Betty are coming, too. Del's going to pop down for a glass of bubbly before she heads to her parents."

"Perfect. It's great having Del upstairs."

"I know. We've gone from opposite sides of the world to a staircase separating us."

"How long until she hands in her notice at work?" asked El.

"She says another six months. They're finalising a marketing campaign in St Ives, and she wants to learn as much as she can before she leaves." Del was planning on opening her own company, specialising in marketing for independently run pubs.

"It's very exciting!" Elowen and Del had spent many hours discussing the pub's marketing plan, during which they'd become firm friends. "Does she have an accountant?"

Mabel chuckled. "She'll be contacting Michael for a quote."

"Good, because The Cornish Vintage Jewellery Shop has a necklace that matches my ruby bracelet."

"Have you told Michael you want it for Christmas, or do you need me to steer him in the right direction?"

"He knows." El shot her a smile before she disappeared into her office to check the lunchtime bookings.

⋙⋘

"Do we still have to go Christmas shopping if Elowen has ordered decorations for the pub?" asked Finn, rubbing sleep from his eyes.

"Yes! It's our first Christmas living together. We should buy a new decoration to celebrate."

"I can't believe it's our second Christmas together," mused Finn.

"It's gone so quickly."

"I know."

"I love you, Finn Hart." Mabel put her arms around his neck.

"I love you, Mabel Appledore."

After a lie-in, they popped into Padstow-on-Sea. Mabel had good intentions when they arrived. She'd planned to buy Christmas decorations and then head straight home. However, she'd soon been enticed into other shops, and then they'd bumped into Zoe and Jada and had lunch with them. It had been a lovely day, but Mabel's feet throbbed and they still had to decorate the tree.

Laden down with shopping bags, they burst into the cottage. Ethel looked up from where she was curled on the sofa, but quickly snuggled back into a ball and fell asleep.

"I'm exhausted," Finn complained, dropping the bags he held.

"Sorry, I didn't expect to spend so long in Padstow-on-Sea."

Finn pressed a soft kiss to her temple. "Shall I make hot chocolate?"

"Yes, please."

Finn made thick, rich hot chocolates while Mabel lit a fire. The flames flickered in the hearth and warmed the room. Ethel mewed from her spot on the sofa but didn't move. Her beady eyes watched as Mabel unpacked the decorations.

"What have you got me for Christmas?" Finn asked, hanging the first decoration on the tree. It was a wooden nutcracker that Mabel had picked up in a charity shop some years ago.

"It's a surprise." Mabel had been working on Finn's Christmas present for a few weeks. He'd shown her pictures from his childhood, and she'd spotted his mother's old vinyl cabinet in the background. It had taken Mabel months to source one similar, and she'd been carefully restoring it since. There wouldn't be enough space for it in the cottage, but Mabel had already earmarked a corner for it at the pub. She'd commandeered Michael's help to move it into place on Christmas Eve.

"Can I at least have a clue?"

"No. What are you getting me?" Mabel was keen to steer the conversation away from Finn's gift before she let anything slip.

"I'm not telling. Although, I'll give you a hint. Belle is helping me choose it." He shot her a wink and turned back to decorating the tree.

Mabel's heart hammered in her chest, and a smile tugged at her lips. She couldn't wait for Christmas Day.

The Cornish Vintage Tea Shop

CHAPTER ONE

Florence bustled her way into the overcrowded train carriage, making herself as small as possible. Hailstones bounced off the windows, and the muggy August air filled the carriage. Fat droplets of water dripped from her hair and onto her shoulders, soaking through her light coat and silk blouse. It was an unpleasant, but not uncommon, feeling. Her expression mirrored the same withdrawn look that everyone else on the carriage was sporting. With some manoeuvring, Florence tucked herself away in a corner by the door, turned up the volume on her earphones to drown out the hum of conversation, and watched as the London suburbs whizzed past. Florence's grandmother, Iris, had always told her that happiness was the most important part of life, yet there was very little to be witnessed on the seven-fifteen to London Victoria.

When the train came to a halt at the terminal,

commuters piled off, and Flo allowed herself to be swept up in the hubbub of the crowd. If she thought about it, she'd feel claustrophobic, so she focused on her music and descended into London's underground. The air was stifling; the crowds hadn't abated, and each step was taken on autopilot.

It was with great relief that she stepped out of Holborn station. The smell of exhaust fumes filled her nostrils, and as she took out her earphones, she could hear the steady thrum of the standstill traffic. Across the road, a coffee shop served her a burnt-tasting latte mixed with overly sweet caramel syrup, which she paid a small fortune for. If Grandma Iris were still alive, she'd have lectured Florence on supporting big coffee chains. They stole customers from the independent shops, and the coffee was never as good. Flo had yet to find a coffee that tasted like the ones her grandmother used to make. However, independent coffee shops were few and far between in central London, and so this burnt, bitter liquid would have to do.

"Morning," the bored receptionist greeted Flo as she crossed the reception area. Every surface was reflective, and the lifts had a tablet to operate them.

Flo's heels clicked across the tiled floor as she smiled at the woman. There was little point in learning the woman's name. She'd have moved on by next week. Flo bypassed the lifts and took the stairs up to her third-floor office.

"I thought you had today booked off?" Carmen, her desk neighbour and work friend, asked.

"Bella cancelled it," Flo said through gritted teeth as she shrugged off her wet coat and switched on her computer.

"Again?"

Flo nodded.

A Post-it note was stuck to a stack of documents. With a sigh, Flo peeled it off and saw that Bella needed the documents proofreading in the next hour. Flo sank into the worn chair. With a wedge of tissues, she dried the wet patches on her shoulders where the rain had soaked through her coat. The chair creaked beneath, and Flo winced. Bella had promised her a replacement since she'd started at the company a few years ago.

"Don't forget those documents," a trainee called as she wafted past.

Carmen clicked her tongue. "Why do you let them talk to you like that?"

"There's a chain of hierarchy." Flo shrugged. "Bella is the top dog, and then her trainees are little minions. As her paralegal, I rank at the bottom. I'm the legal equivalent of fish food."

"You have the same qualifications as they do," Carmen pointed out.

"I know." When Flo accepted the paralegal role at Baker and Harlow, she had grand plans of applying to their trainee program. The first couple of years, she was rejected, then her grandmother passed away, and all plans were put on hold. As each day passed, she became increasingly aware that this career path no longer made her happy. Her life was stagnant, but she didn't have the energy to do anything about it.

The day dragged as heavy rain pelted the windows. It was a gloomy day in London, which reflected Flo's mood. At twenty-six, Flo thought she would have life figured out. However, she couldn't be further from it.

Usually, Flo would stay late to work, but today she left at five on the dot. She joined the crowds as they descended on the station. Her heels splashed in the puddles, and water flicked up the back of her trousers. Once off the stuffy underground, she boarded a Southern train to Surrey. As she left the city and hurtled into the countryside, Flo flicked through pictures on her phone, lingering on one of her favourites. It was of her and her grandmother outside Iris's cafe, The Lavender Tea Shop.

"I miss you," Flo whispered and brushed a finger over the picture before she swiped at the stray tear sliding down her cheek.

Flo checked the time. There was still a while until the train arrived at her destination. She scrolled through her phonebook, her finger hovering over the name 'Victoria'. Gnawing on her lip, Flo pressed the button to call.

After a few rings, someone answered. "Hello?" they said, their voice a high-pitched, sing-song tone. "Who is this?"

Flo pinched the bridge of her nose. This had been a terrible idea. "It's Flo." Her voice shook.

There was a moment of silence on the other end of the phone before Victoria spoke. "What do you want, Flo?" Her tone had shifted to one of frustration.

"It's a year today," Flo muttered, squeezing her eyes shut. The last thing she needed was for her unshed tears to spill down her cheeks on public transport.

"Is it?" came Victoria's cold response. "I thought it was last month."

Anger swirled in the pit of Flo's stomach. "No, this month," she said through gritted teeth.

"It's just another date, Florence."

"A date that means something to me!"

"Florence, it's been a year. You need to move on. It's not healthy to still be grieving."

Flo scoffed. "What would you know about grief or losing a loved one, Mum?"

Before Victoria could respond, Flo hung up. It had been a terrible idea to call, but occasionally Flo craved the love of a family member, and today she'd given in to that feeling, only for it to have caused her further pain. She chewed on her lip and turned her attention to the passing scenery, wishing Iris were there to give her a big hug.

Flo was used to a quick commute, so the journey to Surrey felt as though it lasted a lifetime.

"Aunty Florrie," a small, shrill voice called from the platform. Flo beamed as she spotted her best friend's daughter waving. Poppy's other hand was firmly clasped by her mother, Daisy.

"Hello, Poppy." Flo scooped the girl into her arms, smothering her in kisses.

"Has my daughter replaced me as your best friend?" Daisy huffed, a smile lighting up her face.

"It's so good to see you, Dais," Flo said, shifting Poppy to her hip to give Daisy a one-armed hug.

"You too, Florrie." They'd been friends since school, and even though their lives had gone in different directions, they'd remained close.

Flo swallowed back the lump in her throat at the familiar nickname.

"Mummy's cooked lasagne," Poppy said, realising the attention had shifted away from her.

Flo clapped her hands. "My favourite! Shall we go home and eat?"

Daisy had always been a wonderful cook. She'd started working alongside Flo at The Lavender Tea Shop when she turned sixteen. While Flo liked to bake cakes and be out front greeting customers, Daisy stayed in the back preparing sandwiches and jacket potatoes while dreaming up new flavours for the following week's soup. Everyone had always commented on what a good pair they made. Flo was the sensible, practical one, while Daisy was the creative and impulsive one. Although Flo loved her best friend very much, she sometimes felt envious of her laissez-faire approach to life. At ten years old, Flo had her A-level choices picked out, which were perfectly chosen to support her application to her dream university. She'd never made an impulsive decision in her life.

The three of them squeezed into Daisy's tiny car. Her parents had bought it for her shortly after passing her test. If the car could speak, it would recount many late-night drives and heart-to-hearts about stupid boys.

"I've been thinking of you all day," Daisy said, reaching over to squeeze Flo's hand.

Flo cleared her throat. "Thank you," she mumbled.

"I can't believe it's a year since we lost Iris."

"I know." Flo turned to look out the window, and a wave of emotions hit her as they drove past The Lavender Tea Shop. It looked nothing like it had in Iris's time, but it still sent a pang of pain through Flo's heart.

Daisy's flat smelled of home-cooked food, and Flo felt her muscles relax. She couldn't remember the last time she'd eaten a home-cooked meal or felt at home somewhere.

"I'll pour us some wine. Poppy's already eaten, but I told her she could have some garlic bread with us. Sorry, her dad was supposed to have her, but he cancelled, again."

"You know I love seeing both of you. How are things with him?"

"Don't ask." Daisy's sunny exterior slipped, and the heavy feeling of guilt settled in Flo's stomach. She hadn't supported her friend enough.

Daisy handed her a glass of merlot, and they

joined Poppy in the living room while the garlic bread cooked.

"How's work?" asked Daisy as the dulcet tones of children's television hummed in the background.

"The same. Still no sign of a training contract, and I continue to be everyone's lackey."

"Can't you apply somewhere else? You've been there for long enough that nobody would question you wanting a new challenge."

"I should look," Flo said. She should have looked years ago, but somehow she'd fallen into the monotony of her everyday routine and couldn't muster the strength to leave it behind and search for something new. Then, when she'd lost Iris, all hope for the future had been extinguished with her grandmother's lively soul.

"This isn't the Florrie I know," Daisy commented, concern etched across her face.

"I haven't been that Florrie for a while now," Flo admitted.

"Aunty Florrie, which Spice Girl is your favourite?" asked Poppy, climbing onto Flo's lap and almost sloshing wine across her white silk blouse.

"Is your mummy teaching you about the Spice Girls?" The sadness lifted, and Flo couldn't help the giggle that escaped.

"She's got a lot of energy," Flo commented as Daisy returned from her third attempt at putting Poppy to bed.

"I know." Daisy huffed out a breath.

"How are you, Dais?" Flo refilled her glass.

"No, don't try to turn the attention onto me. I want to know about you. How are you really, Florrie?"

Flo took a deep breath, contemplating how much to tell her best friend. "I'm struggling," she finally admitted. "My job feels as though it's hit a dead end. I'm still living in that awful house share, and even though I've saved a small fortune, I'll never be able to afford a place in London. My life plans have been derailed, and I don't know what to do. It all seems so utterly pointless now." Flo hiccuped as she gulped her wine.

"You don't have to stay in London, Flo. You could go anywhere." Was that a hint of wistfulness in Daisy's voice?

"I can't move back here. As much as I would love to be around the corner from you, the memories would be too painful."

Daisy nodded. "I've got a box of grown-up chocolates in the cupboard. Hold on." Daisy went to fetch them, and Flo pulled out her phone, still considering Daisy's earlier suggestion of leaving London.

With alcohol dulling her sensible side, she chewed on her nail and considered where in the world she would go if she could go anywhere. It didn't take long before she landed on a place. The little village in Cornwall where Iris would take her every year. They'd close the cafe for two weeks in August, pack up the car, and leave. It would be swelteringly hot as they travelled in Iris's old car with its worn leather seats, which always burnt Flo's legs. They'd wind down the windows and let the hot, sticky air fill the car, pretending it was cooling them down. Iris would let Flo choose the music for the journey, so her favourite Spice Girls CD was always blaring out as they sang along. Their two weeks in Cornwall were filled with long walks as they rambled over the Cornish countryside, bracing swims in the bright blue sea, and huge slices of Victoria sponge cake from the cafe around the corner from their holiday let. Iris had always had a soft spot for the Cornish village, which she visited during her childhood. She'd been friends with some of the locals, not that Flo had cared. Whenever Iris began talking to someone, Flo would slink off with a book and find some shade. Flo tapped away on her phone, looking up the village. She gasped at the first search engine find. The cafe they visited was up for sale. Not only was it up for sale, but Flo could afford it.

"What's wrong? Your eyes have gone wild," Daisy said as she held a box of alcoholic chocolates.

"Look at this." Flo almost threw the phone at Daisy as she took the box. She plucked out a dark chocolate and rum truffle and popped it into her mouth, savouring the bitter taste against the tangy alcohol.

"You should buy it," Daisy said, her words

slurred.

"I couldn't."

"You can afford it, right?"

Flo nodded, eating another rum chocolate.

"Call them." Daisy threw the phone back and Flo caught it, squealing as she realised Daisy had hit call.

"There's no answer," Flo said as the ringing ended and an automated voice announced she'd reached the voicemail.

"Leave a message," Daisy instructed, throwing another chocolate onto Flo's lap. This one had a whisky cream middle.

"Hi, this is, um." Flo furrowed her brow. What was her name? "Florence Alden. I'd like to make an offer on the Lavender Cottage Cafe."

THANK YOU FOR READING!

If you have time to leave a review on Amazon or Goodreads I would be incredibly grateful.

You can follow me on Amazon

Sign up to my newsletter at
www.elizabethhollandauthor.com

You can also purchase signed copies on my website

AFTERWORD

Thank you for escaping to Port Isaac with me. I've upcycled furniture for over five years, so I always knew this series would have a vintage furniture edition. I should say, the upcycling depicted in this book is romanticised to save boring you with each monotonous step!

The Cornish Vintage Furniture Shop came to life when I visited Port Isaac in 2024. It was windy and raining, so we found a lovely cafe to dry off in. That was where Fisherman's Brew was created. As I listened to the conversations around me, Gwen's character formed, and I couldn't wait to get home and start writing.

Other books...

THE CORNISH VINTAGE SERIES

THE CORNISH VINTAGE DRESS SHOP

THE CORNISH VINTAGE JEWELLERY SHOP

THE CORNISH VINTAGE FURNITURE SHOP

THE CORNISH VINTAGE TEA SHOP

COMING SOON....

THE CORNISH VINTAGE BOOKSHOP

THE PEACE, JOY AND LOVE SERIES

A MERRY CHRISTMAS AT THE CASTLE

A SPRING FLING AT HOTEL MAYFAIR

Printed in Dunstable, United Kingdom

76712885R00221